The unauthorized reproduction or distribution of a copyrighted work is illegal. Criminal copyright infringement (including infringement without monetary gain) is investigated by the FBI and is punishable by up to 5 years in federal prison and a fine of $250,000.

Please purchase only authorized electronic editions and do not participate in, or encourage, the electronic piracy of copyrighted materials. Your support of the author's rights is appreciated.

This book is a work of fiction. Names, characters, places, and incidents are the products of the author's imagination or used fictitiously. Any resemblance to actual events, locales or persons, living or dead, is entirely coincidental.

Exquisite Redemption

Copyright © 2015 by Ann Mayburn

Published by Honey Mountain Publishing

All rights reserved. Except for use in any review, the reproduction or utilization of this work, in whole or in part, in any form by any electronic, mechanical or other means now known or hereafter invented, is forbidden without the written permission of the publisher.

DISCLAIMER: Please do not try any new sexual practice, BDSM or otherwise, without the guidance of an experienced practitioner. Ann Mayburn will not be responsible for any loss, harm, injury or death resulting from use of the information contained in this book.

Author's Note

While you may think you know Beach and Sarah's story from what you've read in Exquisite Trouble and Exquisite Danger, you don't. Sarah is overprotective of Swan to the point of sheltering her from the world, so Sarah gave her twin sister an edited version of how she got together with Beach…a very edited version. Now sit back, lock the doors and turn off the phone, then grab a cold drink and enjoy another trip on the crazy train that is the Iron Horse MC.

Acknowledgements

I would like to send out a big thank you to my beta readers Meghan Pyne, April Renee Symes, Ann Reeves, and Virginia Swanson for their help in polishing this bad boy up for your viewing pleasure. I'd also like to take a moment to thank Heather Witherell Ray for lending me her mother, Mouse, to use as inspiration for Beach's mom, Mouse. ☺ While artistic license has been taken with the character, in the real world Mouse is just as sassy and sweet as the fictional one and in real life is in fact a kickass catfish tour guide with Santee Cajun Guide Service out of Santee South Carolina.

To my beloved readers, thank you for once again giving me the chance to entertain you.

Ann

Prologue

Sarah Anderson, aka Sarah Kline, aka Sarah Grace, aka Sarah Michaels, Age Seven

Loud, angry voices reach me from where I'm curled into a ball beneath my bed, the lacy white edges of my comforter partially obscuring the line of light coming from below my closed bedroom door. It's cold under my bed and I wish I had the courage to reach up and pull my blanket down with me.

A harsh female scream, muffled behind my door, echoes down the hallway. My muscles tense so hard they ache and I force back a whimper, trying to breathe as little as possible while clutching my stuffed white pony close to me. A shallow breath takes in the comforting scent of his soft fur. Mommy and Mr. Alan are fighting again and I know if either of them sees me they'll yell at me too, so I hide and hope they'll stop.

"Where's my money, you fucking bitch?" Mr. Allen yells loud enough that my body seems to vibrate with his words.

"I don't have your money," Mommy screams back.

"Four *million* dollars is missing from my business bank account, where the fuck did it go!"

"I don't know!"

Goose bumps raise up along my arms at the tone of her voice, a harsh caw that reminds me of the sounds crows make when they're fighting. It's a bad sound, a noise Mommy only makes after she's been drinking her wine and is really mad.

Tears drip down my face, into my pony's fur, as they continue to shout bad words at each other. Their voices are really angry. Soon the hitting will start, and I know I should go help Mommy, but I'm afraid. Mr. Alan is mean, her worst boyfriend yet, and he once hit me hard enough to split my lip open. Mommy made me promise to tell anyone at school who asked what happened that I fell down while playing outside.

If I told anyone the truth they'll take me away from Mommy and throw her in jail forever and ever.

Something crashes and I know my Mommy is starting to throw things.

"You think you can rip me off, you fucking coke head?" Mr. Alan bellows. "I don't know how you did it, but it was fuckin' you and if you don't show me where that money is I'm gonna turn you in to the police. Bet they'd be real interested to know where you are."

More screaming follows and my gaze darts to where the cardboard moving boxes are shoved up against the wall of my bedroom. When Mommy came home with those boxes I knew it was time to leave again, and I begged my mommy to let us stay, but she ignored me. She had said we were moving to Reno where a man named Mr. Jack was waiting for us with a big house. When I told her I didn't want to leave she said I could get a dog and everything would be wonderful. Except she said that every time we moved and I never got a dog and it was never wonderful.

We were in Idaho now, and Mommy had promised we were going to stay, that we didn't have to run and hide from my daddy anymore so he couldn't get us. If he found us he'd steal me away from Mommy and hurt her. We'd been here for seven months, the longest I can remember being anywhere, and I liked it. The school I went to was nice, and I'd become best friends with the girl next door, Beth. Her family would let me spend the night and I loved how nice they were. Beth's mommy and daddy didn't argue, instead they hugged and kissed. Loved each other. I worried Beth's mommy and daddy would come over to see what all the yelling was about, but I don't think they can hear it from across the wide grass field that separates our houses.

They were probably tucking Beth into bed right now, telling her stories or signing her songs. My mommy used to do that, but not so much anymore. The memory of her pretty voice singing me songs in Dutch helps to drown out the increasing noise beyond my bedroom door.

More things slammed against walls, followed by shrill screams, and I plastered my hands to my ears, humming as loud as I could to drown out the hurting sounds. I knew better than to run out there and try to help my mommy. The last time I did that, Mr. Paul, a man I did not like where we used to live, hit me so hard my ears rang and black dots danced around my eyes. My head had hurt for three days and soon after we moved again. Maybe if I stayed here, stayed hidden, we wouldn't have to leave.

Bright light suddenly flooded my room and I gave a short scream before I could help myself as Mommy lifted up the edge of my comforter with her lips curled into a silent snarl. Her eyes were glassy and the smell of wine filled the cramped space beneath my bed as she reached in and hauled me out. Her lower lip was swollen bigger than usual and her cheek was already turning dark with a bruise. Her long red nails sank into my arm and I tried to pull away, but she just yanked hard enough that my shoulder burned like fire.

"Mommy, you're hurting me!"

"Get dressed, quick, Sarah. We have to leave."

It was only then that I realized the shouting had stopped. I looked around for Mr. Alan, but he wasn't there. Still crying, I clutched my pony and watched Mommy jerk down my suitcases from the top shelf of my closet then she began to throw my clothes into them. Red dots were splattered all over her pretty white shirt and pale green pants, and I could see her right eye was all puffy and swollen. I took a hesitant step forward, afraid of making her angry but needing to know if she was all right.

"Mommy, are you hurt?"

She paused with a wad of my socks in her hand. "What?"

"You're bleeding."

She glanced down at herself then quickly back at me. "It's nothing, just some nail polish I spilled."

"But Mommy—"

"Don't backtalk me. Now put some shoes on, we're leaving."

A sob caught in my throat. "I don't want to leave! Please, leave me with Beth's mommy and daddy. They'll let me stay with them, I know they will. Please. Everyone's so nice here."

In two long strides, my beautiful mother with her golden hair and baby blue eyes was across the room. I didn't even have time to shield myself before she slapped me, hard enough that I could taste blood. Pain cut through me and I struggled to control my sobs, knowing if I cried too hard and irritated her, she'd slap me again.

"We are leaving right now!"

All I could do was choke back my tears as she hurried from my room with one of my suitcases in each hand. When she returned I had my backpack stuffed and I was putting my few treasured possessions in it as quick as I could. If we really were leaving that meant we were going now, and if I didn't put it in my backpack I'd never see it again. That had happened twice before and I still mourned the loss of my favorite doll.

Mommy grabbed my hand and pulled me quickly after her, down the hall and into the living room. Red splattered the walls here and I gasped at the sight of Mr. Allen lying in a pool of what I was pretty sure was blood, his green eyes open and unseeing. His face looked weird but before I could study it more, Mommy scooped me up in her arms and carried me out the door before placing me in the front seat of her new white Mercedes.

"Is Mr. Allen okay?"

Mommy gave a brittle laugh that scared me. "He's fine. Now buckle up. I'll be right back."

Shivers vibrated through me as I watched Mommy go back into the house a few more times, coming out with armloads of clothes and stuff. It was all shoved into the car until I couldn't see the backseat. She even put her fur jackets on my lap, a welcome soft weight that gave me a little bit of comfort. I bit my lip hard to keep from crying when she slid into the driver's seat and slammed the door before turning to give me a long look. With her right eye now swollen shut and the shadow of a bruise rising up on her other cheekbone, she looked scary, but her touch was gentle when she smiled at me.

"We're going to go live in a new place now, okay? On a fun adventure where you'll have lots of new friends."

No, it wasn't okay, but I knew better than to argue when she was in a bad mood.

"Yes, Mommy." An orange glow began to flicker out of the corner of my eye and I turned to see fire beginning to flicker through the living room window of the house. "Mommy, the house is on fire!"

"It's fine," Mommy said while she pulled out of our driveway, the engine of the car humming louder as she drove quickly out of our neighborhood.

"But—"

"I said it's fine!"

My cheek still hurt from her slap so I leaned against the car door, held in place by my seat belt and the comforting weight of her furs. "Yes, Mommy."

"Now," her voice held a falsely cheery note that made me wince, "we're going to play a game. Your name isn't Sarah Michaels anymore, it's Sarah Bishop. Can you remember that? Sarah Bishop."

"Why do we have to change our name again?"

I could feel her anger filling the cramped space of the car and right away wished I hadn't said anything. "You know why."

"Because if we don't the bad men will get us."

"They'll take me away from you, Sarah, and if I'm not there to protect you, terrible things will happen to you and they'll hurt me really bad. I'd have to leave you, all alone, and won't be there to tuck you in at night and give you kisses. You don't want that, do you?"

Tears burned my eyes as I slowly shook my head back and forth. "No, Mommy."

"Good." She let out a low breath as we drove onto the highway. "Good. Things will be different now, Sarah, you'll see. We have *lots* of money now. That means we won't have to move for a long time. We'll get a big house, with maids and a huge backyard to play in. We can get you back into doing pageants and ice skating. You love doing that, right? It's going to be different now, Sarah, you'll see, but only if you can keep our secret. Now, what's your name?"

"Sarah Bishop, and you're my mommy, Billie Bishop."

"Good girl. You keep being Mommy's good girl and we'll be safe."

I wished with all my heart that was true and vowed I would be the perfect little girl so we would never have to run away again.

Chapter 1

2 years ago

Sturgis, South Dakota

Sarah Anderson, aka Sarah Star, World Pole Dancer of the Year and Miss March

I was sweating like a whore in church with my ample boobs almost fully exposed by my black leather halter top, tastefully studded and built for maximum support and minimum coverage. As usual, with this amount of cleavage showing, I had guys having conversations with my tits, which were not interested. It was both annoying and pathetic. Thankfully they did it to all of the girls signing autographs, because we were all dressed like biker hoochies to varying degrees.

I couldn't complain because the outfits I was given for free to wear to the biker rally were amazing. Today I wore a custom-fitted Gautier piece that cost as much as some of the shiny motorcycles these men and women rode. The women who weren't riding on the back of a man's bike, that is. Biker guys seemed to love having a pretty piece of arm candy. They'd strut around proud as peacocks with their woman, or women, on their arms. There were some chicks out there who were partying hard, topless, and sometimes bottomless, but they were always with some scary-looking guys who kept them safe.

Scarlet, a beautiful tattooed raven-haired woman with a wicked sense of humor, was one of the girls from *Playboy's* online division who looked like a pinup girl. Wearing a cute pink and white polka dot dress, she had a big laugh and an even bigger smile. Turning to look at me, she gave the universal symbol for "barf me out", pretending to stick her finger down her throat and making a silent retch. I couldn't help but laugh and nod in agreement.

Leaning closer, she said, "I think I need to take a shower after the way that guy was panting. I think he might have spooged in his pants."

"Ewww," I snorted and the guy whose picture I was signing gave me a weird look, but I ignored him as one of the security guys, who were making sure everyone behaved, moved the line along.

"Have any more hand sanitizer?"

I leaned forward and tapped the dark-eyed security guard standing by my table and glaring at everyone who approached me. "I need a quick break."

He looked over at me, his gaze only lingering on my tits for the count of three before he lifted his gaze to mine. "No problem. Take as long as you need, Ms. Star."

I smiled at him, always wanting to be on good terms with people who were trying to keep me alive. "Thanks."

Scarlet took a long drink from her water and I followed suit. It was hot as shit, dry, and I had my final performance tonight. Hell, it might be my final performance ever. It was a melancholy thought, but I also felt an immense amount of relief. I could lead a normal life now. I'd worked my ass off since I was sixteen, on my own, to make it to where I am. Financially independent with a huge savings account and a bunch of healthy investments. I owned my own home, owned my car, and had fought tooth and nail for everything I had.

"Sarah?"

I grabbed my giant Chanel purse—it was really more like a small duffel bag—and dug through it. "What kind do you like? I have coconut scented, or lemon rosewater—but I wouldn't recommend that one. It smells like an old lady but I got it on sale so I'm loath to waste it."

"I know what you mean. I have a bottle of this hideous, cheap, green nail polish I got for St. Patrick's Day one year and I can't seem to throw it away." Laughing, Scarlet crossed her long legs, the cute skirt of the dress she was wearing lifting to reveal the tops of her thigh-highs. "Gimme the coconut one. I don't mind smelling like suntan oil, it takes me away from all this crap and to Iron Horse's Island."

"Where's that at?"

"Down in the Caribbean."

"Wait, Iron Horse the motorcycle club owns an entire island?"

"Yep." she sighed in mock bliss. "It's so peaceful."

Before I could respond, a group of guys came up, elbowing their way through the crowd to the front of the line. They all wore different vests, but the looks on their rough faces invited no bullshit. Dammit, I was a scary-motherfucker magnet. If there was some psychos around with a taste for blondes, I hit their invisible radar full force. They always found me and always seemed surprised when I didn't roll over and offer them my belly when they growled.

People started to yell at the men as they pushed past, but they ignored them, shuffling closer to my table in a tight group. Before I could yell at them for line jumping, they parted to reveal three very scared-looking girls around my cousin's ages. Five, seven, maybe nine-year-old girls, all with big green eyes and dark red hair. All protected by a group of big men with big green eyes and red hair. I didn't understand the family dynamic but there was no doubt these people shared blood.

More security was closing in on my table, but I raised my hand. "It's cool. They brought some young ladies to visit us. We're good, I promise. These gentlemen aren't going to do anything to upset those girls, right?"

The red-haired biker dudes all lifted their chins and I guessed that was the equivalent of a yes.

Not liking it, security backed up just enough that I could see the clearly uncomfortable girls blushing beneath everyone's stares.

Curious as to what brought them, I smiled when an earnest young man with longish and glorious dark red hair walked up to my table. Security was still nervous, but I felt the need to talk with them and I knew in my gut they meant me no harm.

The crowd behind the men who'd shoved their way to the front was getting pissed and I knew I needed to diffuse the situation before things got out of hand. These young girls were already practically shaking in their sneakers and my protective instincts came roaring to the surface. I hated witnessing adults arguing as a kid, my mother's fights with her fuck of the month were often violent and terrible affairs, so I do my utmost to remain in control around kids. I will never be the person they become scared of.

Ever.

"Hi," I chirped and held out my hand, giving him big "I'm not a threat" doe eyes. "Sarah Star, nice to meet you."

The guy was my age, maybe a little older, but he had an edge about him that made me wary. "My cousins would like to meet you."

"And I'd love to meet them," I said while motioning for the girls to come closer.

As soon as I started talking to them, the little girls opened up and I learned they were big fans of my pole dancing. Their mother was a pole dancer who owned a studio in Chicago and evidently she was a huge fan of mine. Now, it *was* a little weird because I'm here for *Playboy*, but at the same time I could easily see how naive and innocent these girls were. Whoever was watching over them was doing a good job and my heart melted at their excited chatter.

"Marley." I turned to the girls and held up my hand to stop the flow of giggles. "One moment please, ladies."

My personal assistant scampered up, her shoulders hunched as if she didn't want to be noticed. Unfortunately for her, we were in a place full of different kinds of predators so her shyness was drawing their attention like tigers to a mouse. I was very protective of her and treated her gently as I relayed my instructions for getting the girls some souvenirs.

As soon as I had them loaded up, the men with them announced it was time to leave because it was getting dark and they didn't want their kids here once the serious partying started. I one-hundred-and-ten-percent agreed the girls needed to get going. Their male relatives all loved me, and I got a couple earnest marriage proposals before they were dragged off by security while I laughed. That's one thing I learned doing this tour. You have to be able to laugh shit off or you go a little insane. Weird shit happened around me a lot and it was either laugh at how ludicrous my life was or cry until I dehydrated.

"That was really nice of you to do."

I shrugged, talking with a fan and signing his poster before returning my attention to Scarlet. "They were a nice family concerned about their young girls. You would have done the same thing."

"Yeah, but *I* know bikers and know they were good guys. You're a civilian."

"A what?"

"A person who doesn't know the MC lifestyle."

Grinning at her, I said in a low voice, "Oh, I'm going to get a taste of that lifestyle tonight. I plan on finding a party, finding a hot and hung biker, then riding him until he can't walk."

Scarlet posed for a picture, then gave me an incredulous look. "Woman, have you ever partied with bikers before?"

"Not really. *Playboy* has me under a tight contract until my final show tonight so I've been stuck on the bus, but I figure there's a first time for everything. Besides, this is Sturgis, it would be a sin to spend my last night here in my bunk bed by myself."

Scarlet's lips pursed and she glanced over her shoulder at one of the guys guarding us. "Unless you want to be passed around by the men, or married to one on sight, I suggest you bypass the bikers. Go for one of your hot *Playboy* security dudes."

"No, they're cute, I don't want them to get fired. And what do you mean, passed around or married?"

Our voices were super soft whispers at this point, both of us cupping our mouths. "Honey, I was with Thorn for a week before he knew he was ready to put his patch on my back and made me his old lady."

"Old lady…" I combed through the biker lingo I'd learned over these last few days. "That's like biker marriage, right?"

"Right, but once you're his old lady, that's it. You are bound by chains stronger than you can imagine for the rest of your life. Even if you break up, in the biker world you'll always belong to him."

"That is bullshit."

"Yep, but that's the way of my world. If you want to live in it you have to accept the local customs, and trust me when I say the payoff's worth it."

Scarlet paused to talk to the person she was signing for and I did the same for the man at my table. Older guy, nice clean white hair, and wearing faded jeans and a cowboy hat. We shot the shit for a minute, took a couple pictures, then I dragged Scarlet back into our conversations.

I could never endure belonging to a man like that, the very thought made my pulse race. "I can't imagine not wanting to cut off some guy's dick if he tried that shit with me."

She smirked. "Thought the same, until Thorn came into my life and healed me, then addicted me to his cock."

"Pardon?"

"Long time ago, and not a conversation for here, but he saved my life and I owe him." For a second, sadness flashed through her gaze, but she buried it behind a glittering smile as she greeted another fan.

We worked for the next hour or so without a chance to talk again. The bikers had been right, as darkness started to move across the gorgeous countryside, the mood at the signing was getting rowdy. Just as I was starting to wonder when they were going to shut down, Marley appeared at my elbow.

With her hair pulled back and her glasses on, she looked terribly young and sweet, but I let her live under the illusion it made her look more professional. Her douchebag baby daddy, who was thankfully in jail for life, had systematically tore her down and isolated her from all sources of support. He'd done a number on her, but I'd taken her under my wing and, more importantly, my parents had taken Marley and her little baby boy under theirs. One day after I'd brought Marley home to stay with them while she recovered, her boyfriend was under arrest for dealing heroine in a school zone. Even though he swore he was set up, and he totally was, he got life because he had a list of priors a mile long.

I quickly stood and waved, blowing kisses before I yelled, "See y'all at the main stage in a couple hours!"

The crowd went crazy and I waved again, my mind switching gears from PR to what I considered my real job. Entertaining. The roar of the crowd gave me an adrenaline high like no other and I knew this audience would be insane.

I couldn't wait.

Three hours later, exhilaration mixed with a tiny bit of stage fright zinged through my blood in a heady strike, like getting ready to snowboard down the side of a steep mountain. With the bitingly cold air frosting your every breath, you know the ride is going to be epic, but man that first step is a doozy.

Adrenaline coursed through me, giving me a high as addictive as any drug I'd ever done, making me want to move. The pulsing beat rattled my bones while I stood next to one of the giant speakers that flanked the stage and I continued to stretch out. Even with my earbuds in the sound was deafening, but it had to be that loud to reach the cheering horde of people watching the stage with drunken, yet rapt attention as the girls strutted their stuff.

A group of women dressed in biker-babe meets slutty-schoolgirl outfits did their dance routine with a crisp perfection that made me proud. They were my opening act and I'd brought them to Sturgis with me from Vegas. Some I'd stripped with, some I'd pole danced with, while others were Vegas showgirls. They all knew how to work the audience and while I was thankful for the energy they raised, I couldn't help a hint of apprehension moving through me.

Ironic that the last crowd I'd perform for like this was also my biggest. And this wasn't a crowd full of tourists enjoying the Vegas nightlife, who had come to watch my act in a show at a luxurious casino theater. No, this was a seething throng of thousands, maybe tens of thousands, of bikers getting their party on with a vengeance. Even the backstage was rife with people whooping it up, but I had a group of scary-as-hell bikers acting as my bodyguards and they'd secured me my own large bubble of space no one violated.

By now my nipples had hardened to bullets behind my black leather-looking sports bra, but not with arousal. Nervous energy zipped through my body, making my skin tingle as goose bumps rose up along my arms. The tight top held my big chest in place while I did my routine, and looked sexy as hell with the shiny studs lining the collar that went around my throat.
Yeah, lots of women gave me shit about the size of my breasts, snide comments about fake tits and being a slut and all of that, but fuck 'em if they thought they had the right to judge me because of how I looked.

Even before I got implants, I had good-sized boobs that had drawn attention, but when I'd dedicated myself to winning the World Pole Dancer of the Year title, I'd gone for it hardcore. By hardcore, I mean working out with the same dedication I showed during my pageant and figure-skating days which had toned me to the point I had very little excess body fat and a lot more muscle. That dedication to getting in shape had deflated my boobs, giving me saggy breasts at almost eighteen, and it looked really weird when I spun fast on the pole. I had to get them lifted and got double D-cup implants that were slightly larger, and a hell of a lot perkier, than my real breasts.

I'd paid twenty-two thousand for them, a crazy amount, but they'd earned me hundreds of thousands of dollars in return and I loved them.

The song blasting through the night began to wind down and I shook out my arms and rolled my neck, trying to burn off my nerves. I swear I could feel the roar of the crowd wash over me as the women on the stage bowed, then waved and blew kisses as they made their way to the backstage area. The hosts of the event went out on stage and talked to the crowd about some charity run they were doing tomorrow while the last of the girls strutted off. When they passed me they all smiled and wished me luck. Kaitlin, my fellow showgirl from Vegas who specialized in the trapeze, bounced up to me and gave me a brief hug then pulled back.

I easily read her lips as she said, "You look amazing! Oh my God, you're going to have guys creaming their jeans. Go get 'em, tiger!"

I couldn't help but laugh and hug her tight. She was cute as a button with her big brown eyes and pigtails that swung as she waved and headed for the trailers. A Midwestern girl who'd moved out to Vegas with a boyfriend who'd tried to pimp her, Kaitlin had been as out of place at the strip club we'd both worked briefly at as could be. While I'd grown up with an evil bitch of a mother and could handle the cattiness of the strip club, she'd been painfully naive. In a way she'd reminded me of my super shy and sheltered twin sister, Swan, and I'd made sure everyone knew if they fucked with Kaitlin, they'd have me to answer to. No one had been there to protect my innocence and tender heart, and I'd be damned if I let someone as genuinely nice as Kaitlin get hurt.

On the stage, the announcer for the evening was pumping up the crowd for me while the bouncers made sure everyone backstage kept their distance so I could focus and get in my zone.

What I was about to do was dangerous, and would require my intense concentration, but I excelled under pressure out of both necessity and pride.

Every inch of my skin erupted in goose bumps as I heard my stage name, Sarah Star, blast through the wild night.

Showtime.

The first strains of "Nothing Else Matters" by Metallica came through the speakers, clean and perfect, bringing a roaring cheer from the crowd. Just like I thought, bikers loved Metallica. I smiled as I closed my eyes and strode onto the stage, mapping the steps out in my mind as I kept my head down, the strobing blue stage lights making everything around me seem super surreal. While I stroked the cool metal of the specially made two-story pole with my fingertips, I turned to the crowd and struck a pose any pinup would be proud of, arching my back before the first crash of symbols hit, changing the tempo of the song. The strobing light stopped and a warm overhead beam illuminated me fully as I nailed them with my trademark pouty smile. I swiftly grabbed the pole above my head and swung myself up, climbing higher as my muscles began to warm.

The song throbbed through my blood, taking me away from my messed-up life, giving me something beautiful to lose myself in. An almost unthinking zone in my mind where my body ruled. Every inch of my skin tingled as I climbed all the way to the top, then stretched out so my body hovered perpendicular to the pole, held solely in place by the strength of my arms. I can bench press more than my own bodyweight and I needed every ounce of that strength to get through the routine ahead.

A soft, melodic part of the song eased the tempo and I exhaled as I drifted down the pole, gracefully moving through the air with one arm and leg extended as I arched my back, my muscles screaming at the strain put on them while I defied gravity.

The melody picked up again and I couldn't help but smile as I ascended the pole in an exaggerated crawl, the noise of the crowd increasing the higher I got. Having perfected my routine with the help of professional choreographers, I slinked up the pole then paused to look over my shoulder at the seething mass of people two stories below me, and winked. Seducing the crowd of wild men through my movements was fun, and I smiled when I got to the very top of the pole. Taking a moment, I tried to see the mass of people as best I could through the lights, before blowing them a kiss.

I paused for dramatic effect, and to center myself, before I threw my lower body off the pole, holding on to it as I whipped my legs around for momentum and begin to rotate, faster and faster, now curling my body in as well. The g-force was crazy as I continued to spin, my abs aching from the strain of slowing my descent while speeding up my spin. My mind, thankfully, remained clear as my heart beat strong and sure. One of the things I'd studied during my figure skating days was physics. Knowing how to work *with* gravity instead of against it was important in learning the different jumps. And, because I was a competitive figure skater, my body had been trained to endure the spinning like no normal person ever could. That particular skill was what had won me World Pole Dancer of the Year, the ability to spin, and spin, and spin without passing out.

With my hair stinging my face, I switched so now I was now fully wrapped around the pole, going fast enough that it was a struggle to draw a breath, drowning in the thrill of speed. Nothing mattered but the rush of the wind, the gentle strains of the guitar, the sensual pleasure of my body flowing to the music. Throwing my head back as I finally slowed, I undulated against the pole like it was my lover, giving the crowd of rowdy men the kind of show I knew they liked. With each roll of my hips, I showed them how good it would be to fuck me.

What can I say, I own my sexuality and I'm not ashamed to flaunt it.

Sure enough, they went wild and I gracefully slid my way down the pole, my muscles burning from the stress of suspending myself for so long. Once I reached the bottom I flexed my bare feet, trying to ease the strain on my weak knee, while turning and giving the audience a good shot of my butt, barely covered by my boy shorts, and pop my booty out then give it a little shake. Or a big shake—I have a lot of booty. The approval of the mass of people hidden by the lights fills the empty space inside of me and I stand up with my blood rushing to my head.

The next song in my set is "Comfortably Numb" by Pink Floyd, and as it begins, I close my eyes, caught up in the lyrics. In many ways this song both heals and torments me, reminding me of the one and only time I've ever done heroine, when I was sixteen. I didn't even know what it was, thought I was just doing another line of coke with my mom while we were at some high rollers party at a casino in Reno. Instead I'd spent the next four hours sitting on a couch in blissful numbness while the world seemed to move at hyperspeed around me.

Morrie, my thirty-year-old lover, had been super pissed my mom had given me that shit, but she'd claimed she didn't know and he'd made me promise never to do it again. Considering I thought I was deeply in love with him at the time, I'd promised and had never touched heroin again. Too bad no one warned me away from *him*, because he was far more addictive and dangerous than any drug.

My legs burned and it removed me from the poisonous hold of my memories, reminding me that at this moment, I was alive and it felt amazing.

The steady tempo in the song guides my movements, drawing me further into the moment, taking me away from my worries as surely as any drug ever had. Holding on to the pole with my good leg, I arched back and moved my arms with the beat, my stomach muscles aching as I began to whip my head back and forth, letting the song guide me. When I reached the midpoint of the pole I began to spin again, not fast, but slow and graceful as a butterfly. The song began to wind down and I slowly returned to reality, the pain of my body exerting itself to the point of collapse, clearing the music from my mind as I finally reached the hard wood of the stage.

My breath is burned my lungs, but I can't help but smile as the crowd's adoration washes over me, filling me with a sense of belonging, of being loved. False though it may be, I drink it in and try to fill the hollow emptiness inside of me that never really goes away, the space that should have been filled with my mother's love.

With trembling legs, I strode to the center of the stage and smiled, giving the crowd a practiced, perfect wave I'd learned from hours of rehearsal with my pageant coach back when my mom had been convinced she could make me the next Miss America.

Bet the bitch never thought I'd be using those skills to win over a crowd of bikers.

The lights blind me to how many people were out there, but the roaring wave of their cheers washes over me, making the hair on my arms stand on end. This was the last time I'd be on a stage like this, the last night for me to be wild, before I finally got to start the next phase of my life as a responsible adult. I was going to have a new life somewhere they'd never heard of Billie Waylan—or whatever the hell she was calling herself now—and where I could begin to live a normal, respectable life along with a normal, respectable man.

That meant this was my final night of partying with abandon before I needed to buckle down and get serious. What better place to find a fantastic, dirty, awesome one-night stand than a biker rally?

With this in mind, I left the stage with the roar of the crowd moving over me like a caress. Pulling out my earplugs once we were far enough away from the speakers, I tried to graciously nod and smile at the people backstage, reminding myself I'm lucky to be here and it won't kill me to take a second to make someone happy by saying a word or two.

As soon as I reach out, my assistant, Marley, is there with a big, fluffy white robe and a melancholy smile. We'd had a lot of fun during the last few months of my publicity tour for both *Playboy* and as a pole dancing champ. Without her organizational skills, I'd be fucked six ways to Sunday trying to keep track of everything. I'm not good at remembering things, my mind is too overactive, like a squirrel on those nasty orange candy Circus Peanuts, and I needed someone to help me stay focused. Thankfully, Marley was everything I'm not—mellow, quiet, and boasting a freakish ability to multitask. She lived in my guest house back in Las Vegas with her little boy and I can attest that the woman is so organized her soda is arranged alphabetically in her fridge.

Wiggling her eyebrows, Marley said, "Ready to party it up?"

Marley knows of my plans to have a wild night and while I know she'll be staying in her hotel room, by herself, she doesn't judge me for my somewhat vast sexual appetites. Sex was something I craved, plain and simple. I know that, my therapist knows that, and I'm okay with it. I yearn for the connection I get from the act, even if it's false, which has led to more than a few heartbreaks. But that wasn't going to happen anymore. Tomorrow I'm no longer pining after bad boys, only mature men who have good heads on their shoulders and were responsible. Someone who had the patience to teach me how to trust, someone I can rely on.

With Marley in tow and two big biker bodyguards in front of me and one behind, I was led through the backstage party. It was packed and I smiled and waved while people yelled congratulations to me on my performance. We made it to where my bus sat in the section of the festival grounds where the VIP entertainers have their RVs and big luxury buses, and I finally relaxed a little bit. The noise level is only slightly less than an airplane taking off, and when I reach the door of my bus, one of the guys escorting us, a hot-in-a-mean-way Latino lover, stopped me. The back of his patched-up vest held the symbol for the Iron Horse MC, an almost tribal-looking horse head with a mane like flames.

Old me, the person my mother tried to make me in to, would have snapped at him to move his fucking ass, but new me had more patience. Or at least I tried to have more patience. Plus this was the MC Scarlet was a part of so I was curious about them, but they were still standing between me and my shower. I wiped my face with the edge of my robe, the sweaty makeup leaving behind a sparkly tan stain. Yuck. Thank God for *Playboy's* kick-ass tour bus that was crazy luxurious with for-real hot water showers—two of them. It sure beat the hell out of trying to clean up with just a sink and a washcloth.

Out of the corner of my eye, I noticed more men materializing around us beneath the portable sodium lights that illuminated this area of the enormous campgrounds, all watching me with expressions ranging from impassive to downright flirty. "What's up?"

The guy blocking my way flashed me a panty-dropping smile, but he was one of those rare hot guys I didn't have any chemistry with. If I was going to spend my last night letting my freak flag fly, it wasn't going to be with this dark-eyed hottie. Arching my brow, I let him know with my less-than-impressed look that his smile wasn't going to make me all starry-eyed.

One of the guys behind him snickered, but the massive Hispanic man ignored him. "Marley was sayin' you want to go out into that mess and party tonight."

"Oh she did, did she?"

I looked over at Marley, surprised she was getting chatty with the bikers. Her flush was highly visible beneath the bright lights and she sucked her lips in. When I narrowed my eyes at her, she blushed harder and kept sneaking glances at one of the bikers behind me. I couldn't tell which one, just that someone had her all flustered. It would have been cute, if Marley hadn't been getting all sparkly eyed over a biker. Unlike me, my assistant didn't have much experience with men and what little she did was horrific. I worried about her getting hurt and gave her a warning look.

Misreading my silent glare, the big Hispanic guy took a step closer to me, his rough hands raised in a soothing manner. "Hey now, don't get mad, she was just trying to coordinate with us so you always have someone with you to watch your back. Trust me, you lookin' like you do is gonna be like throwing a juicy steak to a pack of starving dogs if you head out there on your own. The security they have for you is decent, but they're also busy dealing with a lot of other shit and won't be able to send more than a guy or two with you. That won't be enough to keep you safe. Come party with us and you got 200 brothers makin' sure no one touches you without your permission."

I considered his words, taking another look around me and wrinkling my nose at the surging chaos just beyond the flimsy barriers that sectioned off where the entertainers were staying from the rest of the grounds. That was a big, big crowd and it was a mess. Suddenly I wasn't so sure following through with my plan to find the hottest piece of ass I could was the best of ideas. Yeah, I've been to plenty of wild parties before, but the sheer size of the crowd had little prickles of apprehension skating up my spine. I mentally added my knife to my potential outfit for the night.

Girls gotta be prepared in this world for anything that comes her way.

If my dad was here right now, he'd be tossing my duct-taped ass into the back of his truck and getting me the hell out of here before I could blink.

The doors to the bus opened and the woman who'd sat next to me during the signing earlier, Scarlet, leapt out and into the arms of one of the big guys standing near the entrance with a happy squeal. He had long deep brown hair, a black t-shirt under his vest, and a killer smile with a gold tooth. Not Hollywood handsome, but for sure good looking in his own unique way. Scarlet's long dark hair streamed out behind her like a banner as he spun her around and kissed her.

When they stopped locking lips, he turned and I noticed the patch that said "Thorn" on his chest. Those patches were kinda handy. It was like the badass version of those "Hello My Name Is" stickers they liked to put out at conventions and business functions.

The patch on the back showed the tribal-style horse head with its flaming mane, with the words "Iron Horse MC" on the top part and Austin, Texas, on the bottom.

Scarlet smiled when she spotted me standing next to my escort with a wide-eyed Marley at my side. "Hey, Sarah! I heard you kicked ass out there!"

"She sure did," a sexy Asian guy wearing an Iron Horse MC vest with "Dragon" on the patch said in a suggestive tone.

I met his gaze, waiting for the fireworks that would let me know he was the one, but while there were tiny sparks, it was nothing worth pursuing. "Thanks."

Scarlet laughed while Thorn ran his hands all over her as she tried to smack him away. "Wanna come party with us tonight? I swear *no one* is going to fuck with you while you're with the Iron Horse MC."

So far the guys I'd met had been good looking and nice, so I decided to take Scarlet up on her offer rather than risk being mobbed the second I stepped out of the sectioned-off and well-guarded entertainers' area.

Two hours later, I passed the joint I'd just hit back to Thorn, squinting through the smoke at him. "Are you doubting my ability to kick your ass?"

The men in the circle with us beyond one of the bonfires laughed and I gave them a good glare before turning my attention back to Thorn. I wasn't sure how we'd gotten into a conversation about hand-to-hand combat, but he was irritating me. Smoke and a bunch of the guys in the Iron Horse MC were former military and it was interesting to hear about the different training they'd received in the various branches they'd served in. We were debating the merits of different martial arts styles and Smoke, the hot Latino guy who had been my escort earlier, kept on throwing in comments I knew were supposed to irritate me.

For whatever reason, he seemed to find it hilarious to make me bitchy. While there was no sexual tension between us, and I liked his smartass sense of humor, he pissed me off with his openly misogynistic comments. I whirled around and pointed my finger at him while he shook his head at me and grinned.

Before I could fuss at him, he drawled, "You ain't kickin' no one's ass in that sorry excuse for a skirt."

Lifting my chin, I widened my stance, not letting any of these guys think for one second I was ashamed of dressing in what even I had to admit was a borderline super-duper slutty getup. I blame my current state of dress on Scarlet. She put me in this tight, awesome red sparkly tank top that did amazing things to my breasts, and I'd paired it with a flouncy black leather mini-skirt that played peek-a-boo with my lower ass cheeks. Because it was so dark out beyond the portable lights and bonfires, you couldn't really see much in the flickering lights anyway. Out of difference to not wanting to break my ankle tonight, I wore a pair of thigh-high combat boots that made my legs look kick ass.

Not liking his condescending smirk as he pointedly stared at my super-exposed cleavage, I narrowed my eyes at Smoke. "I'll kick your ass too, buddy. Just try me."

Vance, an older guy I wasn't very fond of, snorted. "Woman, you better mind your place if you don't want a man to shut that smart mouth of yours."

If I'd been a cat, my tail would have just stuck up straight in the air and bristled.

Before I could show that asshole that I could get him in a submission hold, a deep man's voice spoke up loudly from behind me. "Is that any way to talk to a lady?"

Vance ran his tattooed hand over his short dark hair and looked over my shoulder with a blank expression I found chilling. "No harm meant. Just lettin' her know threatenin' a man like Smoke with kickin' his ass ain't a good idea."

"Well…" That deep, sexy male voice came from much closer now and every single inch of my skin sang with the heavy sparks of raw sexual attraction. I really hoped he wasn't hideous. Or married. "That'll never be an issue 'cause Iron Horse don't operate that way."

"Right," Vance said in that crazy empty voice again and I shivered.

Smoke laughed, then said as he walked away, "Careful, Prez, she's a handful."

I wanted to ask Smoke what he was talking about, but strong, warm, rough, *big* hands gently held my shoulders and I sucked in a deep breath, thrown by my insanely intense reaction to this mystery man.

My world narrowed as I spun around and looked up into the rugged face of the man whose voice made my pussy tingle with interest. I took my time examining him while my hormones purred. Letting myself properly drink him in, I stared at his beat-up leather vest covered with a bunch of patches, then my gaze slowly traveled over his broad chest covered in a clean white t-shirt, past the bronzed skin of his neck, and up to his dark-blond bearded face. The white fabric of the shirt set off the deep tan of his skin and I couldn't help but notice how lean and muscled he was.

And, if the bulge in his jeans wasn't lying, he liked me and was packing some *serious* dick.

I was in trouble.

A thrill raced through me and settled right in my rapidly swelling sex. Shit, I was getting turned on so fast it hurt. Older than me, and grown-man sexy with a visible self-confidence that made my knees weak. My own personal kryptonite. It certainly didn't help that I was high as fuck at the moment, and enjoying the courage it gave me to tempt this commanding man.

What can I say, I have daddy issues. Show me a man in a position of authority, more than a few years older than me, and my hormones went into overdrive. I know part of it has to do with the fact that my first real boyfriend was a lot older than me. His name was Morrie and he was way sexier than his name.

I'd fallen deeply in love for the first time and at sixteen, I was putty in his hands. I think in many ways he shaped me sexually. And probably emotionally. Blah, I did not want to think about him right now. Being with him had been the dysfunctional cherry on top of the fucked-up, crazy sauce sundae that was my life. I'd left my mother's house and moved in with him, living a spoiled life filled with shopping, champagne, and lots of high-quality cocaine my mother was only too happy to snort up with me.

The old familiar urge to go find some coke pushed at the mental box I kept it locked up in, but not hard. After a terrible night, during which Morrie had discovered how old I really was (my mom had lied and provided me with ID that said I was twenty-one), I'd almost OD'd, sure my life was going to be shit without him there to guide me, protect me, and love me like I'd never been loved. For the first time in my life I'd felt safe, even if I totally wasn't, and it had all been ripped away from me.

Led Zeppelin started playing from a big set of speakers and I was drawn into the haunting melody as the opening of "Stairway to Heaven" began to roll through the hot summer evening. The weed must have been stronger than I thought because I had no idea how long I'd been standing there, staring at the handsome face half covered by a thick blond beard and lost in my own thoughts. Any normal human being would have said hello by now. The only solace I had to my unusual inability to speak was that the man was as quite as I was, despite how closely we stood together.

He was naturally blond like me, so his thick hair glinted in the light of the fire, casting shadows over a roughly hewn face. In a way he reminded me of the movie star Daniel Craig, but with a beard. His lips were thin, firm, and I just knew he would be a man who took control of a kiss. That invisible aura of authority that I find so sexy? He had it in spades. I was almost afraid to meet his gaze, afraid of the consequences of what would happen if I did. This was one of those times when I could literally feel the course of my life turning, like Fate was adding a twist in her loom that would take me in a whole new direction.

Of course, I could just be high, but when I finally stared up into his dark gaze in the flickering light of a roaring bonfire, I was tempted to put my hand to my chest to see if it was indeed vibrating with the hard thump of my heart as a visceral shock rolled through me.

While I stared at him, his lip crooked up in the corner. "Well, aren't you a sight for sore eyes. What's your name, beautiful?"

Blinking at him, I tried to formulate a thought, dimly aware that Scarlet was calling my name.

I ignored her. Entranced by the tightly muscled man now looming over me, I breathed out, "Sarah."

"Sarah," he purred. "Pretty name for a pretty girl. You come up here with anyone?"

Well, I'd come up with a couple busloads of people, but he didn't seem to recognize me and I liked that. "Nope. Just some girlfriends."

"Not with any club?"

"Nope."

The smile that curved his lips was positively wicked and my pussy tingled hard enough for me to press my legs together.

Oh no, he had demon dick.

That's what I called men who could make me wet, even if it was against my will, with merely a smile. I had a boss like that once. He was a complete and utter asshole, but that didn't stop my body from wanting him. Fortunately, my ex-boss didn't have a very powerful demon dick, but the blond man eye-fucking me sure did. I'd bet my last penny he had a big one and knew how to use it.

Smoke strolled up to us, a woman on either arm and a shit-eating grin stretching his handsome face. "Hey, Beach."

"Beach? That's your name?" I asked, snapped out of my trance by the decidedly unfriendly look the blonde chick on the left was giving me and the odd nature of the delicious blond man's name.

That teasing smile curled the edge of his lip again and he caught my chin then turned my face to his, away from the glare of the tall blonde before dropping his hand and leaving tingles behind. God, how could his eyes seem so warm in the meager light. "Yep, my name's Beach. You wanna go somewhere and talk, *hermosa chica?*"

"What?"

I was back to feeling high as a kite, staring into his dark gaze. He called me a beautiful girl in Spanish. I liked that. A lot. I think his eyes are blue, but if they are, it's a color so dark they almost looked black. Sensual bedroom eyes lined with experience that had my nipples joining my pussy in getting tight and hot. If he kept looking at me with all that sexual tension pouring off of him, I wouldn't be held responsible for jumping him.

"You wanna go somewhere?" he repeated in a low voice. "Just to talk for a little bit, away from all this bullshit."

While I wanted to follow him wherever he wanted to take me, I couldn't make it that easy for him. "Is the party too much for you, old man?"

Instead of getting offended, he full-out grinned and I swear my heart skipped a beat. "Feisty. I like that in a woman. Come with me, Ms. Sarah. I promise you nothing will harm you while you're in my care. You can trust me."

"Trust you?" I meant for my words to come out in a scoffing manner, but instead they were a light whisper. I wasn't even sure he heard over the now wailing electric guitar perfectly complimenting the pounding drums of the music throbbing around us.

He rubbed his thumb against my jaw and I had to resist the urge to step closer to him and run my nipples over his chest to relieve the resulting sting that came from them being unbearably hard. "Yeah, baby girl, trust me. Come with me, I juust want to talk with you."

"I don't think that's a good idea."

As he smiled, the sun lines around his eyes deepened. "Sweetheart, I think it's the best damn idea I've ever had."

Chapter 2

AUSTIN TX

Carlos "Beach" Rodriguez

The gorgeous creature before me swayed closer despite her weak protests, and the scent she wore tore through me. Flowers and peaches, fresh, sticky-sweet and clean. The light from a nearby barrel fire cast flickering shadows over her face, making her appear like an innocent young girl one moment, a knowing temptress the next. She was a total knock-out, the kind of woman men, gay or straight, would stop to look at. Long, pale champagne-blonde hair, light blue eyes, and I was pretty sure she had freckles.

So damn cute.

I needed something to refresh my soul after all the shit I'd had to do the last few months. Not only did I have to deal with business back in Austin, I'd also been spending a lot of time up in Denver with the Iron Horse MC chapter outside'a the city. They were the newest chapter of Iron Horse MC nationally and I was a personal friend of the new President, Khan. Crazy fucker, but a good man and a solid leader. Once he got his feet under him, he'd have no problem dealing with club issues on his own, but I don't think he realized how far he'd have to go to protect his position in the MC.

Thankfully, Khan practices the same flavor of practical violence I do. We don't seek the shit out, but if you want to fuck with us, you'd better kiss your loved ones goodbye now because we will come for you and we will find you. Always.

In the second it had taken for these thoughts to flicker through my head, the woman's attitude had changed, a bit of sass and fire coming through in the way she lifted her chin at me. Either she didn't know who I was, or she was one ballsy bitch trying to stare me down.

I liked it—a lot.

To make sure I knew where I stood with her, I said, "Name's Carlos Rodriquez, but everyone calls me Beach. I'm the National President of the Iron Horse MC."

When she burst out laughing I didn't know what to make of her, and a curiosity I hadn't felt in ages flared deep in my gut.

"Well lah-di-dah," she said in a teasing voice as she rolled her eyes, clearly unimpressed.

In that instant I knew she was trouble, big trouble, but I also knew she was gonna be mine.

She had no idea who she was talking to, or the fact that she was unknowingly insulting me. If I was a different kinda man, I might throw some attitude at her for not respecting my position, but that wasn't how I operated with females. If a woman had fire, all the better. I liked my women to have some attitude, they couldn't survive in my world if they didn't. 'Sides, my dick liked that naughty gleam in her wide eyes, the way her full lips curved into an easy smile while she openly studied me. While we stared at each other, I had the weirdest feeling of anticipation, something I hadn't felt in a long time when it came to a woman. Shit, with as busy as my life was, I hadn't had time for a real relationship in years, just an easy variety of pussy whenever I wanted it.

I studied her closer and figured she was in her early twenties, but something about the way she held herself made her seem older. Like she'd seen and done some heavy shit. If I was any kinda decent, I'd walk away from the temptation of this sweet young thing, but that was already impossible. She was my every wet dream come to life, and if her sass was any indication, she had a quick mind. Don't care what anyone says, fuckin' a stupid woman sucks 'cause eventually you're gonna have to talk to her, and if she doesn't have a brain in her pretty head it's a short conversation.

Her gaze flickered down to the name patch on my worn leather vest, then back up to me, eyes a blue so light they seemed mercurial in the light of the fire and scattered lanterns.

"Why do they call you Beach?"

Unable to help myself, I gently grasped her chin in my hand, running my wind-roughened fingers along the delicate slope of her jaw. Jesus, her skin was so soft I got off on just touchin' her face. Even as distracted as I was by the unusually strong attraction between us, I decided to shelve that question for later. No way in fuck was I tellin' her the origin of my name involved my favorite way to kill people, so a little diversion was necessary. Time to switch her thoughts to other, more pleasant things.

"Like it when you say my name. Gonna like it even more when you scream it while I take care of your no doubt soft and sweet little cunt."

She might have blushed a little, but her gaze was all fiery challenge as she said, "Only if I get to return the favor."

"Baby, it ain't gonna be no hardship to watch you wrap those pretty lips around my cock, that's for damn sure."

The way her eyes locked with mine, her breathing hitched, and how she leaned into me told me one thing for sure—she wanted to fuck me. I could read it in every line of her smoothly muscled body, and my dick was more than ready to explore her no doubt fantastic cunt. I had no idea who she was, if she was one of the other clubs' sweet butts or even someone's old lady or wife. To be honest, I didn't give a fuck. She was gonna be mine soon, every delicious inch of her. Those legs of hers went on forever and they led right up to a tight but big ass that taunted me to spank it like her panties asked.

And those freckles killed me, a light dusting over her cheekbones and nose, almost totally covered with makeup, with more on her shoulders. Women do the weirdest shit, trying to hide parts of themselves from the world that they deemed flawed. Like those sweet freckles that made her seem younger than she was. At least physically. She had old eyes, the kind of weight to her gaze you can only get from experiencing some sorrow and heartache. It bugged me to see that darkness deep in her gaze, to sense a dangerous vibe coming from her that was at total odds with her California-sun-bleached-blonde, hot-girl-next-door look.

Christ, the sexual chemistry between us was intense. I'd never felt anything like it, and I found myself dangerously distracted. Some motherfucker could pull a gun on me at this moment and I still wouldn't be able to tear my eyes from all her glowing, tanned skin. She had these sexy thigh-high combat boots on that filled my mind with images of having those boots wrapped around my hips. I could all too easily imagine sliding myself between those smoothly muscled thighs of hers, and I wondered if her pussy was pink or dusky. Tart or sweet.

From her mile-long legs encased in those boots, to her tiny skirt and incredible tits, she was the essence of sex. The things I'm going to do to this girl… My cock got uncomfortably hard and punched at my fly. She studied me back with open interest, and I liked how bold she was with me. A confident woman was a sexy woman, and I wasn't the only one who noticed. People walking by stared at her, and the macho side of my personality loved knowing they wished they had the privilege of having all that beauty to themselves. Too bad I got her first.

Movement came from my left and I turned, my hand straying to my side where my gun was holstered before I realized it was just Smoke with two sweet butts on his arms. While Smoke may be one of my best friends, he was also a ladies' man. He loved the women and they loved him. I watched him close, waiting for him to hit on Sarah, but he merely grinned at her, and I didn't like it one fuckin' bit when she smiled back. Liked it even less when he blew her a kiss and she laughed, a wild and free sound that tugged at something deep in my gut. The only thing that kept me from pounding on my Master at Arms was the fact that there was no heat in either of their smiles, just a friendly vibe that calmed me down enough to get ahold of my territorial anger.

What the fuck was wrong with me? I never lost my shit over a bitch.

"Hi, Beach," the blonde, Tila, said with an obvious purr while hanging off Smoke's arm. My Master at Arms was now busy mouth-fucking the topless brunette next to him while Sarah made a soft gagging sound at the sight. "I've missed riding your *big* dick. Let's party."

I'm used to sweet butts having no qualms about poaching men from each other, and I normally didn't give a fuck about their drama, but I did *not* like the way she was glaring at Sarah one bit as she said this, or her disrespect. And Sarah was no sweet butt, I was sure of it.

When I glanced over at Sarah to measure her reaction, I found her glaring back at the other woman, giving Tila a murderous look I don't think the drunk bitch even noticed. If she'd been sober, or it had been daylight, she would'a probably realized Sarah was the kind of woman you didn't want to fuck with.

Despite the savage nature of Sarah's rather impressive glare, I found myself giving Tila a hard look of my own that clearly told her to fuck off. If the bitch was smart, she'd pay attention to the message I was sending her 'cause no one fucks with me, and there was no way I was letting this used-up piece of ass cock-block me.

"Baby," I murmured to Sarah and was gratified to see her easily dismiss Tila then turn her mesmerizing gaze back to mine.

The sweet girl staring up at me like she wants to eat me alive was a quality woman, the absolute top of the line. Underneath all that smooth skin she had a strong, athletic frame despite her large breasts, and I really wanted her lean thighs wrapped around me while I slammed my cock into her. Bet her pussy would suck me deep, hold me tight.

Shit, I needed to shut those thoughts down before I snatched her up and threw her over my shoulder.

Ignoring Tila, I stroked the back of my fingers down Sarah's neck, noticing the way goose bumps followed my touch. I needed to get her away from all this bullshit in order to give her the kind of attention and privacy she deserved. I'd soon have her screaming my name and that wasn't for anyone's ears but my own. Normally I didn't give a fuck who watched me, but I'll be damned if the idea of anyone seeing her take my dick didn't make me murderous.

Continuing to stroke her, I wrapped my hand around the back of her delicate neck and pulled her unresisting body closer to mine. "Let's get out of here."

Her full mouth parted and I stifled a groan when she licked her lower lip.

"I'm still not sure that's a good idea, Mr. Beach." There was a teasing tone to her voice when she said that, but I liked the way her hips shifted as she rubbed her thighs together. "For all I know, you could be some psycho who wants to take me out into the desert and make a sculpture out of my bones."

A surprised laugh escaped me and I grinned down at her. She was kind of weird, but I liked that too. Been a while since I had a bitch who didn't fall on my dick on command, and I found myself enjoying talking with her. "Fine, we'll do the get-to-know-you bullshit. Where you from?"

Sarah smiled at me, her full lips parting to reveal a million-dollar smile. "Las Vegas."

"Ahhh, Sin City."

"Yep," she took a small step closer, a flirtatious smile curving her lips. "What about you? Where do you hang your hat?"

"I'm not too far away from you out in Austin." I noticed her gaze scanning my chest again, reading my patches. I'd bet my left nut she had no idea what most of them meant.

She perked up and the light in her eyes drew me. "Austin, huh? I have a sister in Houston. I've driven through Austin a couple times. Neat city, lots of energy and culture."

"Small fuckin' world."

She gave me a bemused smile. "Yeah, it is."

Without thinking, I grabbed her hand and tugged her over to one of the benches set up around the perimeter of the fire. Her fingers were slender, the back of her hand soft, but her palm was rougher than most women's and I wondered how she'd gotten those callouses. Another throb of want tightened my balls as she lightly stroked my hand with her thumb. As soon as they saw us coming, the people who were sitting on the bench cleared out.

I straddled it then sat down, surprised when Sarah did the same so our knees were almost touching. I took a quick look down to make sure she wasn't flashing the crowd, that damned greedy streak rearing its head again, and my dick appreciated the sexy black panties she wore that almost looked like tiny shorts. Her skin glowed with good health and I loved drinking her in.

She was the kind of woman a man could look at every day and be happy. No matter how hard and ugly things got, if I had beauty like this waiting at home for me, I'd be happy. Shit, just looking at her brought me the kind of pleasure that sent a surge of energy through me. A cool beauty for sure, with her icy blue eyes and white blonde hair. Like staring at the stars out in the desert on a clear winter night.

Jesus, I sound like some horny thirteen-year-old with his first crush.

Fucking pathetic. I needed to get my shit together and stop being distracted by the sexual tension building between us. Still, her large tits moved with every breath she took and I wanted to rip her top down and get my lips on her nipples. I wondered if they'd be large or small, if they'd be sensitive or if I could put clamps on them. Yeah, fucking jeweled clamps that would sway on her constricted nipples while she rode me.

"So what do you do, Mr. Beach?"

Snapped out of the porno running in my head, I ran her question through my mind and hesitated. I didn't want to go into detail about my job, not when we'd just met. It might freak her out, or she could be one of those bitches who would fall to her knees as soon as she figured out just how much influence I have in the world. And how much money. Unfortunately that kind of easy pussy didn't do anything for me for beyond a fuck and I'd reached the point in my life where I wanted more from a woman than sex.

Still testing the waters, I answered her question with one of my own. "How 'bout you, sugar. What brings you to Sturgis?"

She rolled her eyes with a grin. "Evasive much?"

Smirking, I had to resist the urge to run my hands along the endless expanse of her toned thighs. This woman seriously had a body better than anything I'd ever seen. Add to that her drop-dead gorgeous face, and my desire to have her moaning beneath me had me edgy. When I returned my gaze from her amazing tits, again, to her eyes, I found her smirking at me.

Playtime was over.

Staring her down, studying each nuance of her expression in the flickering light of the fire, I leaned closer, liking how her breath caught. "Why don't you ask me what you really want to know?"

"And what, exactly, do I really want to know?"

I'm sure she meant those words to come out snarky, but instead they came out all husky with arousal. "You want to know what it's gonna be like to fuck me."

Her long lashes fluttered and she pursed her lips, obviously trying to decide if she should be offended. "What makes you think I want to fuck you?"

"Right now, your nipples are poking out of your shirt, beggin' me to suck on them. Your pulse is bangin' in your neck and your pupils have almost swallowed the beautiful blue of your eyes." Leaning forward, I took an audible sniff, my hands instinctively clenching on her firm thighs. "And I can smell your pussy. Bet if I touched it you'd be wet for me, your clit nice and swollen. I'm gonna make you come until you pass out in my arms, then I'm gonna fuck you in your dreams."

She licked her lower lip and I was dying to taste that plump flesh myself. Without a doubt, she had the most perfect dick-sucking lips I'd ever seen. The more I studied her, the more obsessed I became with her, until I could have been in the middle of Niagara Falls, 'bout to go over the side and plunge to my death, but I still wouldn't have looked away from her until the Grim Reaper took me.

Her fingertips rested against my thighs and I swore I could feel the heat burning through the thick denim of my jeans. "A lot of guys say they can go the distance, but few can. What makes you think you can even make me orgasm once?"

The gleam of mischief shone in her gaze and I liked the sparkle it put there. No fucking way did she not feel this insane connection between us. Besides, if there was one thing I was confident about, it was my ability to please women. "I make pretty little girls like you beg for mercy, make them please their *Papi* before I give them my dick."

"*Papi?*"

"Love it when you call me that."

"*Papi*?" Her eyes widened. "You mean like you enjoy women calling you essentially Daddy in Spanish?"

"Yep. Nothin' too crazy, I just like to take care of my woman." Well, actually, with sweet butts I didn't give a fuck, but with the rare woman I'd dated, it was different. Sarah was different. "It satisfies me to know my baby girl is taken care of, that she lives an easy life."

She jerked her head back and frowned. "Are you into age play?"

"What?"

"You like me to call you *Papi*, and you sure call me baby a whole lot, you're not into that absolutely wrong and foul incest play?"

"No." My gut clenched at the very idea. "Fuck no. It's a cultural difference, the slang meanin' way different from the direct translation. Like when I call you baby it's not 'cause I think you're a baby, not with those tits-"

Giving my arm a soft smack, while laughing, she said, "Hey now!"

"Just trust me, I am more than aware you are a woman."

She stroked my shoulders with a gentle touch. "Sorry, didn't mean to offend you. I've run into some guys with some super-weird fetishes and I just wanted to make sure. I have an identical twin sister and some men have a sick thing about it. Fucking nasty and it pisses me off. Especially when it happens to her. My sister is the sweetest, nicest, kindest, most naive woman in the world. To hear someone talk to her like that is offensive. I've kicked more than one guy's ass because of it and let me tell you, I bet they're too scared to even *think* about us when they jerk off anymore."

It took some effort, but I managed to keep the laughter off my face as she scowled at me, so fucking cute. "I don't blame you. I don't have any brothers or sisters by blood, but I have 'em by friendship and I'd do the same damn thing. No one talks to family that way, you did the right thing."

"Thank you!" She threw her hands up in the air, her breasts lifting and moving as she gestured wildly. "Some people don't understand that just because we're conventionally pretty, doesn't mean we're inanimate objects with no feelings. When you say those things to my sister, you're not talking to someone like me who can handle your shit. You're talking to a high-functioning, brilliant autistic woman who is a way better person than you can ever hope to be."

Her hands finally settled back on her lap and she let out a little huff as I examined her. "Sounds like you love her a lot."

"I do." Tears suddenly filled her eyes and she abruptly sat straight up. "She's special, innocent, and it's my job to protect her. Too bad I screwed that up as well. Shit."

Not liking the utter desolation that filled her face, I couldn't resist reaching out and smoothing her hair back. "What happened?"

For a moment I thought she was going to open up to me, then something flashed through her eyes too quick for me to identify, and she shook her head while laughing softly. "Fuck, that weed is really strong. Thorn said it was strong, but wow, it's strong."

I allowed myself one touch of her cheek with the back of my knuckles, unable to be near her without wanting a physical connection. "You okay?"

"Yeah, yeah I'm fine." She gave me a brilliant smile that didn't reach her now cool and guarded eyes. "Sorry, I get really chatty-ranty sometimes when I'm high."

"Chatty-ranty?"

"Yeah, you know, go off on a tangent and babble. Swear to me right now you will never, ever talk politics with me when I'm high. It really isn't pretty and I tend to get a little heated."

"Alright," I said with a chuckle while she relaxed further. "Though I happen to like it when you rant. Your tits shake when you start swingin' your arms around. No man is gonna give a shit what you're sayin' when he's got those beauties in his sites."

For a moment she stared at me, then burst out laughing when I winked. "Dick. So basically if a woman is naked she can throw a fit and you wouldn't notice?"

"Oh, I'd notice. Then I'd spank her and fuck the shit out of her until she calmed down. Give a woman enough orgasms and you can screw the bitch out of anyone."

Giggling, she smacked my leg lightly. "You're such an asshole."

"Why? You know it's true. And you know just as well as I do that when a man is in a shitty mood, nothin' will turn it around like a hard fuck."

"Mmmm." Her gaze went a little hooded and the coolness thawed from her icy eyes. "Good point. And sometimes a *man* needs a good spanking in order to behave."

I couldn't help the growl that escaped me. "Let me make one thing clear right now. I like control, I like to lead. It is who and what I am, and that extends to the bedroom, sweet Sarah. Doesn't mean I won't let you have fun, doesn't mean I won't let you tie me up once in a while if that's what gets you off, but it does mean I'm gonna take you how I want and make you come so fuckin' hard, just the brush of my breath on your overworked clit is gonna make you see stars."

The shiver she gave me lit me up inside as arousal brought a flush high on her soft cheekbones.

Grinning, I slid my hands up her thighs until they were beneath her skirt, my thumbs resting close enough to her pussy that I could feel her heat. "And I'm gonna punish you when you've been bad."

Instead of being offended, or disgusted, her fair brows rose up and a tremble ran through her. "Seriously?"

I couldn't help but grin at her interested yet apprehensive expression, then leaned forward and whispered in her ear, "I like to take care of little girls who need a firm hand."

She jerked back as if I'd breathed fire on her skin, but her hands now gripped my thighs tight. "You're seriously into that kind of stuff? BDSM?"

Leaning closer, her perfume once again teasing me, I murmured, "*Corazón,* I like all kinds of stuff, but I don't label it. I like what I like, and that's to have control."

She dropped her gaze to where her hands were now stroking my legs, playing with the muscles there. I kept myself in shape to keep me alive, not to look pretty, but that didn't mean I wasn't aware bitches liked a guy who took care of himself. Her continued quiet tweaked at my self-control, but I had to let her figure this out for herself. I had no idea what was goin' on between us, but it was powerful and I wondered if she knew how unusual our connection was.

And fuck me, she was hot.

For this girl, I'd try vanilla if it was the only flavor I could get her in and fuckin' love it.

What I wasn't expecting was for her to look up at me, bold as hell, and whisper, "A man after my own heart."

My cock jerked in approval. "Is that right?"

"Mmm-hmmm." She lightly ran her nails up and down my forearms. "And I'm not afraid to ask for what I want, either."

I couldn't help but grin, loving the hell out of her ability to surprise me. "And what do you want?"

"I want a good, hard fuck. Think you can help me out with that?"

"Absolutely." Then I forced myself to play this right, even if I wanted to just drag her off right now and screw her bowlegged. "How hard you want it?"

She looked up at me through her lashes and I groaned low in my throat as she gave me this somehow super-cute yet totally seductive pout. "As hard as you can give it to me, *Papi*."

That word coming from her lips hit me right in the dick. I wanted to throw her down right on this bench and strap her arms to it with my belt, but that wasn't the best idea I'd ever had, no matter what my dick said. "You better mean that, little girl, because I'm the kind of man who will make all of that happen."

"But only for one night."

I'd play her game, agree with her, but she was crazy if she thought I was gonna be satisfied with one evening in a hotel room with her. I live by my instincts and they're telling me she belongs to me. I gently grasp her slender throat in one of my hands, amazed at how unblemished and smooth her skin looks compared to my scarred and tattooed skin.

"I'm gonna fuck you so good you're never gonna want another cock again."

"Promise?"

She knew just how to goad me, exactly what to do to make my already strong need for her turn savage.

My voice came out rough as I said, "Promise."

Instead of speaking, she slowly nodded and her hips twitched as she wiggled with desire. Fuck yeah, she felt it. I swear even though we were a good inch apart, I could still sense her body against mine as if we were pressed skin to skin. In my thirty-two years on earth, I've been with my share of women, but I've never felt this kind of chemistry with anyone.

I closed the distance between us, the front of our bodies pressed lightly together. She sucked in a quick breath and shifted slightly, rubbing her breasts against my chest. "Let's go."

"Where?"

"I've got a hotel room."

Her lips curved into a smile that slammed into me like a burst of sunshine in my chest. Damned if I wasn't grinning back at her like a fool. A quick glance confirmed we were being watched closely by the crowd and I inwardly snarled. They were staring at us as if we were some fucking reality show for them to observe. Sometimes, being President sucked as far as privacy went. Everyone wanted a piece of me all the time. Even now I could see some high-ranking members of some of our affiliate clubs partying with us, and I should go shake some hands and drink some beers, but nothing short of a nuclear war could draw me away from the exquisite Sarah.

"Prez," Hustler, one of my Enforcers, called out.

I didn't even bother to look at him, just yelled back, "Not now."

Obviously not catching my mood, Hustler strode up to us with a dark look twisting his face. His hazel eyes were a little glassy and his black hair messy, but his usual joking smile was missing so I knew whatever was going on was gonna be a fuckin' pain. "We got a problem."

"Handle it."

He stroked his short goatee, a sure sign of anxiety. "No, we got a *problem*."

He didn't even look at Sarah, something that instantly set me on alert. Hustler loved beautiful blondes and they didn't come any better than the stunning creature nearly sitting on my lap. Normally Hustler would be eye-fucking her up and down instead'a staring at me.

Out of the corner of my eye, I noticed Smoke heading my way, minus the bitches and now accompanied by Thorn and a few more of my officers, along with some of the Wyoming and Montana members of the Iron Horse MC. The hard rush of impending danger made the hair along my arms raise up and the skin of my back prickled like someone was starin' at me.

In Spanish, Hustler said, "Los Diablos is partying across the way and a little down from us with a couple of their affiliate clubs. Fat Perry and Suds are over there as well, and one of the brothers said he saw Digger earlier."

The mention of the former Iron Horse brothers had me instantly pissed. "They fuckin' dare? They fuckin' dare show their face around me? Have they forgotten the only reason they got to live is with the understandin' I'd never fuckin' lay my eyes on them again?"

"Yep. Haven't looked at or said shit to us, but just them bein' so close is a fuckin' insult."

When I'd taken over the Iron Horse MC position as National President, we'd cleaned house of all the dipshits Red, the former Prez, had surrounded himself with. We'd gotten rid of every single man who'd been loyal to Red, and most of the ones we didn't kill had ended up over with Los Diablos, a rival club of ours whose members were known to do anything for a buck. Sell their sisters, kill their mothers, pimp out their wives or children—you had the money, they'd make it happen. And now former Iron Horse members wore their fucking colors. Shouldn't be surprised; reason I killed Red was because I found out he was into human trafficking on the side, and Los Lobos dealt heavily in that terrible shit.

Having them set up this close to us, out of all the fucking space here, was deliberate.

I put my fingers to my lips then whistled sharp and loud, "Yo, Rock."

The dark-haired, older man still built like a brickhouse ambled over to us with a few of his Enforcers flanking him. Rock was the Vice President of the Rochester, New York, chapter of the Ice Demons, a club we were affiliated with, and also a personal friend. The Ice Demons had a few mutual business associates between them and Los Diablos, so while they weren't friendly with Los Diablos, they kept the peace.

"Beach, good to see you, man." Rock clasped my shoulder and squeezed, his craggy face lighting up with a smile.

"Good to see you too. Mind doin' me a favor?"

Instantly his gaze sharpened and the men standing behind him tensed. "What's up?"

"Los Diablos has a party goin' close by and we need a little buffer between us and them. Got some old brothers from back in Red's day who're wearin' Los Diablos colors now."

"I can't believe those stupid fucks would push their luck like this." Rock shook his head. "That's some bad blood right there. I'll pull my people into neutral territory. Got a lot of brothers with me tonight so it won't be an issue."

"I appreciate it."

Lifting his beer to me, Rock took off into the night, his Enforcers tagging other Ice Demons and their women as they passed.

With that shit show handled, I turned to check on Sarah, finding her pretending to look at her nails while she peeked at me beneath her long lashes. My dick urged me to get back to that fine piece of ass as quickly as possible and I bit the inside of my cheek. Fuck, those legs of hers were gonna be the death of me.

Grinning at me, Smoke said in Spanish, "What, you only doing one bitch tonight? Feeling tired, Prez? Brandy and Sandy wore you out?"

"Fuck off, Santos."

Smoke chuckled, enjoying the opportunity to mess with me. Asshole. "Can't remember the last time you didn't need at least two bitches at once to get you off. You on Viagra now?"

"You wish you had such a fine piece waiting for you. Any of you shitheads would trade your left nut for a chance with her."

Crossing his arms over his chest, Hustler smirked. "Gotta say, she's hot enough I'd tag team her with your ugly ass in a heartbeat. Damn, she looks like the kind of bitch who can take more than one dick. After you're done with her, pass her along to me, yeah? I don't mind your sloppy seconds. You train 'em up right."

Before I could tell Hustler to fuck off, knowing he was screwing with me because that was Hustler's fucked-up sense of humor, Sarah said in decent Spanish, "Sloppy seconds? Are you kidding me? Like I'd ever let a no-class, nasty-ass piece of monkey shit like yourself ever come near me. You know what—fuck you all, I'm outta here."

Her spectacular thigh muscles flex enticingly as she stood then started to move away from the bench. She's taken no more than a step before I'm up as well, eyes glued to the irritated twitch of her sweet ass. Shit, even walking away from me she's so sexy my dick hurts.

Inwardly wincing while my brothers laughed as Hustler sputtered, I turned, ready to do damage control, before gunshots filled the air and the night erupted into chaos.

The booms were still echoing in my ears as screams and shouts muffled my hearing further, the panic of the crowd so thick I could feel its sting against my skin.

Another couple gunshots, this time to the south of us, launched me into action.

"Smoke," I shouted above the noise, "get everyone safe then grab some brothers and take these fuckers out."

"But—"

"Fuckin' do it!"

Hustler lifted up high enough to flip over the bench we'd been straddling. A solid piece of wood wouldn't do shit against bullets but would at least provide us some cover for return fire.

Hustler and myself had just crouched behind it when a woman's sharp scream rang out and I glanced over my shoulder to find two men in black t-shirts and black jeans attempting to snatch up Sarah.

Without thought, I lunged from my cover and took off across the packed earth of the campground, firelight throwing crazy shadows among the surging crowd of people. Hustler yelled for me but I ignored him, intent on getting to her. I knew that if I lost sight of her she was gonna be heading for a fate worse than death.

The gunshots had ceased, but a full-on stampede had started up, people pushing and shoving their way through the crowd in an effort to get away from the violence. At 6'3", I could see over most of the people there and it wasn't hard to spot Sarah's bright blonde hair and sparkling red shirt in the surging mass. Looking pissed, she struggled against the two men who were obviously trying to drag her off somewhere.

No, she wasn't struggling, she was fighting.

As I elbowed my way through the crowd, I saw one of the men slap her and my temper snapped. I was pushing through when the mass of fleeing people parted again and I had a perfect view of Sarah turning the tables on the men who were attempting to get control of her.

In a perfect move any of my Enforcers would admire, Sarah let her weight drop forward so the guy behind her was off balance, then twisted her hip and threw him to the ground. The other guy snarled something at her but she didn't bother to respond, instead giving him a punch to the throat followed by a swift kick to his face that left me gaping. This bitch could fight.

Unfortunately for her, the fucker she'd thrown off her back was up, and I could easily see the gun in his hand aimed at her.

I was almost to them now, but still too far away to intervene. He motioned with his gun while his friend remained slumped on the ground, obviously knocked out by Sarah's roundhouse kick to his head. Now, most females I know would be crying, begging, and pleading for their lives if some guy held a gun on them, but Sarah did none of those things. No, that ballsy bitch was pointing her finger at him like she was the one who held the gun, as fierce as any mythological Valkyrie who'd ever confronted her enemy.

I got shoved from behind by some bearded drunk dude running past me with his bitch then I glanced over my shoulder to see what was headed my way.

My gut tightened as I spotted a group of five men in the distance briefly illuminated by a big set of portable lights and random fires. They weren't wearing cuts, and their lower faces were covered by the kind of mask I wore while riding to protect my lower face in dust storms. It obscured their features and in the low lighting, I had no idea who they were, but they were armed and they were carefully sweeping through the area where Iron Horse had been throwing their party with a military precision. Hit squad for sure. So far they seemed to be shooting to wound, and I knew they were on the hunt.

A gunshot sounded loud enough behind me that my ears rang with it. I shoved my way through the fleeing people, fully expecting to see Sarah either dead or seriously wounded, and instead I found her shooting out the guy's knee-caps—with his own gun.

Then she shot him right in the dick.

Right in the fuckin' dick.

Talk about insult to injury.

The casual brutality of the act, the cool and precise way she'd placed those shots, made me proud. Yeah, it was fucked-up to find the fact she was a stone-cold killer exhilarating, but a strong man needed a strong woman. I'd had more than one relationship fail because the woman couldn't handle the violence of my life. The beautiful blonde I was starting at wouldn't blink at some of the shit I had to do in order to keep my people safe. I knew this because she smiled down at the man screaming in agony and appeared to be telling him something while he writhed in the dirt.

Jogging now, I quickly made my way to her, intent on sweeping her up and getting her the fuck out of here. As soon as I got close, she whirled to face me in a shooter's crouched stance, and I was pretty sure I was staring death in the face. An exquisite death for sure, but I wasn't done enjoying my life yet.

"Easy, baby, it's Beach. I'm friendly, yeah?"

The gun lowered and she gave the downed guy to her left a kick in the face with her sexy-as-hell boots that made the unconscious man moan in reflexive pain. "Yeah, but I got this, so off you go. I'll email you or something. Later."

"What?"

"I said I got this, so *largate*."

"You want me to leave you alone? Here? Are you for fuckin' real?" I threw out my arm. "Take a look around you. Bad shit is going down and you do not fuckin' need to be here."

Waving the gun at me, her finger carefully off the trigger, she sneered. "Really? Bad shit is happening? I didn't notice because I was too busy being kidnapped by these soon-to-be-dead motherfuckers."

I momentarily forgot the hit squad behind me, until a loud bang followed by a burning line of heat across my calf had me shouting out in surprised pain while Sarah dove for cover.

"Fucking shit," I hissed as I scrambled to the dubious safety of an overturned chair and checked my leg.

My calf had been grazed from the side, and while it burned like a bitch, I didn't think it was too deep. Gunfire roared through the night and I lay flat while Sarah sheltered herself behind a couple stacked kegs for minimal cover, then shot back at the advancing men like some bitch out of an action movie. There was a series of roars of pain behind me, along with a shout that someone named "Gilov" was dead.

Dust pinged around her as they returned fire, but it was far less than earlier. Anger roared through me and I pulled out my own gun, returning fire as I tried to limp my way to where an RV stood. I know I managed to hit at least one of them, and the gunshots ceased. My ears rang from all the explosions and I couldn't hear shit outside my pounding heart. Dancing lights from the fires flickered over the mostly deserted area as I grit my teeth against the pain of putting weight on my leg. When someone grabbed me beneath my arms and began to drag me, I almost put a bullet into the person's chest until I realized the body pressed up against mine was female with big round tits.

Sarah.

She hauled me across the open space while I favored my injured leg. "Woman, get the fuck out of here and get safe. I didn't come back for you so you could get yourself killed. Now go, run!"

Ignoring me, her breath coming out in harsh grunts as she continued to take a good deal of my weight, she paused when the way became obscured by people who were terrified and running. I could see some Iron Horse men in a large group coming our way in the distance, and movement here and there that could be random people or hitmen. Either way, I needed to get her the fuck out and safe before I went back out to regroup with my brothers.

"*Mija*, let me go. Get safe and I'll come for you."

"Shut up. You're beginning to sound like an ungrateful little bitch. I am not leaving you behind, and you're going to help me get your heavy ass to cover before they regroup. Someone's going to die soon, and I'd rather it not be us."

Doing everything I could to help us move faster, I grit out through the pain, "I'm gonna spank your ass—"

Gunfire thundered through the air now from somewhere to our left with an ear-piercing boom and I struggled to stand up, but she had some kind of fucking hold on me that kept me confined in her grip, as helpless as a baby kitten.

If I didn't think it was impossible I'd say she had some kind of Special Ops training, but a style I wasn't familiar with.

My ears rang and I had to shout, "Sarah, fuckin' listen to me, you need to get out of here, men are—"

"Trying to kill me," she panted. "I know."

"Kill *you*? Why the fuck would they do that?"

She gave a bitter chuckle that cut right through me. So much pain there. "It wasn't anything I did, at least I don't think it was, but I've got a relative who gambles and some think threatening me will make her pay up."

In the distance, bike engines roared and I scanned the area around us. We'd reached the side of a huge, tricked-out RV by now and she propped me up against the door. The interior of the vehicle was dark and the door was evidently locked because it didn't open when she tried. Muttering a curse, she gave me a quick head-to-toe sweep, her gaze lingering on the gun still in my hand and the blood-soaked cloth of my jeans over my injury.

"You're a liability. Stay here."

"You are fuckin *loco*—"

Before I could finish my statement, she'd assumed a modified shooters stance and was crouched down, sneaking quick peeks around the side of the vehicle with a deadly intent that fascinated me.

Her smooth voice carried easily to me on the cool evening breeze. "Don't shoot the guys with the Iron Horse patches, correct?"

There was no more gunfire so I didn't have a hard time hearing her at the other end of the massive RV. "Don't fuckin' shoot anyone. Shit, woman, get back here."

Completely ignoring me, she kept her gun at the ready. "Damn it, I can't see anything right now. All those people running stirred up the dust."

Totally thrown by the pretty young thing acting so completely blasé about the whole situation, I grunted as I stood on my good leg, fighting off the dizzying sensation as my body tried to cope with the shock of being shot. "I *said* get the fuck over here."

She looked at me with her brows raised and such a sarcastic expression it made my hand ache to spank her. "Oh, I'm sorry, you must have confused me for one of your bitches that you say suck, and they say how hard. That shit is not going to happen with me. Now, considering I just saved your ass, wouldn't the polite thing to do be to back the fuck off and let me take care of business? Or maybe you should be saying 'Thanks for saving my ass, Sarah' instead of being a dick? God—men. You're all alike. Little too much testosterone and you turn into belligerent assholes. I'm not putting up with that shit, you hear me? If I had something dangling between my legs you'd treat me like I had a brain in my head, but because I have boobs you instantly peg me as dumb. In case you haven't noticed, I know what I'm doing. So pardon me if I tell you to fuck off." Her nostrils flared and the lines around her mouth deepened with her displeasure. "Shit. You made me monologue. I hate that."

Not many things, or people, surprised me anymore but this pretty girl and her rambling had totally thrown me for a loop. A thread of humor cleared my head and I had to resist the urge to laugh. Fuck, I think I could love this woman.

"Baby, come here so I can kiss that sassy fuckin' mouth of yours."

Her response was cut short when I felt the unmistakable kiss of the barrel of a gun pressed against my head as someone got me in a chokehold and someone else grabbed my gun.

As I struggled, Sarah started to raise her gun but another man came from around the side of the RV and pistol whipped her hard enough that her eyes rolled back into her head and she went down in a heap, with me following her down not long after.

Chapter 3

Sarah

"*Mija*," a man's voice said gently as big hands stroked my face.

I scrunched my nose then frowned, my head pounding in a way that wasn't like a headache, but still hurt.

"What?" Well, I intended to say "what", but how it really came out was, "Waz?"

"Sarah?"

Swallowing was difficult with my throat being as dry as a hundred-year-old nun's kitty. "What's going on?"

"Open your eyes, baby."

Someone shifted me around and it was only then that I realized I was being cradled in a strong man's lap. I forced myself to open my eyes and blinked in the almost complete darkness, seeing just the faintest hint of a bearded man's profile. While I didn't recognize his face in this light, I remembered his scent and relaxed enough to think.

"Beach. What the hell is going on? Where are we?"

"No idea and no fuckin' idea. Far as I can tell we're in a holding room of some kind. No windows, door is fuckin' solid. Hear some voices occasionally, but nothin' else. We haven't been here long, less than an hour."

"No windows?" I tried to keep my growing panic at bay, but my claustrophobia was creeping in.

"Don't worry, I'll get us out."

My rational mind was quickly receding, no match for my phobia of being in anything resembling a closet. "We have to get out."

"I'll get us out."

My voice dropped to a ragged whisper as my phobia screamed through my mind. "We have to get out."

"Baby." His voice was firm and his arms tightened around me. "Easy."

Pushing at his chest, I began to tremble. "We have to get out!"

His whole body tensed and he pulled me tighter to him. "Honey, relax. Shhhhh, gotta keep quiet, sweetheart."

"Please let me out! I don't want to be in here, let me out. Please, not the dark, don't leave me alone, please. I'll be good, I pinky swear, please let me out!"

Dimly, I knew I wasn't really in a closet, but to my battered mind I was nine years old again, screaming to be let out of the punishment room in my mother's mansion. It was in the basement, a utility closet near the sauna, that the maids were forbidden to open. Just a bare room, four paces by four paces. Smooth walls, concrete floor, a bucket in the corner to pee in, but no escape and no one could hear me scream. Time became distorted in the dark and I desperately clung to Beach, fearful moans escaping me.

"What's wrong, Sarah?"

He removed my clinging hands from his shirt and wrapped them around his neck, repositioning me so I was straddling him. Right away I shoved my face into his throat, feeling his pulse beneath my lips, the scratch of his beard on my face, surrounding myself with the reality of him. I wasn't alone in here, someone was with me, I wasn't alone. Not alone.

"No, *mi corazón*, not alone," Beach whispered into my ear. "Breathe with me. In…and out."

I tried, but it was so hard to do anything when my anxiety was through the roof like this. My therapist and I had been working on overcoming my phobia, but the mental wounds from my past still had the power to enslave me. In an effort to focus on the here and now, to not feel the phantom thirst and hunger pangs that came from my triggered memories, I rubbed my face against Beach's neck, the scent of him somehow pulling me out of my nightmares enough to talk.

"Claustrophobic, bad. And I don't like the dark."

"All right, sweetheart." He began to stroke my rigid back. "What can I do to help?"

"Distract me, help get me out of my mind."

I'd thought, silly me, he'd talk to me some more, but his distraction was much more effective.

He seduced me.

And he didn't fuck around doing it.

The words had scarcely left my lips before he jerked my top down with a low growl.

My nipples were already rock hard, and I willed myself to only focus on him, to give him everything I had.

Right before his lips wrapped around my right nipple, he whispered, "You must be quiet, *mi corazón.*"

Warm breath washed over my nipple for a brilliant instant before his lips wrapped oh so softly against the tightening nub, the opposite of what I thought he was going to do. My expectations of a rough bite left me unprepared for how intense the soft sucking sensation was, how his beard brushed my breast as he made a low hungry noise. I bit my tongue to keep from moaning at the gentle suck of those soft lips, my hips rubbing a tight circle over his rigid erection. My whole body lit up beneath his touch and I lost myself in the blessed relief of his caress, grateful for any escape from the darkness trying to destroy my sanity.

As I swiveled my hips with the experience of a former stripper, Beach grasped my ass with both of his big, long-fingered hands and dug in.

"I want to fuck you so bad," he growled. "Want to slide into that hot, tight little cunt. You gonna give it to me? Spread out for me pretty and hold those long, long legs open? You gonna show me what's mine?"

He could have asked for my soul at that moment and I would have gladly traded it for an orgasm. I was insanely wound up with fear and tension, yet so beyond aroused my legs were shaking with it. The throb of my clit as I rode his jeans-covered cock had me clutching his thick hair tight. That made him hiss and I smiled when his hips rose to meet mine in perfect rhythm. This was beyond amazing and approached "oh fuck I'm in trouble" land really quick.

"Tell me, Sarah."

"I will, I'll show you what's yours," I answered without hesitation.

I'd never been with a man quite this dominant before, and as I sank deeper into his touch, all I could do was still, then tremble as my orgasm hovered just out of reach. This was because he held me tight to his lap, his thick length throbbing against my pussy. At some point, when we weren't being kidnapped, I was going to rub myself against his cock until I came all over it. Hell, he was long enough to give me a G-spot orgasm. As soon as we escape from this coffin of a room.

The grind of his hips chased that thought from my mind and my clit throbbed with the beat of my heart, each rub pushing me closer to the cleansing oblivion of orgasm.

"You come when I tell you to," he ordered in a soft but authoritative voice, as though he had every right in the world to make that demand of me.

"I'll do whatever I want, including orgasm, thank you very much."

He gave my pussy an incredibly long, slow slide over his cock and I bit back a mew as the fat head pushed into my panties. "You want this cock inside of you, you take it however I give it."

A hard bolt of lust almost knocked the breath out of me. Who knew I'd get off so much on a guy being bossy? "Whatever."

Well, that wasn't my most eloquent response, but it would have to suffice because he'd begun kissing my neck, his lips doing that devastating soft thing again, so at odds with his harsh voice and almost cruel grip on my hips.

"I promise you, nothing you can do to yourself will be better than what I can do to you."

"You're crazy," I scoffed, which would have sounded more convincing if my words hadn't come out in a breathless whisper.

"Most beautiful fuckin' thing I've ever seen. Swear to God my heart skipped a couple beats the moment I saw you," he whispered into the shell of my ear. "You're gonna come for me now, Sarah. Put your hand over your mouth and muffle yourself. Be a good *mija* for your *Papi*."

He rubbed himself against me as he sucked my nipple into his mouth, hard enough to sting, and it sent me rocketing to the edge. With ease, he built the need for release in me, my body screaming out in pleasure at his experienced touch. I had enough time to slap my hand over my mouth before I was tensing all over, everything inside of me so tight as heat blossomed through me. My back arched and I nearly choked on my suppressed cries while Beach rocked me against him, the muscles of his big thighs pushing against my butt when his hands worked me back and forth. I hung limp in his grip, too busy coming my brains out to do anything else.

Slowly I came back down to earth, my harsh breathing filling the echoing space around us.

Okay, there was an echo, so it meant it was big. Suddenly I wasn't that scared anymore. Amazing what a really good orgasm could do for a panic attack. I'd have to keep condoms on me in the future so I could jump a random hot guy if I felt too much anxiety.

Beach's voice came rough and low as he murmured, "I really fuckin wish I could have seen that. Bet it was spectacular. In the future you're gonna masturbate yourself to multiple orgasms for me before I'll give you my dick. I'm getting you a giant box load of toys off the internet and you're gonna use every one of 'em for me."

Panting, I rested my head against his shoulder, barely moving when he pulled my tank top back into place. "I have my own toys, thank you very much."

"I bet you do," he whispered while continuing to rock his hips sensually against mine, his cock still rock hard. "But I promise it'll be more fun to share with me than play alone."

I wanted to call him crazy, but I had panties that were soaking wet with my climax, which said otherwise. "Oh, I know it would be, but we have different lives. Not to mention the fact we're currently hostages. That might put a slight crimp in your plans."

"When I get us out of here, you're comin' home with me and you'll see what I'm talkin' about."

"Are you on drugs? When *I* get us out I'll make sure you're safe, then I'll be on my merry way."

He gripped my hair and slammed his mouth to mine, kissing me into submission until I lay limp against him. "Listen up, Sarah. You need to know right now that this shit between us is not normal. This is something more, something worth fightin' for."

"Something more?" I tried to scoff but instead whispered sadly, "Look, now that I'm no longer acting like a crazy person, we need to figure out how to escape."

Instead of being angry, he stroked my face with a soothing affection I fought. It wasn't real, this wasn't real, he was just another guy. I'd thought in the past love and sex were the same thing, but they're vastly different and I'd learned that lesson the hard way.

Then again, maybe we were both insane, because him touching me felt like magic.

Even though I longed to melt into his caress, then suck on his tongue to get more of his glorious taste, I stiffened when he growled out, "I will get us out of here."

I wanted to push out of his arms, to explore the room for an exit, but the thought of leaving him had as much appeal as letting go of a buoy and falling into a sea full of Clive Barker's savage monsters, all whirling fangs and slashing teeth.

Pulling my phone out of my boot, I pressed the on button and grimaced when I saw that I had no bars on it. Wonderful. I tried moving my arm around, hoping for a signal, but I knew wherever I was, I wasn't getting service. As quickly as I dared, I shone it around the space we were trapped in, revealing we were in some industrial concrete room with a strong-looking black door. I quickly turned my phone off and put it away, not willing to alert anyone outside I had it.

"No signal," I whispered.

"Nice hiding spot."

I took a deep breath as my eyes readjusted to the dark, hating the tiny bit of panic trying to invade my thoughts. "Thanks."

Before either of us could say anything else, the door to the room swung open and the lights turned on, blinding me. I raised my arm to cover the glare as I rolled away from Beach. I'd only been still for a moment and was just rising to my knees when Beach let out a pained groan.

I would have looked to see what had him making that pained sound, but I was too busy being Tasered until I passed out, grateful to leave the nauseating pain of being conscious behind.

Chapter 4

AUSTIN TX

The painful throbbing of my head tore me awake and I tried to bring my hand to my face to brush away my annoying hair from my eyes, but for some reason my hands seemed to be stuck together. A humming rumble came from the floor beneath my ear and a metallic taste filled my mouth, my whole body aching like I'd just done a twenty-mile hike with my dad. It took me a few more moments to realize my hands were bound together and there was a strip of tape over my mouth. Unfortunately, I also wasn't being held safely in Beach's arms, and I instantly worried about him as a strong, breath-stealing pain filled my chest.

My immediate impulse was to open my eyes and search for him, but this wasn't the first time I'd been kidnapped so I managed to keep still. True, it was the first time I'd been for-reals taken, but my father had staged enough mock kidnappings that his insane training kicked in. The distracting heat of my anger threatened to overwhelm me and cause me to act rashly, but my mind had been trained by a master manipulator to deal with a crisis. The only thing that could derail me was my phobia, but the danger was so great that my well-honed survival instincts took over and I gathered myself.

A calm washed over me, clarity returning as I dove into the deep parts of my mind where fear couldn't touch me. I needed to evaluate the situation and know what I was dealing with. The feel of rough carpet beneath my face combined with the sensation of moving indicated I was probably in a car of some sort, maybe something bigger because I wasn't feeling anything like a seat. The scent of cleaning chemicals and cigarettes was strong, but that didn't help me out in any way. It was still dark, or I was in a space with no light because I couldn't detect any illumination coming through my eyelids. This indicated I'd probably only been out for a little bit, or I was being held in a box of some kind.

Panic tried to claw at me at the thought of being trapped in a small space, but since it was a vehicle and not a room, I was able to push it back without too much effort.

Focus, Sarah, those who lose focus lose their lives, my father's voice whispered through my mind.

I opened my eye closest to the floor a little bit but couldn't really make out anything in the dim light through the curtain of my hair. I debated blowing it out of my way, but that would for sure alert whoever had taken me that I was awake. The vehicle rocked slightly and I used the opportunity to roll with it, allowing my head to flop like I was still unconscious and the bulk of my hair to fall to the side of my head. This gave me a little bit of a better view, but all I could really make out was the metal ceiling of what had to be a van. Whatever road we were driving on didn't have streetlights and a faint glow came from the front seat, probably from the dashboard.

A zing of adrenaline rushed through me as I realized my hands were duct taped in front of me but my legs were still free.

Inside of my boots was one of my throwing knives, a gift from my stepmother Mimi that went with me pretty much everywhere. And to think I'd initially been disappointed I hadn't gotten a car for my birthday instead of knife-fighting lessons from Mimi. I also had my phone but I'd send an SOS out to my dad after I took care of the immediate threat. If I did otherwise, he'd make me go rock climbing up the brutal wall he'd built as punishment when I was younger. It was three stories tall and hard enough to challenge even a seasoned climber. Even worse, I wore a safety harness so if I fell, I'd just swing safely out over the huge, Hollywood movie stunt-scene worthy crash pad. If I didn't grab the wall when I swung back, he'd lower me to the ground and I'd either have to admit defeat or start over again.

I never admitted defeat, and a couple times Swan had to climb up there with me to help me finish, but I always beat my Dad in a battle of wills. And for once I was happy my dad was this crazy, scary arms dealer who was good friends with some of the greatest mercenaries in the world. It meant when I called him, he'd come get me with everything he had, so I just had to stay alive long enough for him to get here.

I wanted to reach down and yank one of my knives out and take care of business, but I had to know what I was up against. Letting my head rock to the side slightly, I listened for the sound of breathing. Someone was nearby but their breaths were low and shallow. Trying to hear over the pounding of my heart, I could only make out the occasional murmur of a male voice from the front area of the van.

Moving as slowly as possible, I looked as much as I could without lifting my head and saw the unconscious figure of Beach trussed up like a Christmas goose not too far away from me. While they'd only taped my hands and gagged me, they'd bound his hands, arms, and legs with enough duct tape to subdue a lion. In a way, I was kind of insulted they didn't view me as a threat.

He had a small trickle of dried blood coming from his nose, and the duct tape covering his mouth made me internally wince. It was stuck to his beard and I knew it was going to take some of his facial hair with it when it was removed. I didn't dare try to wake him, not that he could do much of anything right now, so instead focused on gathering my courage enough to steal a look at the front seat.

Shit, this was not good. If only I wasn't a fuckup like my mother; I'd never be in this situation. I'd allowed my weakness to distract us from escaping earlier when we had a potentially better chance at survival. It was all my fault we were here.

Guilt tried to keep me immobile, tried to force tears into my eyes, potentially blurring my vision, but my dad's training helped me to center myself and I clung desperately to the memory of him, refusing to relive my past with my mother.

I need strength, not weakness.

When I was fourteen and my mother allowed my father to see me again—unbeknownst to me at the time, only after a huge payment and promise of no retribution from my father—I finally got to meet him and he was not what I had prayed for. I was disappointed to quickly learn my dad was as irrational as my mom. He loved me, I could tell that from the start, but he got so pissed off so easily I hesitated to talk to him about anything. In many ways he reminded me of some of the men my mother had hooked up with over the years, scary men who I kept as far away from as possible. Trust me when I say it took me a while to warm up to my farther.

Initially I'd hoped I would be reunited with my twin sister and she would be my soulmate, my other half in all things. Instead of being my instant best friend, my sister Swan was as different from me as possible, a high-functioning autistic introvert who hated attention and had no interest in anything I was into, namely sex and drugs at the time. In my self-involved state, I didn't even realize at first she had social issues. I was too busy wallowing in my own pity party to realize she had been trying to reach out to me in her own way, I was just too dense to see it.

I was such a shit to her at first, jealous she'd been able to live in the same house all her life, envious she was so sweet and smart, that she had my father's love. In short, I was a total bitch to my twin and I deeply regret it to this day. That first summer I spent with my father, he sent Swan and me to a really nice camp in Montana together. It was out in the middle of nowhere and they kept the boys and girls camps strictly separate. I didn't belong there, and I certainly didn't fit in or understand all the fourteen- and fifteen-year-old girls I shared a cabin with. Their innocent conversations about letting boys kiss them were completely silly to me because by that point, I'd already had sex and regularly partied it up with my mother in Reno, thanks to a fake ID.

At first I'd broken all the camp rules in an act of stupid rebellion, negative attention and all that, but when I realized how much Swan absolutely hated camping, how hard it was for her to survive with all these people around her constantly, I had to get her out. Even then I knew she was too proud to ask for help or admit how uncomfortable she was, so in order to help her escape, I made sure we were booted. That led to us returning to my dad's place, where for the next two months I learned the fine art of kicking ass from a psycho.

When I returned home to my drug-addict mother after visiting my dad, I fell right back into partying with her. She and my dad had an agreement that there would be absolutely no one spying on us, something my dad had surprisingly agreed to. I think he did it because the only person he knew who was crazier than himself was my mom, and that's saying something.

My father isn't normal, in any sense of the word. He's a survivalist who was determined to turn both me and Swan into mini-commandos. For real. Instead of sitting on the couch on Sunday afternoons when I was visiting, and watching football with my pops, we went through hostage-situation scenarios followed by running through obstacle courses while shooting at targets.

The only instant love I felt was from my stepmother Mimi, and it was overwhelming.

I sucked in a deep breath through my nose, willing myself not to give up and cry.

I, unfortunately, had been a complete brat to her at first, poisoned against her by my mom. If I'd been dealing with a lesser woman, I'd have driven Mimi away within a day. Instead she'd taken me for a horseback ride with her at sunset, and had talked to me as if I was an adult instead of the child my father wanted to treat me like. To this day I fondly remember that life-changing ride, during which I realized I finally had someone in my life who wanted to be everything a mother was supposed to be. Mimi's love for my father and sister was unconditional, and she swore one day we'd grow as a family to the point where I loved them as well.

She'd been correct, as usual, and right now I took every drop of their love I could and used it as fuel to force myself into action.

Lifting my head the slightest bit, I glanced towards the front of the van and saw two men sitting casually, nothing visible in the dim lighting except the backs of their heads and the black of the sky through the windshield with just a hint of dawn on the horizon.

Okay, there were two of them and they weren't paying attention to me at the moment; this was good, I could work with this.

Unfortunately they weren't playing any music so I had to draw my legs up as slowly as possible, rolling again as we took a turn. With my hands bound, reaching down into my boot was harder than I thought it would be, and my sweaty, slippery fingers weren't helping me get a grip on the thin hilt of the knife. I inwardly cursed as the vehicle began to slow and we hit a rough bump in the road.

From the front seat came a man's lightly accented voice. "Call the buyer, let him know we're about an hour out."

The other man grunted and I froze, turning my head enough so I could keep an eye on the men while I desperately dug for my knife. I managed to shove my hands as far as I could into my boot and caught the tip of the hilt between two of my fingers, stifling a sigh of relief as I pulled it free. With half an ear, I strained to hear what the guy in the front was saying on the phone, but he was speaking in a language I was unfamiliar with. I had my knife, but I quickly realized it was going to be a complete bitch to try to use it to cut through the heavy tape around my wrists without slicing myself to ribbons.

He continued to speak into the phone as he left his seat then crouched down next to Beach, pushing his unresisting body over so he was lying on his back. Something flashed beyond the curtain of my hair and I realized it was the flash of a camera, taking pictures of Beach. Another flash came, bright enough that I could still see spots behind my closed eyelids. The man began to speak again and the driver replied with a grunt.

The guy moved back to the front and he put the phone on speaker. "Kyle is listening, Chief."

A man's voice, sounding slightly metallic and distorted, came out in a furious growl. "Why the fuck did you take that gash?"

Gash, a charming slang term for women that was as disgusting as it was derogatory. Despite how much the word irritates me, it looks like I wasn't the target of this kidnapping so that's something positive. That meant they didn't know who I was and what I was capable of if backed into a corner. Perfect.

"We're takin' her with us," the guy driving replied. "Don't worry 'bout her. You get your man and we'll deal with our new friend."

"You idiot," the strange man seethed through the speakers. "You're risking everything for a piece of ass?"

"Nope, risking everything for a million-dollar payday. There are buyers who would pay that without blinking to own such a beautiful woman."

"You're aware she's going to be missed, right? That it'll be all over the news by tomorrow?"

The driver grunted, then said, "What're you taking 'bout?"

"That bitch you have in the back is Sarah Star, a *Playboy* Centerfold and this year's headliner at Sturgis."

I hoped maybe that news would somehow sway them to release me, but instead of being upset, both men cheered. "Fuck yeah, payday! This bitch will be on her way to Russia by tomorrow."

The stranger's oddly modulated voice cut through their glee at the thought of selling me for a bunch of money. "Just make sure she's gone."

"No worries, this bitch is about to become a ghost."

"Good."

The stranger must have hung up because the guy driving angrily said, "What a motherfucking dick. Hate that asshole. Thinks just 'cause he ranked high in the military it means jack shit."

They bitched about him while I tried to get a good grip on my knife, my fingers straining in my limited range of movement.

Glancing over at Beach, I was surprised to see he was awake, his dark eyes glittering with rage and concern as he watched me. I returned his gaze and tried to evaluate how aware he was. For all I knew, they'd drugged him before tossing us in the back of the van after Tasering us.

Moving as slowly as possible, I inched closer to him and tried to communicate for Beach to turn over so I could reach his hands. His brows scrunched down in confusion at my subtle head movements, then I moved my hands so he could see the knife. Right away his eyes went wide and he jerked his head but didn't turn so I could have him hold the knife.

The guys up front were talking now in that foreign language again while a third person, a woman, chimed in, and I realized they'd put the speakerphone on again. They sounded as if they were arguing and I heard my name, but I couldn't stop to listen. Knowing they were distracted—the chick on the phone sounded seriously pissed—I took the opportunity to use my knee to try and shove Beach so he'd roll over to his side.

It took a couple subtle pushes, but eventually he got the idea and rolled.

His hands were almost completely covered in tape but I managed to wedge my knife in there, praying we didn't take any abrupt turns or I'd get that razor edge right in my gut.

Moving as quickly as I dared now, I began to saw through the edges of the tape holding my hands together. I was almost free when the vibration of a heavy foot hitting the floor had me freeze. The guy in the passenger seat from up front was coming back to us and I fought back a tremble of fear.

If he turned me over now, I was fucked.

Sweat beaded on my face as I struggled to control my fear, my overactive imagination painting images of him shooting me in the head as I lay here, almost free. Adrenaline coursed through me and the need to jerk my hands and break free of the tape gnawed at my self-control.

Cloth shifted and I held my breath as he moved, waiting for him to touch me and expose the frayed tape, but karma was on my side at this moment and instead he returned to the front seat.

Sensing time was running out, I managed to free my hands, burning the skin of my wrists in the process. The moment I was free, I froze, waiting for the men to raise the alarm, but they continued to talk—no, argue—with the woman on the phone. Beach remained on his back so I reached beneath him, his big body jerking at my touch, and took the knife from him. I sucked in a deep breath and debated if I should try to free him or take out the threat.

My father's voice whispered in my head that I knew what needed to be done, and even though the tender part of my heart I'd managed to protect from my mother's cruelty protested, I shut it down. The men in the front seat went from being people who had families and loved ones, to my enemy.

No way in hell could I take both of them at the same time, so I had to get rid of the passenger first. If I went after the driver, he'd most likely crash us and I wasn't sure if I'd survive it. Fortunately for me, the argument up front was becoming heated and I could feel the anger from them both filling the van. That sense of time running out sent adrenaline coursing through me and my muscles trembled with the need to move.

I glanced over at Beach, who was clearly telling me to cut his bonds, but I subtly shook my head before looking away. My nostrils flared as I tried to take another deep breath and I wanted to rip the tape off my mouth, but I couldn't risk any more delays.

I got a better look at the passenger as I rolled to my feet and crept towards him. He was in his late forties, maybe early fifties, with dark-tanned skin and black receding hair. His face was craggy and he wore leather gloves—but that was all I noticed before I moved behind his seat and slit his throat.

Hot blood splashed over my hands and I choked back the bile rushing up from my stomach at the hideous gasping, gurgling sound he made. The man driving shouted something as I lunged for his throat then he whipped the van to the right, making me lose my balance and smash against the side of the van. My head rang and a dizzying rush of pain dimmed my vision as I scrambled to my feet. The knife, slippery with blood, fell from my grip and I let out a muffled shout of dismay as I ducked to grab it as a loud bang shook the interior of the van. Glass rained down on my back and I scrambled for the blade, the realization I'd almost been shot threatening to send me into a blind panic.

I managed to scoop up the knife and got a better grip on it as the driver slammed on the breaks. Instead of fighting the momentum, I allowed it to carry me forward and reached out blindly in the direction of the driver, stabbing over and over at the mass of his body as my ears rang and my vision continued to dim. Faintly I thought I heard the man screaming but I was only focused on one thing—killing him.

The van struck something and I flew forward, hitting the dash with my side hard enough it knocked the breath out of me.

I tore the tape from my mouth, the sting of my lips nothing compared to my ribs. Each breath I took sent a wave of pain through me and I shoved my hair from my face, trying to see what had happened. The sky had lightened to the point that through the blood-smeared passenger window, beyond the corpse of the man slumped against the glass, I could see a dim line of pink and gold on the distant horizon.

Steam escaped from the front of the van where it had run into a boulder and a quick glance confirmed the driver was on his way out. Blood covered him and his eyes were already glassy with death as they locked on mine. He was young, maybe in his mid-twenties, and the shock that contorted his features made him appear even younger. My mind tried to focus on the fact that somewhere right now a family was about to lose their loved one. The pain of taking a deep breath cleared my thoughts of anything but the fact I was hurt and these assholes were going to sell me to the fucking Russians, whatever that meant.

Muffled sounds came from behind me and I forced my numb limbs to move so I could go check on Beach. He was crammed against the wheel well, his gaze locked on me as I crawled to him, my breath coming in short pants. I had to wipe my hands on his jeans to get the blood off enough so I could grip the handle of my knife without it slipping as I cut his hands free. From the front seat, the driver exhaled his final breath in a death rattle.

It took some effort, but by the time Beach was able to move, the smell of gasoline was overpowering. He gave a shout as he ripped the tape from his mouth and sure enough, some of his facial hair came with it.

Having had my kitty waxed a couple dozen times before I got most of the hair permanently lasered off, I could empathize with his pain.

My mind was going kinda floaty at this point and I didn't resist when he grabbed the knife from me and began to saw through the tape binding his legs with a fierce grimace.

"Are you okay?"

I gingerly touched my side, pressing down lightly on my ribs and whimpering at the pain. "I think my ribs might be bruised, but not broken."

The scent of smoke reached me as Beach grunted. "We gotta get outta here."

I was in complete agreement because the air inside the van was rapidly fouling and I knew once the fire reached the fuel, we were fucked.

Luckily the back of the van wasn't damaged and it opened from the inside. Beach got out first, his gait unsteady as he helped me out as gently as possible. We stumbled away from the smoking wreck, Beach's face pale and drawn as he took most of my weight with his one good leg and helped me stumble across the sparse grass of the deserted plains. The one-lane road was completely empty as far as the eye could see. I had to hold back my tears as the realization we escaped a terrible situation filtered through the chaos of the last few hours. Training for a situation like this was one thing, but actually living through it was something else entirely.

Beach sat against a large reddish boulder near the side of the road and I pretty much collapsed next to him.

"Fuck," he muttered. "Let me look you over. Where you hurt?"

"My head, and my ribs and my shoulder."

He gently lifted the side of my tank and made a pained noise. "You're banged up pretty bad. Thought for sure you were gonna go through the windshield."

"I'm pretty sturdy." I gestured to my right boot. "My cell phone's in there. Inner pocket. Call my dad."

For a moment he stared at me, then shook his head and loosened the laces of my boot with unsteady hands. "Take it easy, sweetheart, I've got it from here. Don't think callin' your daddy would be the best idea at the moment. I'll get us safe, *corazón*."

I wanted to argue with him that calling my dad would guarantee a quick rescue, but the adrenaline rush was fading and I began to shake, a chill invading me from the inside out.

Beach gave me a concerned look as he began to thumb through my phone. "Sendin' texts first to my SOS network."

Blinking at him, I belatedly looked around and wondered where the fuck we were. There were trees around us, not too thick, but within a mile or so the land stretched out into a proper forest. Our position was exposed from two sides and I didn't feel safe here. We were bound to have company sooner than later, and even though it looked like we were in the middle of nowhere, all it took was one person with a cell phone to see us and call us in to the police.

No, no cops. I didn't want to have to explain I was just an innocent bystander at an outlaw biker party who got snatched, then killed her attackers. This whole situation stunk of some type of organized crime and after a lifetime of my mother scamming people left and right, I'd had my fair share of run-ins with really bad people. Hell, I still had a scar on my chin from where one of the mafia's thugs had kicked me in the face, passing a message along to my mother that she needed to settle her debts.

All that shit changed after I met my dad and it took me a while to realize it, but he'd given me the greatest gifts he ever could. Real self-confidence and the ability to effectively defend myself and those needing help against pretty much anything and anyone. He gave me the skills needed to kick my mom's infrequent boyfriends' asses when they got inevitably rough with her, and to fight off any man who thought because I played up my sexuality rather than be ashamed of it, I was a whore.

Best of all he'd given me the skills to save Marley's life when her ex-boyfriend had beaten her with a baseball bat. I took that bat from him and beat him to within an inch of his life, then called my dad for help with the cleanup. When he found out what happened, that it was some drug addict trying to hit a pregnant woman with a baseball, he became personally involved. My dad doesn't fuck around and Marley's ex found himself in a whole new world of hurt.

"You need to call my dad," I repeated. "Him or one of his buddies will find us quicker than you could believe."

Leaning over, Beach gently cupped my cheek and looked at me with an intensity that cut through the unwanted memories of my past. "You don't get it, *mi reina*. Your life ain't safe to return to right now. Whoever these fuckers were, they'll be pissed we got way and you ain't safe until I figure out who they are and deal with them."

"Beach, listen to me. My dad can take care of it. Seriously."

His eyes got soft and I wondered if he was mentally unbalanced. "I admire your confidence in your father, but truly, you don't want this shit touching him. I'm gonna protect you. I know you don't believe me 'cause you have no idea who the fuck I am, but you'll learn I'm a man of my word."

A secret, stupid girlie part of myself I thought had died years ago latched onto Beach's words with a desperate hope. I wanted to trust someone enough to take care of me, to hold me in the darkness so I wasn't alone, but it was tough. The world was a harsh place filled with predators who blinded those they intended to devour with pretty words. Instead of finding safety in the arms of my boyfriends, I'd found traps, and I was determined not to fall into another one.

I tried to fight the tiny pinprick of hope in my chest, telling myself Beach wasn't good boyfriend material, that he was bad news. Still, what he'd said sank into me and softened the pain flowing through me. I resisted the forbidden temptation of trusting a man, yet he seemed so earnest. And he'd taken care of me back in that horrible room. He'd fought through the crowd to reach me. He said I was the most beautiful thing he'd ever seen and meant it.

He called me his queen.

My temples throbbed and I raised a hand to the back of my head, probing the goose egg there where I'd been pistol-whipped.

"Why," I bit back a wince as I probed the wound, my hair all matted with dried blood and super nasty, "do you have a Spanish accent and yet you look like a really tanned Swedish guy?"

Humor danced in his eyes and I realized it had gotten bright enough that I could tell their true color, a blue so deep it was almost black, midnight blue in the truest sense of the words. Add to that the thick lashes framing those amazing eyes, along with his light copper skin, and you had a supremely hot man. The tense lines around his eyes eased a bit and he gently ran his scarred and tattooed knuckles down my cheek, leaving tingles in their wake.

"First-generation American," he said with a small smile, "on my father's side. He was Mexican, a professional dirt bike racer. My mother's a lovely Texas lady who runs catfish tours. Spent the first six years of my life down in Mexico before we came back to the States with my dad. He passed away few years back, and my mom still works 'cause she loves her job."

Blinking, I cocked my head to the side and grinned. "Your mama runs catfish tours?"

"Yep, her name's Mouse. She'll like you."

"What?"

"She'll like you 'cause you saved my life, and 'cause I like you."

"Did you hit your head too hard?"

Smiling down at the phone while he sent another text, he murmured, "Boys are on their way. ETA fifteen minutes."

He stared at my lips and I thought, despite our mutual battered state, he might kiss me, but the phone rang and Beach looked at me with a raised, blood-flecked dark blond eyebrow.

"Your dad is calling."

Chapter 5

AUSTIN TX

Carlos *"Beach"* Rodriguez

I watched Sarah closely as she answered the phone, wondering if it was just a coincidence her daddy was checking in on her.

With a huff and an eye roll that made her momentarily appear younger, less jaded, she answered the phone. "Delta six eight breaker times two I'm happy-dappy Daddy-o, now calm the heck down. It's not good for your heart."

Baffled, I wondered if she had a concussion, but her pupil response was normal and she seemed coherent. Still, it worried me and I examined her closer, noting the line between her eyebrows deepening as a man yelled hard enough through the phone it made her wince. Caller ID had said "Dad" calling, but now I was wondering who the fuck was going off on her.

"Put Mimi on," she said in a tight voice. "No, I'm not listening to you when you're like this. I get you're scared, and I appreciate you telling me that—your honesty really shows you're working hard with your therapist, but that does not excuse you for losing your shit. Now put Mimi *on*."

Well, it didn't look like she'd have a problem standing up to her dad.

Made my life easier to know my woman could handle herself, not that I'm gonna let anything touch her. Easiest way of that happening was her coming home with me. For a moment I considered she might balk at going anywhere with me, past few hours haven't been good, but I'd treat her so nice she'd never want to leave.

My lower back ached and, fuck, between getting shot, then knocked out, Tasered, then tossed around the back of a fucking van, I was running on fumes and needed my boys to get here quick.

Sarah sat up straighter and touched her side with a grimace. "Hi, Mimi, what the hell is going on?"

For a moment she was quiet, then her expression went downright pissed. "That asshole! He promised me, swore, that he wouldn't put any trackers on my phone."

Trackers? What the fuck kind of father put trackers on a phone? I mean, if I had a daughter as pretty as Sarah, I'd do the same, but it made me rethink my first thought that Sarah came from some nice, normal home in suburbia. Then again, no girl who spent most of her teenage years in the mall spending her dad's money could take out the two men in the van with the efficiency that she did. I hadn't been able to see much due to my bound position, and it happened fucking fast, but I had a few clear seconds of watching her snarl as she ended a man's life. Savage and so sexy it made me fight my cock getting hard.

My brain was still addled from being knocked around, but I was chagrined to realize I'd been so blinded by her beauty that I hadn't looked too far beyond her sweet and spicy exterior.

I wasn't going to underestimate her anymore.

"It was just an app?" She looked slightly mollified, then stiffened. "Yeah, my ribs hurt like a bitch. I'm okay, but Beach was shot in the leg and probably hit over the head like I was. And I think he might have racked his back pretty good. Yes, I said his name is Beach. He's a biker." Even I could hear her dad yelling through her phone. "Tell Dad to calm down, Beach took a bullet meant for me. I owe him, so I'm not going anywhere without him. Yeah, there was a riot at this huge biker party and he fought his way through the crowd to get to me."

I liked the way her expression softened before she said, "Mimi, I'm okay. Seriously. Dad has a friend on the way and Beach says his guys are coming. I've got my knife and he's a good guy. No, seriously—he is. Look, I had a flashback and he pulled me out of it…I know."

Trying to keep my interest hidden, I pretended to check over my injuries, wondering if she was talking about her freak-out back when we were in that holding cell. She'd been terrified, so completely undone that her body had radiated her fear, making my instincts roar for me to protect her. I'd never felt anything like it and I'd been desperate to somehow take away her terror. Thank fuck she'd responded to me.

"Yeah, touch therapy worked…he held me and made me feel safe."

Something eased deep in my gut at her words, a sense of rightness.

She frowned, then looked up and scanned the area, blood still drying on her arms and face. "Shit. Okay, Beach isn't in good shape but I'm going to get us deeper into the brush. Tell whoever is coming out on Dad's behalf to give me warning that they're in range or they'll end up with a knife between their eyes."

She said a few more words, but I was trying to bite back a groan of pain as I stood with the help of the rock and tested out my leg. It had started bleeding again after I'd hit it when the van crashed and Sarah was right, we needed to get under some kind of cover, but the vegetation really was sparse. My respect for her grew as she got me into a firm hold and helped me move as quickly as possible. I could feel the hard muscles of her shoulders shift beneath her silky skin as we made our way across the rocky dirt. In an attempt to take the worry out of her eyes, I gave her a light squeeze then kissed a part of her head where her hair wasn't matted with blood.

"Anyone ever tell you you're the most beautiful thing they'd ever seen?"

Her pale blue eyes cut to mine and some of the tension left her full pink lips. "Sweet-talk me when you're not bleeding."

We didn't make it very far before we had to stop so I could catch my breath. Even though squatting clearly pained her, she knelt before me and whipped out her knife, quickly slicing my jeans so she could look at where I'd been shot. Her touch was light, but it hurt as my adrenaline began to fade. I looked down and watched her slender fingers gently examine me with a distracting grace.

"You have a nice slice, maybe a little bit of muscle damage, and you could do with some stitches, but you're not going to bleed out on me. That would be inconvenient. Plus my dad would never let me live it down, a man dying on my watch."

Not sure if she was joking or not, I sucked in a long breath then stood again. "I'm takin' it your dad isn't a suburban dentist or some shit, is he?"

Standing slowly, she lifted her chin to the left. "There's a thicket of bushes, if we get in there we'll be cool."

I nodded and we moved again, each step sending a wave of hurt through me, but I sucked it up and tried to put as little pressure as possible on Sarah. I noticed the way she favored her side and I hated that I couldn't immediately fix this situation. We settled into the bushes and I grabbed her phone, sending the guys a quick text about where we were, and that we were injured.

As soon as it was sent she grabbed it back and quickly dialed someone's number. "Gotta call to make sure they don't think I've been abducted."

A big smile lit her face, but didn't reach her eyes as she talked. "Hey, sugar, I'm hooked up with a biker hottie and I'm gonna hang out with him for a little longer. You know, my last hurrah before I enter the real world. This guy is so good I need another night or two of being bad. Might even take him down to Cozumel with me." She gave a fake laugh that was totally at odds with her pained expression after listening for a few moments. "Huge. Yeah. Like Long Dick Dong."

I rubbed my face as I tried to get my leg into a more comfortable position, keeping an ear open for company even as she chatted like she was layin' in the fuckin' sun somewhere with a margarita in her hand and a dental floss bikini.

"Just bring my stuff home with you and handle any business crap that comes up. I'm gonna hop a flight tomorrow to go visit my dad for a few days before returning home, you know how crazy he gets if I don't check in. Maybe after that I'll head down to Houston to see Swan." She winced when I put some pressure on her ribs, but allowed me to feel for anything broken. "I know I'm never home, and I miss you too, but you should be happy you have a nomad for a roommate. Means you never have to put on a bra while you're at home if you don't want to."

Her cheeks lost color as I touched a sore spot and I hated having to watch her in pain. Fucking killed me that I couldn't heal her. Satisfied nothing was broken, I leaned back and closed my eyes for a moment, exhaustion hitting me hard.

She laughed and this time it had a real feel to it. "Fine, I'll bring you back those coffee cups you love. Don't worry about setting me up with a hotel in Houston, I've got my ID and credit card with me so I'm good."

After a long goodbye, Sarah hung up and visibly sagged. I pulled her against me as gently as I could, leaning back on my arms. "Come here, put your head down."

Her shoulders firmed and she lifted her head slowly. "I'm okay."

"Just relax. I've got you."

"Beach?"

I glanced down at her. "Yeah?"

"Thanks for uh, holding me and stuff back there. I'm sorry I lost it."

"Hey, none of that shit. You got nothing to be ashamed of. You saved my worthless fuckin' life, ain't nothing weak about you. Nothing."

"Okay," she whispered back, soft and sweet, with her big, bloodshot blue eyes staring up into mine.

"Mean it, *mi riena*, I'm gonna change your world for the better, take care of you and treat you right."

She closed her eyes and placed her forehead on my chest. "Once again, save the sweet-talk for when neither of us are bleeding."

Looping my arm around her shoulders, I pulled her deeper into my side and she resisted at first, then let out a hitched breath and finally gave me more of her weight. Stroking her blood-and-sweat matted hair back from her face, I rested my head lightly on hers, relishing her warmth. Though she was tall for a woman, she was still small compared to me, the perfect size for me to hold and cuddle.

I placed my lips against her temple. "Gotta say, baby girl, this is a hell of a first date."

A snort of laughter escaped her before her hand went to her side again. "Don't make me laugh, it hurts."

"Sorry, sorry. So you wanna tell me who your daddy is?"

Her body stiffened and she tried to pull away, but I wasn't letting her go. "Not really."

"Well, if one of his boys is on his way, it might be a good idea if I knew who I was dealin' with."

From nearby came the low hum of chopper blades drawing closer.

A text came through, letting me know Smoke was flying in with a helicopter ride outta here for me and Sarah.

"Come on, it's my brothers."

"The helicopter is your brothers?"

"Yep. Need to hustle as much as we can and get airborne."

She hesitated, "Where are we going?"

"To Denver to rest up, then on to my home in Austin."

"Uh—no."

"Babe, you can't stay here."

She frowned. "I should wait for my dad's friend. They're going to be pissed if I bail."

"He'd want you safe, right? Well waitin' for his friend at the still-burning scene of a crime ain't safe. My men will clean it up and the cops won't get involved, but we gotta go. He'd want your ass on that chopper." I caught her gaze and let her know I wasn't going to put up with any of her bullshit. "Now get over here and let's move."

For a half second she paused, then ducked her head and muttered, "Annoying."

Shoving her shoulder beneath my pit, she took a hitching breath and I knew she was hurting.

I hated to see her struggle, so I tried to take her mind off the pain and found myself being far more honest than I intended. "When I woke up I thought I was gonna find you dead, or worse. You have no idea how much it relieved me just to see you breathin'. Then the way you took those guys out, pure beauty."

To my surprise, she visibly swelled with pride at my kind of fucked-up words of praise and stood straighter. "Thanks."

Heartened by this, I kept up a constant stream of compliments to her as we hurried out to the road. One thing good about being on the plains was I could see for miles on either side. There was a dust ploom racing towards us from the direction of the rising sun, and the copter coming from the opposite direction. Thankfully I knew the chopper would make it here first, but I wondered who the fuck was speeding our way.

The big helicopter set down in front of us and the side door opened up as the blades slowed. Smoke appeared and jumped down, running over to us while Vance got out and provided cover with an AK-47. Both of them were deadly and completely capable of protecting us.

Smoke shouted, "Got company coming from the east. Three big-ass black SUVs."

I didn't bother to waste time or effort shouting back, grateful when he helped Sarah into the chopper before me. Vance was the last in and as soon as he shut the door we were airborne. Smoke handed out headsets, but the noise wasn't too bad in here. Normally I liked my luxury helicopters, but Smoke could have flown in on a fucking blimp and I'd be happy. My anxiety levels went down and I turned on my headset while everyone else did the same after strapping in.

"Situation?"

Smoke shook his head. "Not good. Lots of bodies to get rid of at once and tensions are high. Took a multiple club effort to clear that shit. Plus, a couple women were shot. Thank fuck they were all women who're loyal to their respective clubs and know how to keep their mouths shut. They're being treated at a top-of-the-line hospital down in Mexico now, chilling in the sun at their private villas for the next month while they recover. Cops know something went down, but not what, and those women are not talking. All the clubs are working together to smooth this over. No one wants the kind of attention this bullshit could bring."

"Do we know what happened?"

"Ambush, but it was kind of fucked-up. We got a couple guys Khan swears are Los Lobos from the Denver area, but we also have some mystery bodies with no type of identification. Gonna run prints. Can you tell us anything about the people who took you?"

"I didn't see much. The driver of the van clocked Sarah over the back of the head with his gun, but he's a crispy critter right now, along with the passenger and any evidence. I was out most of the time in the van, and my memory from. And they have my cell phone and gun."

"Assumed that when you called from her phone."

Sarah casually added, "Before you woke up, they talked to a man with a weirdly modulated voice about you. I think he was the one who ordered the kidnapping. I was an unexpected bonus to the guys sent after you, and got taken along for the ride with the hopes of selling me into sexual servitude for a profit."

We all stared at her as she calmly said these words and I had to bite back the fury that tore through me at the thought of *anyone* forcing her to do *anything* she didn't want. "That will never fuckin' happen."

She rolled her eyes at me and I simultaneously wanted to spank and kiss her.

"I know it will never happen, because I will kill any motherfucker who tries it." Then she graced us with a smile that almost looked genuine. "But really, I'm a nice person."

Vance stared hard at her while Smoke laughed then looked at me with a shit-eating grin. "You're fucked."

Ignoring my Master at Arms, I continued to look at Sarah. "You think you could identify that voice if you heard it again?"

She pursed her lips then smacked them together in a way that made me want to kiss her senseless. "Probably. I can describe it to you if you want, but I don't know if it will do much good. Like I said, his voice was disguised."

"We'll talk about it once we're outta the air."

"Where are we going again?" Sarah asked while looking out the window.

I looked over at Sarah and found her leaning her head against the glass while her shoulders slumped.

Exhaustion lined her face and her eyes were a little glassy. I wanted to pull her into my arms, but this wasn't the time or place.

"Denver," Smoke replied. "Got a guy and a nurse there who'll take care of you. Shit, they've got a whole medical suite."

She rolled her forehead on the glass. "They have a shower?"

"Yep." Smoke gave her shoulder a squeeze. "Don't know what went on, but Beach said you saved his life, so I owe you a debt I'll never be able to repay. Not only is he my Prez, he's also one of my best friends."

"She sure as fuck did." I kept my eyes on her, drinking in the slight changes in her guarded expression as I spoke. "Bravest woman I've ever met."

Her gaze darted to me and a pink flush hit her cheeks. "I was saving my own ass, you just happened to be there."

Smoke chuckled while Vance looked out the window, but I shook my head. "Right."

Smoke looked down at his phone, then frowned. "Change of plans. Source at the airport where we were gonna land says cops are there. We're heading to Golden instead."

"What?" I leaned forward, pissed beyond belief. This was not a coincidence; we picked a way-the-fuck-out-there regional airport to come in. It was in the middle of nowhere and isolated from civilization. It was so against the odds that I knew someone had ratted me out. No way a cop was gonna take one look at our blood-caked bodies and not wanna question us. "Are you fuckin' kidding me?"

"No." Smoke met my angry look with one of his own.

"How many people know we're coming?"

"A lot," Vance quickly said. "When you got snatched up, people lost their minds. Had to let them know we found you and you were alive before people sought vengeance. Got a bunch of the Austin chapter at a hotel in Golden, waitin' on your arrival. Shit has seriously gone down while you've been missing."

"Not too much longer," Smoke said while checking his phone. "Instead of having you stay with Khan, we're taking you to the hotel where the rest of our people are staying. The cops in Denver seem a little too interested in us right now. Nothing to do with that shit that happened back at Sturgis, that scene got cleaned up so well even the FBI couldn't find shit."

"Good to know."

Picking up a hank of her blood-crusted hair, Sarah said, "Look, right now I don't care where we go as long as it's got a bed and a shower."

I reached out and held her slender hand. "Baby, you're mine now, which means you can have whatever you want. All you gotta do is ask."

Her gaze got hard and I had the feeling I'd insulted her somehow. "I don't need a man to buy me stuff. I have—well, I *had* a good-paying job, I have a healthy bank account and investment portfolio, so I can buy anything I want on my own, thank you very much."

Both Vance and Smoke gave me surprised looks at my public declaration of ownership, but I kept my attention on her. "This is not the time or place for this discussion but I suggest you get used to the idea of me spoilin' you. I know we're new—"

"We?" she said in a disbelieving voice.

"Yeah, we're new and it's gonna take some time to get to know each other, but you need to understand I'm in your life now and shit is gonna be different—better in ways you can't imagine."

Most of the women I knew would have been jumping up and down with joy right now, but she looked suspicious. "You're delusional."

I only winked at her, then turned back to my men. "I want her taken care of. Whose gonna be on the ground?"

"Khan, Hulk, and Frame."

"Hulk is her primary bodyguard when you're not around."

"Excuse me," Sarah said in an irate voice. "I don't need a bodyguard."

I turned to her. "I'm gonna have to handle some shit as soon as we land. Might have to be separated from you for a little bit."

"Oh." She looked upset, then quickly hid it. "That's fine, whatever. I just want a shower and food."

The bright sunlight beaming through the window against the side of her face highlighted the dirt and blood marring her gorgeous features and made her pale eyes glow. "Like I said, anything you want. I promise."

The moment our feet hit the tarmac, I spotted Khan, along with Hulk and Frame. I held Sarah's cold hand tight, noting the tension filling her and the way she scanned the area around us as if anticipating an attack. Her unease set me further on edge and by the time we reached Khan, my tolerance for the current situation was getting dangerously thin. If I didn't calm it down soon I was gonna go on a rampage and *no one* wanted that.

Khan, a solid guy in his sixties with a black and grey Fu Manchu mustache stepped forward. "Prez, wish it was under different circumstances, but we're glad to have you with us. Hulk'll take care of your girl, we got shit to discuss."

Out of the corner of my eye, I noticed Sarah was giving Khan her "eat shit and die" look, which he was ignoring and further pissing her off. Now, I might not be an expert on women, but I knew with the trauma she'd been through and the lack of sleep, her ability to maintain her self-control was thin, and I had a feeling people died when she got fed up with their shit.

In an effort to keep her from slitting Khan's throat, I took a step forward and put myself between her and Khan, earning an irritated huff from behind me. Thank fuck she didn't plant a knife in my back. My skin prickled and I swore I could feel her gaze hitting me like daylight on a sunburn.

"Let me get one thing straight real quick. This is Sarah. Not only is she my old lady, she saved my life. Any man who disrespects her will answer to me. Am I clear?"

"She's your property?"

"Yep."

"Excuse me." I inwardly groaned as Sarah added from behind my back, "First, I want a fucking shower. Second, crazy man with the rockin' mustache, I am not a thing or parcel to be passed around at your whim. I go where I want, when I want, and no man will ever tell me what to do."

Smoke, the asshole, busted out laughing and I shook my head at Khan. "She's cranky when she's tired."

"No," Sarah added with so much snark it made my cock fight to get hard. "I'm cranky when I'm dirty; I'm homicidal when I'm tired."

At that Khan smiled wide. "She's gonna give you a run for your money, buddy."

"Don't talk about me like I'm not here," Sarah said and poked my back, like I was the one irritating her.

Hulk cleared his throat and I shifted my attention to him. We've been good friends for a while and I'd been up here 'bout ten months ago for his young daughter's funeral. Terrible shit, the kind of stuff that'll mess you up forever. Hulk was hanging in there, but he'd been quiet, withdrawn. For the first time in months, a smile curved the corners of his mouth as he moved around me to directly address Sarah.

"Hey, sweetheart," he said in a smooth voice as he gave her a smile bigger than I liked, even if it was good to see it on his face. "Name's Hulk, I'm Denver's Master at Arms, and I'll be taking care of you."

"It's nice to meet you, and thank you for the kind offer, but I don't need anyone to take care of me."

Instead of arguing, he nailed her with that bright smile and I remembered how much pussy he'd scored before he met his ex-wife. "Then my job will be a hell of a lot easier. Vacation time. All you wanna do all day is relax at the pool in a bikini, I'm down for that. Then again, I know I'll have to beat motherfuckers off with a stick so maybe we'll stay indoors and play Monopoly or some shit."

Her soft, bright laughter had everyone turning to look at her with an appreciative eye. Even exhausted, covered in dirt and blood, and as irritable as a wet cat she was fuckin amazing. Stuff dreams were made of. Hulk, to his credit, held her gaze and didn't let his eyes wander down to where her big breasts jiggled as she laughed.

"You, me, and margaritas sounds like a plan. But can we do some video games instead of Monopoly?"

"Place we're goin' doesn't have game systems, but it does have a nice, big shower."

She stepped away from me so quick I could still feel her body heat even though she now stood next to a grinning Hulk. "Right. Let's go. And, just so you know, I will gut any man stupid enough to get fresh with me right now."

"Gorgeous, it's not you I'm worried about slitting my throat," Hulk said as he led her over to Frame while giving me a quick look over his shoulder to make sure it was okay to touch her. When I gave him a chin lift, he turned his attention back to my weary girl. "Let's get you checked out then I'll take you to the hotel so you can clean up and relax. You hungry?"

"Very."

"Like fried chicken?"

"Do whores like premature ejaculators?"

Hulks deep laughter rang through the air and I stepped back and watched as Frame quickly looked her over, his red hair burning in the sun and his face going serious as he examined the extent of her injuries. A small portion of her ribs was bruised up and she had various small cuts and scrapes. It killed me to see that perfect body injured and I wanted to go over there and kiss every exposed bruise.

"Old lady, huh?" Khan asked in a low voice.

I kept my eyes on Sarah, ready to step in if she showed a moment of unease. "Yep."

"How long you known her?"

"One day."

Sarah started to walk away with Hulk, then stopped and spun on her heel. She quickly made her way back to me and wrapped her arms around my neck. Deep circles bruised the flesh beneath her red eyes, and her normally pink lips were paler than usual. "I just wanted to say thank you. You didn't have to come back for me when I was taken, but you did."

I wanted to kiss her, but both our lips were crusted with dried blood. "I'll always come back for you."

Her arms dropped. "As much as I appreciate the sentiment, I doubt the veracity of that statement."

With those odd words she was off, leaving me staring after her as Frame came over to treat my injuries and Khan began to fill me in on everything I'd missed.

Chapter 6

Sarah

After we landed at a small airport, I'd been checked over by some redhead biker medic who cleaned my head wound and gave me a strong shot of antibiotics. He agreed my ribs were bruised, and that they would hurt for a few days, then he offered me some painkillers but I declined. I could suck it up right now and would rather save them for when I really hurt. That left me with Hulk, a beautiful black man with massive slabs of muscle and kind green eyes.

We were currently in his truck and he'd asked me a few gentle questions before I made it clear I really didn't want to talk.

After we drove for a bit while listening to some soft R&B, he said, "You'll be staying here at the hotel until we can make sure the current shit show with the cops is handled. Pain in the fuckin' ass."

"Do they bother you guys a lot?"

His hands tightened on the wheel, thick silver rings gleaming on two of his fingers. "Not usually. We got an understandin' with them of sorts. They leave us alone and we keep our territory free of street-corner pimps, drug dealers, and gangbangers. Plus, we…influence some politicians. Have some friends in high places."

"Huh." I yawned and right away winced. "Fuck."

"Should'a taken a pain pill," Hulk muttered, a point he'd made repeatedly over the last twenty minutes.

"I'm fine," I snapped. "Jesus, I'm not some delicate fucking flower that's going to die from a chipped nail."

"Right," Hulk said with a barely hidden smile.

Irritated, I turned back to examine the building surrounded by pine trees that we were pulling up to, my humble abode for the next few hours.

It was three stories high with open walkways leading to the different rooms, which had brass numbers on their doors. The hotel was u-shaped and opened to a lovely view of the mountains. As soon as we pulled into the lot, men and women began to fill the courtyard, enough that I was soon gripping the armrest between Hulk and myself. There were a few cars and trucks with motorcycles in their beds, but even if I hadn't seen all the bikes there I would have pegged the people moving quickly towards us as bikers.

Most of the men were rough looking, some big, some small, but they all had a total "don't fuck with me" vibe going on. The women ran the same gamut, from a gorgeous brunette in a bikini top that could have passed for pasties and denim shorts small enough to be thong panties, to a blonde woman who was probably in her late seventies with skin as wrinkled and tanned as an old leather couch. That older lady wore a bright purple kimono with Jack Daniel's bottles all over it and a pair of old-fashioned high-heeled shoes with pink feathers on the toes. I liked her on sight.

They converged on the truck while Hulk came quickly around to my side and helped me gently out, his touch polite but his stance protective.

A tall woman with her dark brunette hair in braids sauntered up. Then a woman with a shellacked helmet of hair wearing a black tank top and great legs gave me an up-and-down look, then glared—so I glared right back. If she thought a mean look and attitude were going to intimidate me, she had the wrong chick. I had no idea who the hell these people were, but I'd had a rough night and I was struggling to keep my considerable temper under control. Jesus, I stood here obviously covered in blood despite my efforts to clean up with baby wipes at the airport, and I was getting catty looks? These people were weird.

I knew my bitch glare was more powerful than hers, and gave her a taste of it while a group of older men came up to us with grim looks. The sun was warm on my skin and I hoped we'd get to someplace I could sleep soon. The performance, the drinking, and finally killing a couple men had caught up with me, even if I didn't show it on the outside. I'd perfected hiding my pain, hiding my discomfort. Probably because my psychopath of a mother occasionally liked to see me suffer along with her when her bipolar was on the downswing.

"Beach okay?" an old man with a long, white Santa Clause beard growled out.

Unlike the real Santa, this man's blue eyes weren't merry, they were cold and furious. I was unable to help myself, my muscles tensed, ready for violence. It was a knee-jerk reaction when I felt threatened, a flood of flight-or-fight chemicals consuming me and 99% of the time I chose to fight. What can I say, I'd been molded in a world filled with violence, my innocence taken away far too soon, and I'd survived those hard times because I was a fighter. A survivor. I didn't need anything or anyone to get by, but damn it was a lonely life.

Startled by my unexpectedly melancholy thought, I glanced over at Hulk while he gave the men a rundown of what had happened.

Hulk put his hand on my shoulder and I shrugged it off with a glare, irritated how the men were giving me openly disbelieving looks at the mention I'd saved Beach's life. Hulk studied me for a moment, tension tightening the fine lines around his eyes, but whatever he saw on my face seemed to calm him. A dimple popped out in his cheek as he gave me a wide smile, handsome enough that he made me blink, and I've been around some unbearably hot guys in the entertainment business.

"Ms. Sarah," he said in a voice loud enough to echo in the courtyard, "is going to be our guest for a bit. Our honored guest. She got our Prez safe when he got shot and taken and he's in her debt. He also claimed her, so I suggest you treat her with respect or you'll be hearin' from Beach, and you do not want that."

Everyone looked at me now with expressions varying from disbelief, to open welcome, to scary blank face. The scary blank face was mostly on the guys, but there were a few women who looked like they could hold their own gazing back at me with no expression. I didn't mind; my father was one of the most suspicious people in the world and I was used to people treating an outsider like…well…an outsider. My dad, stepmom Mimi, and twin sister Swan all lived on an honest-to-God prepper commune in Texas. They, along with about five thousand plus other families on various compounds, made up their own town on a shit ton of land in the Texas Hill Country. Being self-sufficient, they rarely left the compound and all visitors were looked at like potential invaders.

With this in mind, I gave the bikers watching me a bright smile that I'd practiced for hundreds of hours for the various pageants I was in as a kid. "Hey."

Okay, I probably looked creepy as shit giving a merry wave and a smile while looking like roadkill, but it was the best I could do at the moment.

A few said hey back, but the guy who seemed to defer to was a handsome Spanish guy in his thirties with a short mohawk and tattoos all over. He wasn't wearing a shirt so I got a nice view of all that intricate ink stretched over thick muscle. The tattoos crawled up to his neck in some Aztec-looking pattern, calling attention to how thick his muscles were. He gave me a deliberate inspection, staring me up and down, then smiled.

"Well, well, well, never thought we'd have Miss March as the Prez's old lady. Beach does not disappoint, but darlin', you're lookin' a little rough."

"I don't have time for your bullshit. I need my own room to crash in and a laptop." I cracked my neck then yawned again. "With all due respect, I'm past exhausted and I've been up for almost two days. Can I please get a shower then collapse somewhere with a clean bed?"

"She's staying in Beach's room," Hulk said quickly.

"He's such a lucky fucker, always takin' the best women for himself." The hot guy with the mohawk winked at me. All the men laughed and the guy with the mohawk handed the gun off, then stuck his hand out. "Name's Sledge, I'm the National Vice President for Iron Horse. Good to meet you, Sarah. Saw you work that pole back at Sturgis. I'm a big fan."

I shook his hand, wanting to wrap this up and get inside. A migraine was beginning to threaten and already the light was bothering me. I knew the stress combined with getting my head banged around triggered it, but I left my pills back at the campground in *Playboy's* RV, which meant Marley had them. Crap.

"Can I get a phone?"

"Why you need a phone?"

"Beach still has mine." Closing my eyes against the glare, I sighed.

"Rosco," Hulk bellowed over his shoulder to the watching crowd. "Burner, now."

Before I could draw a breath, a short and beefy guy with a good dark pornstash and an easy smile handed me a phone.

"Right," Sledge said and turned his attention back to Hulk. "Drop her off in Beach's room and come back down. We got shit to discuss."

The crowd began to disperse a bit and I was grateful Hulk quickly led me up two flights of stairs to what was evidently Beach's room. While I was pissed over the way Beach had talked about me with his buddies back at the party, I had to admit the fact that he shoved his way through a stampeding crowd of people to get to me made my heart flutter a little bit. He took a bullet for me. If he'd been hideous, I wouldn't have a problem telling him to piss off, but he was so unfairly sexy. He was the kind of man women dreamed about, but never saw in real life. Well, maybe not exactly what women dreamed about; he could be a prick, but God I wanted to see him in all his naked glory.

My semi-benevolent, mostly horny thoughts about Beach came to a crashing halt when Hulk opened the door and the first thing I saw in the dim light filtering in through the heavy curtains was an older bottle blonde with thick eyebrows lounging on the bed.

How did I know she was a bottle blonde? She was nude and the carpet didn't match the drapes.

At the sight of me, she sat up, her dark eyes narrowed as her overinflated lips stretched into a pissed-off pout. Now, I'm not one to cast stones for cosmetic surgery, if it makes you feel better about yourself by all means go for it, but this bitch had a really shitty doctor and her growing sneer pissed me right the hell off.

"Who the fuck is that, Hulk?"

The big man at my back made a tired sound. "Naomi, get the fuck out of here. Have you lost your damn mind?"

"But Beach always asks for me," she whined, and any happy horny thoughts I'd had about Beach died a quick death.

"Don't fuckin' bullshit me," Hulk growled as he tossed what I assumed were her clothes at her. "I don't know who the fuck let you in here, but I can guarantee you it wasn't 'cause Beach wants to see you. Now get the fuck out."

Snarling at Hulk, the woman jerked on her uber-short white skirt. "Beach will be pissed when I tell him how you're talking to me."

Letting out a deep, not-so-nice laugh, Hulk took a menacing step closer. "If you think he gives a fuck about how I talk to a club whore, you are out of your damn mind. Now, last warning, get the fuck out before I tell Beach about you bein' a pain in my ass."

"Fuck you," she snapped.

When she walked past me, she pushed me back and my injured side hit the wall, sending a wave of pain through me that snapped my self-control.

In a blind rage, I grabbed her by the back of the head and smashed her face against the wall hard enough to make her nose gush blood. She gave a terrified scream and I threw her away from me.

"Hulk, get her the fuck out."

"Stupid fuckin' bitch," Hulk muttered. "Damn, girl, you went all ninja on her and shit. Nice moves."

He shoved the sobbing woman out the door and I paid him no mind when he returned a moment later, without the bloody woman. "So, in the future, if you have a problem with someone, let me handle it."

"So, in the future, if you fuck up and someone hurts me, I'm supposed to stand there and pout while the men handle it? No." My eyes stung with unshed tears and I lifted my hand in his direction. "This discussion is over, time for you to leave."

"Hey now, I'm sorry 'bout that, girl. I had no idea she'd be here and I can assure you Beach don't want nothing to do with her. And you're right, if someone hurts you, don't fuckin' wait for a rescue, handle that shit yourself if you can."

Hating how quickly I was becoming debilitated and the fact that I needed to ask for help, I said through gritted teeth, "Don't care. My head hurts. Migraine."

I staggered forward until I felt the edge of the bed with my knees, then crawled onto it with a low moan. Everyone needed to shut up and let me curl into a ball of agony and zone out. Nothing touched the pain of a migraine, not even when I'd blown out my knee during ice skating, and that shit had hurt. I pulled one of the thin hotel pillows against my stomach and curled around it.

"Sarah." Hulks voice came from nearby, but I didn't even lift my head. "You okay?"

"Yeah, migraine, go away. Need quiet."

"You need some medicine?"

"Yeah, but my pills are back home in Vegas with Marley, my roommate and assistant." The pain made me want to snap at him, but I forced my anger back and struggled to breathe evenly. "It's okay. Just need dark and quiet."

"Okay." He sounded doubtful. "You sure?"

"Yes. Just go."

I think he left soon after, but I wasn't sure. Pain is a funny thing; when it hits you hard, time doesn't act like it's supposed to. A minute can take centuries, an hour goes by in an agonizing blink. When the bed next to me depressed and a rough male hand stroked my hair back from my sweaty face, I struggled to push past the throbbing in my head enough to speak.

"*Mi corazón*," a deep male voice as smooth as honey whispered, "I need you to take these pills."

I was so desperate for relief I would have done anything at that point to feel better. Nausea gripped me and I couldn't help but cry as I lifted my head enough for Beach to place the pills in my mouth. A moment later he lifted a glass to my lips and I took a couple big swallows of cold milk, the pounding in my head so bad I could only moan in pain. Everything throbbed, there was no rise or fall to the pain, it was just constantly bad.

"Gotta rehydrate you. Need you to drink a little more for me."

I wanted to weep, but I moved my head enough to guzzle down some water before I couldn't bear the pain anymore.

Beach lowered me back down then began to very, very gently stroke my body, his touch soothing me on some base level, helping me to relax enough that my muscles weren't constantly tensed up. If I had a really bad migraine I'd be sore the next day, like I'd done a triathlon. As either the pills or his touch began to work, I couldn't help the low moan that ground out of me as I stretched my arms and legs on the comforter.

The comforter that the stupid bitch had been lying naked on. Yuck.

"Beach?" I whispered. Opening my eyes at this point wasn't happening. Any change in light seared through me and I wanted to pass out into the peace of unconsciousness.

"It's me, sweetheart. You okay?"

"Better, thanks." I moved as slowly as possible, trying to sit up, which made my head pound again.

"Hey, hey, where you goin?"

"I'm not lying on skank."

"What?"

With a groan, I collapsed back down again, having to take a moment to gather my breath before speaking, my eyes still closed. "Some chick was in here, naked on your bed waiting for you. Her cooties are all over it."

His hand, which had resumed its slow circling of my back, froze. "Who was in here?"

Realizing no one had told him, I tried to play it off. "I don't know, some woman."

"She was naked, here, in my room?"

Oh boy, the temperature of said room just plunged a few degrees.

"Uh—yeah. Hulk got rid of her." Without even looking at him I could feel the anger coming off him in icy waves. Wanting to distract him, and get him back to doing that wonderful stroking that helped take the pain away, I rolled over to my back with a grunt. "Can you get my boots off, please? And can I get another drink of water?"

He blew out a huff of air, then unzipped my boots and drew them down my legs, making me sigh in relief once they were both off. "Be right back, babe, gonna have these cleaned."

I kept my eyes closed and tried to relax as he opened the door ten spoke to someone in a low voice. I knew he'd returned when the bed dipped and his warm, jean-clad thigh pressed against my hip. With Beach watching closely, I drank more water and I swore I could feel it slowly hydrating me. He was quiet for a couple dozen heartbeats, but I didn't say anything. My relief was a precarious thing and I didn't want to do anything to piss my brain off. It was time to get another round of Botox shots, something I put off because of my touring. Looked like I was paying for it now.

Without asking, Beach removed my socks as well, then ran his hands up and down my legs before rubbing my feet. As his thumb pressed into the sole of my foot, he spoke quietly. "My mom used to get bad headaches. After she'd work all day, sometimes she'd come home with a pounding head. Hated that I couldn't take her pain away, couldn't take care of her. Looked up everything I could about how to treat headaches. Tried 'em all but found out that for her at least, a foot rub helped to ease the pain."

His words resonated with me. Like Beach's mom, mine would often come home from work with a headache, but that was because she'd be coming down from being either drunk or high as fuck.

Things got worse after I reconnected with my dad. I can remember dreading going back to my mom after staying with him because I knew she went on benders when I wasn't there to keep her grounded. In many ways I'd been the adult in our relationship, the one relied on to keep it all together despite my mother's ever-increasing spiral of self-destruction. At one time she'd been the best mother in the world, but those days were long gone. She was weak and her already fragile mind had fragmented beneath the crushing weight of years of heavy drug use.

The calming stroke of his rough hands on me as he slid me beneath the sheets was nice and I sighed when he got into the bed behind me.

At first he didn't touch me, then he let out a heavy groan and rolled over, his weight on me comforting. He wore what felt like a t-shirt and boxers, and he smelled divine. He was so tall that his feet had to be almost hanging off the edge of the bed, and broad enough to make me feel sheltered by his presence. Even so, I stiffened when he wrapped one arm gently around my lower belly and curled the other beneath my pillow so my head was resting on his hard biceps.

"Easy," he murmured against my hair. "I just want you to get some sleep while I hold you, okay? Nothin' more. Don't like seeing my baby in pain so give this to me."

"'Kay," I whispered back, the drugs now working through my system having totally taken away any pain I may have been experiencing and replacing it with drowsy pleasure.

The sensation of the rough hair on his legs felt nice to my addled mind and I rubbed my leg over his. "Scratchy."

He chuckled and soothed his lips over the sensitive skin behind my ear. "Smooth. Soft. Delicious."

When his tongue darted out to lick my earlobe, I pushed my butt back into the very, very generous erection pressed up against me. "This is nice."

He nipped my earlobe then released it. "What is?"

So sleepy that I could barely form words, I stretched out, then settled back into him. "We fit. Click."

"What?"

"Puzzles pieces, made to fit."

He sucked in a deep breath, his broad chest pushing against my back. "Yeah, we do."

Somewhere in the back of my head I knew I should be asking some important questions right now, or calling my dad, but I was helpless to resist the drugging warmth of Beach holding me close and tight, like I'm something extraordinary.

"Sleep, Sarah," he whispered against the top of my head. "Swear you're safe with me."

Anything he said after that was lost to me as darkness sucked me under.

Chapter 7

AUSTIN TX

Waking up brought a stunning clarity that made me really wish I still did coke. I know it sounds ghetto as hell when I say that, but I'd been a coke head between the ages of fifteen and sixteen, during a really dark time in my life. Judge all you want, but with my mom's dysfunctional guidance, I'd discovered early on recreational drugs could dampen the pain associated with living. Unfortunately, they also helped blunt the good parts of me that recognized what my mom did was wrong, what I did to help her was wrong, and that we were hurting people. When I was high it didn't matter that my mom worked at a brothel outside of Reno, that she disappeared for weeks on end, and that I was beginning to realize how many people's lives she'd ruined with her scams while using me to do it. The only way to escape my guilt over hurting people by participating in her schemes was to get obliterated.

I'd done things that were flat-out wrong, and had the slap down from karma to prove it. It was only after I'd changed my own selfish ways that my luck finally began to turn around. I didn't always get it right, had fucked up major with my twin sister while trying to help her see the truth about her douchebag boyfriend, but I swear I was coming from a good place.

Behind me, a very large man shifted on the bed, then curved his bare, furry, muscled arm under my waist and settled against me with a sigh and a sleepy rumble.

Beach.

The situation I was currently in was not the safest. I knew it, my soul knew it, yet my body didn't give a fuck. It was thrumming in delight at the sensation of a big, bad, scary, *powerful* man curled protectively around me. He slid one thigh forward, pressing between mine until I was straddling his leg as he pretty much covered me from the top of my head to the tips of my toes. The warmth of his breath against the back of my head felt good, comforting, and tingles raced from my nipples down to my clit. Even though I was sore as hell, his body cradling mine in warmth and comfort was amazingly delicious.

I've had my fair share of sex, in some cases more than my fair share, but I'd never experienced the kind of attraction I felt for this man. To make matters worse, I was rocking myself, ever so slightly, against the hard male thigh pressed against my needy sex. Warning bells rang in the back of my mind that I needed to get out of this bed, away from the drugging influence of his body, and think.

As tempting as it was to lay here in his arms, I needed to check in with my parents then hit the road and get back to Las Vegas.

A twinge of unease went through me at the thought of leaving Beach behind, but I forced myself to ignore it. This, whatever it was, between us was never going to happen. My ten-year plan does not include being a biker bitch, no matter how much Beach made my libido purr. And I was sure he didn't mean all that stuff he said about taking care of me. He probably hit his head too hard in the van.

Besides, he just thought he wanted me, wanted the carefully crafted illusion of Sarah Star. In truth I was horrible at relationships, just terrible. Watching my mother manipulate, use, then destroy men over and over again had screwed up my ability to form a lasting romantic attachment to anyone. My therapist said I chose the wrong men to start relationships with because I knew they were doomed from the start and sooner or later the guy would give me some excuse to break it off with him and never look back. Dumping and forgetting men was easy for me. After all, I'd watched my mom devour any man foolish enough to ever care for her over and over again. Memories of all the men, good and bad, that she'd wronged raced through me, killing any lingering desire I felt for the massive biker holding me so close. If he knew how damaged I was inside he'd leave me, so it was better if I left first.

With a soft exhalation I shoved myself off the bed, fighting his hold when he tried to drag me back into the warmth and safety of his arms. He made a surprised grumble when I easily twisted out of his arms and evaded him, but I had to get some alone time, now, to process this and figure a way out. As much as I'd like to just vanish, as much as my animal mind was urging me to flee, I didn't want him to worry about me. He seemed like a good guy, in his own way, and I didn't want to hurt him.

"Bathroom," I muttered.

I noticed for the first time that Beach had shaved his beard off, revealing a super-sexy man who made my who body tingle. I hit the hot guy jackpot, sexy both with and without a beard. Rugged, experienced, totally drool worthy. Another shiver raced through me between my thighs, making my sex clench as I allowed myself to indulge in staring at him. Damn, it would have been a lot easier to resist the urge to jump him if he'd been butt ugly beneath his whiskers. Other than having a good-sized bruise on his temple, a couple scrapes and a healing split lip, he looked fine. No, more than fine, he looked amazing, and I wanted to sink my fingers into his thick, clean golden hair.

And I really wanted to rub up against his golden chest hair.

Nice.

Leaning up on one arm, his tribal tattoos flexing enticingly against his big biceps, he gave me a very slow once over that made me aware I'd stripped down at some point in my drug-and-exhaustion-induced sleep. Not unusual; wearing clothes to bed made me feel claustrophobic. A quick look down confirmed I still had my sparkly red tank top on, and my "spank me" panties were in place, but that was it. Then I raised my hand to my hair and winced. Fuck, it was all windblown, blood-matted and a huge rat's nest.

"Where's the bathroom," I repeated, my skin itching with the need to wash.

"To the right," Beach said as his dark blue eyes blazed with need, making my skin feel tight and in need of his soothing touch.

Feeling like a coward for running away, I growled when he evidently read the rear end of my panties and laughed out loud. "Baby, I'll spank your bad little ass anytime you need it, but why don't we wait until you heal up first."

After shutting and locking the bathroom door behind me, I looked in the mirror over the old green sink and winced. My makeup had melted down the side of my face I slept on, and I had dark circles beneath my eyes. A quick sniff of my shirt confirmed I smelled like a nasty combination of sweat, my faded Burberry perfume, and blood. Not a nice smell at all. With a shudder of revulsion, I stripped off my clothes and tossed them into the corner. No way I was wearing those things until they'd been washed like a dozen times. My belly churned as I turned on the water, not even waiting until it was warm to jump in and grab the little bottle of liquid soap the hotel provided.

I had to get clean, now.

The water heated up as I used a washcloth and proceeded to scrub my skin with shaking hands until it was pink. I have a thing about being dirty and smelly. At one point in my young life, my mother had been forced to leave me home, alone, for over a week when I was six. No doubt she'd screwed someone over and was on the run, burying her tracks, or she'd been on a drug binge. She'd also "forgotten" to pay the water bill and it got shut off three days into her absence. There was plenty of bottled water to drink, we had one of those big water bottles in the kitchen, but I couldn't flush the toilet or bathe, and soon the apartment and me had started to smell really bad before my mom finally came home.

As a result, I'd developed an aversion to being unclean, to things being dirty and smelling bad. It reminded me of the fear I'd felt at being alone, being too scared to ask the nice neighbor lady who always gave me cookies for help. If I did my mom said they'd take me away from her and put me in "the system", a terrible place where pretty girls like myself were hurt in bad ways.

With a harsh breath I forced my thoughts back to the present and tried to only think about the decadent pleasure of a warm shower. Right here, right now, I was safe, and I had to enjoy these moments of quiet while I could, knowing all too well how quickly the illusion of peace could be torn to shreds. I ran my hands over my smooth legs, loving how they stayed bare thanks to laser treatments that removed all of my body hair except for a thick landing strip. What can I say, I like my partner to have something to pet.

Once I was finished with my cleaning ritual, including spending what felt like twenty minutes working the tangles out of my hair with conditioner, I relaxed and let the warm water loosen my muscles, gathering my thoughts. I killed three, maybe four people last night. The only worry I had was getting caught, but I knew if worse came to wort my dad would cover my tracks. As far as having a mental breakdown over ending their lives? That wasn't going to happen. I was an instrument of Lady Karma last night and as I can personally tell you, she can be a bitch.

Grabbing the bottle of citrus-scented lotion from the small basket on the faded vanity, I slathered myself up before opening a toothbrush that had been left on the counter. While brushing my teeth vigorously, I took another look at my bruises, testing the ones along my ribs and wincing a bit. They looked terrible, and I had other black, yellow, and purple splotches blossoming on various parts of my body. Including a nice one shadowing the right side of my jaw.

I pondered for a moment if I should put my old clothes back on, but they were so nasty they should be burned. So I wrapped a towel securely about myself then I stepped out into the hotel room, bracing myself for seeing Beach—then puzzled and strangely sad when I noticed I was alone.

There were a pair of jean shorts left at the foot of the bed that was pretty tiny and a skimpy black tank that would expose half my stomach and half my breasts. As I held them up, my lip curled in disgust at the sheer trashiness of the outfit. Wear this to a club in Las Vegas? Sure. Out in daylight at a hotel in Bumfuck, Colorado? Um—no. Look, despite the fact I enjoyed dressing sexy, I understand there is a time and a place for everything, and that your kids don't need to see my bottom biscuits and major cleavage. Besides, wearing an outfit like this among a bunch of strangers, testosterone-fueled biker strangers at that, wasn't a good idea. I could handle any guy who got too frisky, but I really wasn't in the mood to fight, and especially not in a shirt where my tits could pop out.

While it was nice Beach had left clothes behind for me, no way in hell was I putting them on.

For all I knew, one of their…what the fuck had Scarlet called them…the women who were like free-range pussy to the bike club they belonged to? Oh yeah, the sweet butts had contributed it. These skintight clothes could have been worn by one of them and I was not putting it on. Not happening. I was all nice and clean at the moment, and I planned on staying that way. With this in mind, I went over to the battered brown leather duffel bag sitting on the dresser then opened it up. I was momentarily surprised to see a loaded Ruger SR40 pistol lying atop a pile of what looked like clean t-shirts, but I was more interested in covering my ass with the clothes beneath the weapon.

Moving the loaded weapon aside, and marveling at Beach's stupidity for leaving the gun where it could be easily found, I pulled out the first black t-shirt of his I saw, gratified to find it smelled of fabric softener. With no bra I had to be careful of wearing thin t-shirts, but he was such a big man that it wasn't skintight and fell to the tops of my thighs. There was no way I was going out there in just a t-shirt and my thigh-high combat boots, so I dug through his bag again.

I found a pair of Armani black boxer briefs lying atop a couple pairs of jeans. For a moment I studied them, wondering at the kind of biker who would wear such expensive underwear. Men's voices came from outside so I quickly pulled them on, smiling when I saw they actually almost looked like yoga shorts on me, other than the fly.

Trying to act nonchalant, I finger combed my wet hair, grateful once again that it would dry bone straight. My stomach growled as I studied myself in the mirror over the chipped dresser and wished I had my makeup bag to help combat the "survivor of the zombie apocalypse" look I had going on.

As if in answer to my empty belly's prayers, the door opened and a warm breeze blew into the room, bringing with it the scent of delicious, greasy fried food.

Automatically, I did a quick mental calculation of the calories I could afford to spend on the meal, something second nature to me, then let out a little huff of relief as I realized I wouldn't have to do that anymore. For the first time in my life I could have a belly pooch if I wanted it. I would never give up working out, it helped staved off depression, but I could indulge in foods I'd forbidden myself for far too long. Calorie-laden meals that were so delicious, but after first the world of beauty pageants, then competitive skating, and onto stripping then pole dancing, I'd never had the opportunity to be in anything other than top physical shape.

But now that I was leaving that world behind and starting my career as an interior designer, I no longer had to worry about how my abs looked in a string bikini.

Instead of forcing down another salad, I could have anything I wanted.

I could even have dessert.

Awesome.

With this new truth settling into my mind, I looked up from the bags of food Beach was carrying and sucked in a quick breath as his gaze met mine. I was kind of hoping he wouldn't be as hot as I remembered, with his golden-blond hair and deep navy blue eyes, would be easier to resist, but fuck he was so good-looking I could feel my breasts swell in a painful rush. As if my chest had some kind of secret ESP with him, his gaze zoomed in on my erect, thick nipples, which pushed against the thin fabric.

Crossing my arms, I glared at him. "Hey, buddy, my eyes are up here."

From behind Beach came an unfamiliar man's voice. "Don't get fuckin' lippy with the Prez, you stupid cu—"

Whatever he was going to say ended abruptly when Beach, without looking back, said, "You talk about my old lady that way again and I guarantee you'll be breathin' outta tube before sundown."

A hard tingle zapped my clit at the possessive way he said "my old lady" and I inwardly berated myself for being a moron attracted to violent criminals. Beach kicked the door shut behind him with his foot, and I couldn't help but notice how long his legs were, and how he had really nicely muscled…well—everything. The package he was packing behind his jeans was not small by any stretch of the imagination and my body wanted him inside of me, bad. My gaze drifted to his face as he set the bags down on the dresser, taking in the lines around his eyes, the self-assured way he moved.

"Hungry, *mi nina linda*?"

I frowned at him, not sure if I dug him calling me his "pretty little girl". "Yes."

"See you're wearin my clothes instead of the ones left for you. Been goin' through my stuff?"

He said it like I was snooping on him and I gave him a frosty glare. "Look, I'm not wearing some strange hooker's clothes."

"What?"

I pointed to the bed, not touching the items lying there. "I have no idea who wore these, or what kind of personal hygiene they had."

A dimple popped in his cheek as he smiled. "But you'll wear my clothes?"

He looked strangely pleased by that and I marched over to his side, as best I could with no bra and barefoot, then grabbed a paper bag and let out a little moan when I opened it and found thick French fries and what smelled like cheeseburgers. Snatching the fries out, I also grabbed one of the cold bottled waters he'd brought with the meal. The first bite of the golden fried potato goodness was so divine that I sighed and closed my eyes, savoring the greasy, salty nummyness.

"Oh man, yum."

Amusement rang clear in Beach's voice. "That good, huh?"

"You have no idea." I shoved another one in my mouth, not caring they were almost too hot and burned my tongue. "What else did you get?"

"Bacon cheeseburgers with the works."

"Awesome."

Focusing on eating was one way to delay any inevitable conversations, so I scarfed my food down like a starving woman. The cheeseburger was even better than the fries and I had to admit, diet mayo tasted nothing like the real stuff. Swan, my twin sister, ate junk food all the time and I often stared on with longing while she dug into sour-cream-laden mashed potatoes and I had my steamed vegetables. I laughed to myself as I thought about how shocked she was going to be when we did lunch again and I ordered fried cheese sticks for an appetizer.

A pang hit me low in the gut as a I realized how much I missed her and I really wished I hadn't fucked up with her.

While Swan and I are, in theory, identical twins, we are vastly different. See, when we were born, Swan was the weaker twin. I hogged up all the resources in the womb and she was smaller than me. My mom said I starved Swan while sharing a womb and that's why she's autistic. Of course I didn't believe her, but she'd planted that evil seed of self-doubt inside of me that had taken root despite my best efforts to weed it out.

Shit…Swan.

"My sister."

Beach put his food down. "What's that?"

"My sister, she's alone in Houston. You need to send someone to watch over her. She's my identical twin and I don't want someone thinking she's me."

"You give me her information and I'll put some boys on her."

I hesitated, knowing she'd hate for me to reveal her weaknesses to a stranger, but needing Beach to understand. "She's a high-functioning autistic, so whoever keeps an eye on her needs to understand she is to be left completely alone. Do not approach her unless she's in real danger. This is the first time she's left my parents' house and I don't want anything to make her run back there. I'm afraid if she does, she'll never leave the safety of their home, and that's not a bullshit fear. She…she doesn't process things the same way most people do, but she can be incredibly dangerous thanks to my dad's batshit crazy training. If she finds out I have people watching over her, she will freak out that I betrayed her privacy, and our relationship is already shaky, so whoever goes will have to be skilled."

"Why is your relationship shaky? Sounds like you love her to death."

"I do. I…well, I fucked up, bad, and I'm still trying to win my way back into her life. If she knew about any of this shit," I circled my hand in the air, gesturing to our surroundings, "she'd flip out so I need to keep everything that happened on the down low. Tell your guys if she spots them to say you and I met in Austin when I was checking into a design school there. Keep it simple but believable."

"Not sure I like lyin' like this."

"I'll tell her the truth, eventually, but I don't want her worrying about shit she can't fix right now."

He frowned then took a drink from his soda. "Won't your parents clue her in?"

"No. She'd overreact and want to come rescue me, guns blazing, then she'd retreat back into her shell and any hope she had of a normal life would be gone.

Beach, she deserves to be happy, without my family's shit spilling over into her life. She deserves to be able to be the person she wants to be without having to pay for my sins. Just make sure whoever watches over her knows what to say." I put my almost-finished burger down and met his gaze, willing him to understand how important this is to me.

Reaching out, he threaded his fingers through my hair, gently working out any tangles he encountered with a soft touch. I could only sigh as he pulled me into his arms and rested his head atop mine. The scent of his delicious cologne filled me, cloves and some kind of earthy spice that reminded me of the smell of autumn. Beneath that lay his unique scent and it calmed me to breathe him in.

"I'll put some guys on her, men who know how to stay hidden and to watch from a distance. Won't be 24/7 guard, but I'll have Smoke set it up."

"Thanks," I said before gently pushing out of his arms and returning to my meal, my heart and head lighter.

By the time I was done, I was feeling really mellow and appreciative of the fact that Beach had allowed me to eat in silence. It wasn't an uncomfortable silence. He'd spent the time staring at me while I avoided his gaze. In a way, I liked him staring at me. No matter how screwed up, the truth was I enjoyed having a man think I was beautiful. I know it's a leftover thing from my pageant days when I'd been objectified to the point of being a living doll, but just because I was aware of a character flaw didn't mean I could change it. I had to survive so my mind adapted in a way that kept me sane. Or should I say, sane-ish.

That sanity was being questioned as I sat back against the headboard and crossed my legs, meeting Beach's gaze as he cleared off the bed before returning to my side. He didn't try to grab me, but he did lay down next to me with about a foot of space between our bodies. The soft material of his grey t-shirt clung to his well-built chest and I couldn't help but reach out and run a finger over one big pectoral muscle, testing to see if the fabric was as smooth as I imagined.

A low rumbling sound came from him and he wrapped his big hand around the back of my neck, urging me closer.

Stupidly I asked, "What are you doing?"

"Kissing you."

"We shouldn't do this," I whispered.

"Yeah, we should."

"I need to call my dad."

"You can call him in a little bit," he breathed against my mouth and I softened into his touch.

"No, really—I don't think we…"

My voice trailed off as he ever so gently brushed his firm lips over mine, a slow rub that sent my hormones into overdrive with electrical sparks. A whimper escaped me when I opened to his soft mouth and rubbed my tongue along his, tasting him and relishing the way his grip on my head tightened. Shit, he really knew how to kiss, and I was no slouch in that department. His tongue slowly stroked along mine and I groaned at the taste of him, my skin growing sensitive to his every touch. He held me gently as we kissed, his hand rubbing along my back slowly, taking his time exploring me.

It took a monumental effort on my part, but I managed to jerk my head away from his dangerous lips. The feel of him echoed through my pussy in a burning wave of heat that had my body hating me for stopping the fun. Denying my sexual needs has never been one of my strong points. When his big hand cupped my ass and jerked me closer, he took the opportunity to roll partially on top of me, his expression serious even as his long cock pressed into my pelvis.

"So pretty," he murmured while stroking my face. "So fuckin' pretty. Know if I have you to look at for the rest of my life I'd be a happy man."

"Beach."

It was a protest, but I wasn't sure what I was even arguing with, totally thrown by the way he made my entire body light up.

I couldn't help but notice the beginning of a colorful tattoo on his inner biceps that I couldn't quite make out. His thick, golden hair gleamed in the light coming in from around the edges of the curtains, and motorcycles revved outside. I could also hear the occasional laughter of women mixed with the loud shouts of men. Oddly enough, everything happening outside held no importance at the moment. My gaze had been captured by his and I struggled to remain strong against his magnetic pull.

"I need to call my dad, then I need to get back to Vegas."

"Not safe, you're comin' with me to Austin."

"Umm, no." I put my hands against his chest, telling myself I was pushing him away instead of groping him. "While this has been fun, I have a life there I need to get back to."

"Not anymore. It's common knowledge you saved me, and baby, you are not inconspicuous. Can't say I was surprised to learn your gorgeous ass was a showgirl and a *Playboy* bunny. The people who lost out on takin' me will target you. We both know it, and while I know you can handle yourself, the thought of harm coming to you in a brief unguarded moment is not good. You're coming back to Austin with me, end of story. Now call your dad and tell him you're *my* responsibility now, my woman, so he can relax."

End of story?

What a dick.

The arrogant tone of his voice made my hackles rise. No one, absolutely no on, told me what to do. It was why my relationships—if you could call having regular fuck buddies relationships—ended quickly, when the men I'd been having sex with realized they couldn't control me and they couldn't win my heart.

My stomach, unused to such greasy food, churned uneasily as I realized Beach was entirely serious about keeping me with him.

"I don't know what kind of La La Land you live in, but I'm leaving and if you try to stop me, you will be a very sorry man."

His gaze narrowed and I glared right back at him, not intimidated in the least.

After a long moment of this, during which neither of us backed down, Beach finally smiled then began to chuckle as a soft look that took my breath lightened his deep blue eyes just a bit, like hints of sky blue shining in the depths of a sapphire.

A dimple popped out in his cheek as he smiled wider and I knew his boxers that I was wearing were growing damp from my arousal. "Fearless little thing, aren't you. *Mi reina*, I have a feeling life with you is never gonna be boring."

"I want boring!" I glared harder. "There is no us and I'm not your queen."

A laugh escaped him before he was able to control himself. "You are so wrong about that. Know you and I are new, but you need to understand that I'm gonna treat you like my queen, *mi reina*. Don't fight it, let me take care of you and I promise I'll make you happy. You've got a temper on you so I'm sure we'll have spats, but we'll fight and then fuck each other's brains out and shit'll work itself out."

I was a little panicked at how smoothly he said that, like it was a forgone conclusion, and I tried to slip out from beneath him. Unfortunately, this time he was ready for me and easily pulled me back against his body with a good grip. I could probably get out of it, but I wasn't in the mood for a wrestling match. Especially when he bit the tender spot where my shoulder and neck meet, making my nipples painfully hard and my clit pulse. It was so fucking unfair that I had to have this kind of intense chemistry with a man who was a delusional misogynist.

Dammit, Beach had managed to fuck me stupid without having actually fucked me.

"You are out of your mind," I squeaked out as he pressed his ginormous, hard cock against me, carefully keeping his upper body light over mine.

"Listen real good, Sarah. Yesterday you showed me you're something special, something I want to hold on to, and I always get what I want. 'Sides, I owe you for saving my life, and I don't take that kinda shit lightly."

Right away, I groaned. My father, bless his insane heart, is a scary motherfucker, as were all his friends. Former super-secret assassins for the US military, able to kill a man a hundred and fifty ways in five minutes and all that bullshit. While my dad was now king of a series of vast prepper compounds out in Texas Hill Country, he'd never lost his savage edge. Being that I was familiar with badass-men behavior, I knew Beach feeling like he owed me was not good. Badasses paid their debts, always, and if his way of paying it was by watching over me, I'd never get away from him.

"Well you can repay that debt by letting me go."

"They'll come for you."

I turned over so I could look him straight in the eye. "I can take care of myself."

"I'm not sayin' this to be a dick." He huffed out a breath that warmed the skin behind my ear. "But no matter how good you are, my brothers and I can give you more protection than you would have on your own. Even you, my lethal beauty, gotta sleep."

"They have better things to do than babysit me, I'm sure."

"*Mi riena*, you saved the life of the National President, which means they owe you."

I could tell he thought I should be impressed or something by that, but in this case, ignorance was bliss and I sighed. "I told you, I can take care of myself. You don't need to worry about me."

"Bullshit."

"Excuse me?"

His expression hardened and anger flashed through his gaze, speeding my pulse in response. "Bullshit. You need someone watchin' over you. Fuck, woman, you're a danger to *yourself*. Your decision-making skills are shit, and you're far too trustin' for your own good. Case in point, how we met last night. What the fuck were you thinkin', coming by your fuckin' self to a one-percenter party not knowing shit about the MC life?"

"Hey now," I gave him a good glare and tried to ignore how much I wanted to suck on his lips. "Scarlet and Smoke invited me, two people who I happen to like, and I have no fucking idea what a one-percent party is. I was just trying to have fun before I have to change my life."

His body lost some of its tension on top of me. "Change your life? What're you talkin' about?"

The stress caused by our conversation was getting the better of me and I ended up being way more honest than I intended. "I'm worn out, Beach. Maybe not on the outside, but on the inside I'm so tired of the bullshit I've had to endure. I want to be normal. I want to settle down, stand on my own feet, and work a job where people don't instantly judge me for my profession. I want to go to sleep knowing I don't have to worry about people trying to kill me. All I want is to have a safe home to raise my family in."

"Family?" His eyes widened and I swear grew a lighter blue.

"Don't freak out, I don't want a kid right now. I can't."

"Can you not get pregnant, honey?" he asked in an incredibly gentle way, his worry for me cutting through my anger.

"No, I'm sure I can, but I've been on the shot since I was fourteen. Cramps,"

I bold-faced lied. I went on the shot at fourteen because I was curious about sex, hormonal, and had a mother who was only too happy to ensure I wouldn't get knocked up. Having a pregnant daughter would have messed with her plans.

"The point isn't about having kids for me right now, the point is to have a stable home. A slice of the normal life for whatever children I may have far, far in the future after a ring is on my finger and I have a husband I love." I rubbed my forehead. "Can we drop it?"

"Honey, no matter how hard you try, you'll never be normal. You're exquisite, funny, and so fuckin' adorable I just want to hold you against me like this all day. I get wantin' to make your own way in the world, Lord knows I've had to fight for everything I got, but you will never blend in. No matter where you go, you're gonna shine like a diamond among pebbles. 'Sides, I know that life wouldn't make you happy."

My reply was saturated in sarcasm. "Right, 'cause you know me."

Instead of getting offended, he ran his fingertips down my cheek, affection obvious in his touch.

"I don't have to know your favorite color to see your wild spirit. Woman like you always want to be as free as the wind, needs to spread her wings in order to grow, and I can give you that. You're also the kinda woman who'll need a man strong enough to satisfy her and keep her safe—and, *mi nina linda,* I got that in spades. Most important, you need someone to trust your heart with and I can promise you'll never find someone better than me to give it to." He gently kissed my temple and I tried to resist the lure of his touch even as my stupid soft heart swooned for Beach. "You don't know me, but I promise you, I will give you the life you need to make you happy in ways you can't even imagine."

"The life I want and what you think I need are two different things. Get off of me so I can go home."

"Nope." Another gentle kiss, this time to my cheek. "You're not leaving my sight. Gotta take care of my girl, make her happy, and I can't do that from another state. Come on, Sarah, give us a chance. Swear it'll be the best decision you've ever made."

My whole body softened at his words and I drank them in, starved for affection. That was another addiction of mine, the need to feel loved. It had led to more than one regrettable hook-up, but my mother's love had been a conditional thing and I was often deprived of it.

Considering the way she tried to isolate me from the world, she was my everything, and when she shunned me for some insult, imagined or real, I'd been utterly distraught. Thanks to my therapist, I was aware of how this shaped my psyche and made me vulnerable to assholes, but that didn't mean I wasn't utterly taken with the sincerity ringing through his rough voice. Yes, he could be an accomplished liar, but my gut told me he was serious.

"I won't say I'm not tempted, you could talk a nun out of her panties, but I can't just run off with you, Beach. I have a life in Las Vegas, a roommate who has a young son I help out with. I can't abandon Marley."

He said gently, "You go home, they're gonna take out the people around you to get to you. Don't worry, I'll make sure Marley's got someone to help her out, but you can't go back to Vegas, baby. If they can't get to you, they'll take out someone around you instead."

I stiffened.

Shit, if I went home and people came after me, my dad and stepmom would exterminate them before they got within a mile of the house. As fun as that would be to witness, my father would overreact and I'd be lucky if he didn't lock me in his bunker for the rest of my life. My dad was protective to the extreme and tried to treat me like I was ten. If he thought biker gangs were after me, I'd either be forced to move home with him or be surrounded by his badass buddies acting as unwanted bodyguards 24/7.

"I won't drag this mess home with me. I'll take off for a while and let things cool down, but I need to take care of some things first."

He frowned, obviously not liking my answer. "Not gonna happen. Besides, you said you wanted to start a new life. You are, but you're doin' it in Austin, *mi riena*, and you're gonna do it with me having your back."

"I don't need you at my back."

This man had the patience of a saint, 'cause most guys I know would have been ready to strangle me by now. Instead of getting angry, he got gentle, which had a much more devastating effect on me. I could be pissed at him if he was being a jerk, but not when he was being sweet…in a kinda jerk-ish way.

The lines of his face relaxed as he continued to drink me in, a peace I'd never seen before softening his constant glare against the world. My stupid heart wanted to believe I was the only one he'd ever looked at this way, but that was impossible. He was too old to have not loved someone deeply, at least once.

He rubbed his thumb over my lips and the urge to suck it tormented me. "Baby, you have no idea what you need, but I'm gonna take great pleasure in showin' you."

"You know, your cryptic remarks are getting seriously annoying."

"Then let me be a little more direct." His large, warm hand cupped my breast and I froze, his thumb just inches below my nipple, which strained against the thin fabric of the t-shirt. "I'm gonna fuck all that stress and sass outta you until you walk around with a permanent smile on your face."

I tried to sound offended but instead words came out in a breathy, "Pardon me?"

He leaned forward, placing gentle kisses over my face with soft puckered lips as he said, "I'm gonna fuck you so good you'll be nothin but happiness in my arms.

Got lots of jagged ice surrounding you, warnin' a man off. Most guys wouldn't have the temperament to love you like you need to be loved, but I do."

"Whatever."

The soft rumble of laughter came from deep in his chest as he resumed touching me. I swear I wanted to purr like a spoiled cat and it irritated me that he had me so far under his spell. For whatever reason, the dirty daydream of rubbing my nipples against his furry chest came to me and I mentally bitch-slapped myself.

"I've had a brief taste of the incredible warmth of your heart past all those barriers, and I want it. If I need to destroy you with orgasms to get you there, I will. And once you let me in, you'll know that there's no one on earth better for you than me."

I should not have felt that right in my clit. Certainly not in my nipples as well. I knew I was staring at Beach's mouth, wanting so bad to kiss him again, to feel those gentle, puckered sucks on my sensitive breasts.

I wiggled onto my back beneath him and he lifted enough to allow my movements. As soon as I was settled, he slid one hand up to cup my breast, his long fingers squeezing gently. His thumb made a brief pass over my nipple and I shivered at the way that touch made my pussy clench. Our eyes met and I found myself leaning closer to him, holding his gaze the whole time.

A banging thumping came from the front door. "Yo, Prez, time to go. Got company on the way of the blue variety. Seems someone tipped them off 'bout you bein' in town."

Cursing, Beach rolled out of the bed and winced a bit as he hit his bad leg, then held his hand out to me. "Come on, babe, neither of us want to be here when the cops arrive."

Panic hit me hard as I stared at his rough and tattooed hand, the promises he made me battering my self-control. This was all too real, too serious. I knew if I took his hand, I'd be sealing my fate with him.

A pain pierced my chest as I forced the words, surprised by how much it hurt to spit them out, to turn my back on the dubious promise of happiness he offered me. "I'm not going with you."

He shook his head and gave me a look I couldn't quite interpret. "You wanna argue with me here so we can hang around long enough to get arrested, or you wanna get out of here and onto my jet? Promise you it's more comfortable than sittin' in an interrogation room. It's waitin' for us at a private airstrip."

"Are we wanted for what happened up at Sturgis?"

My worry must have shown on my face because he slowly softened before my very eyes. "I told you I'd take care of that shit, and I did. No one is comin' after us from law enforcement for what happened."

"Um, you mean multiple homicides just somehow vanished?"

"Yep. We don't want trouble, and neither do any of the other clubs. You'd be surprised how loyal people can be when you got their respect. Now, enough with this shit. Time to go."

Having no interest in being questioned by the police, considering my Sarah Star alias was totally made up with forged documents, I allowed him to haul me off the bed with a huff. He threw his shit into his bag from the dresser, but when he pulled the gun out, he put it into his saddlebag.

When he handed me my boots, cleaned and with my knife and phone back in their respective pockets, I couldn't help but sigh in relief. "Fine, but if I don't call my family ASAP we're fucked. Lead the way, *Presidente*, but I really need to make this call."

He nodded, still going through his stuff. "Do what you need, I'll take care of everything else."

His constant harping about taking care of me was both irritating and enamoring me. I think I might be emotionally bipolar. Wouldn't be a big surprise considering my family. Thankfully, the person I was about to call was super cool. Mimi wouldn't give me too much shit.

I hoped.

Her phone range once before she answered with a snarl. "This better be Sarah, safe and sound."

"I'm hunky-dory."

"You are not, in any way, shape, or form, hunky-dory."

Well, maybe I'd ticked off Mimi a little bit with my lack of communication. "I'm sorry! I'm safe, but things have been crazy. I would have called you but I was down for the count with a migraine."

"Oh, *tesoro*." Her voice went soft right away. She understood what that meant, having nursed me through more than a few. "Are you all right? How bad was it?"

"I'm fine, Beach took care of me."

There was a moment of silence, then her voice came out bland. "You're still with him?"

On the other side of the room, Beach smiled wide, his dimple winking at me. "Yeah. Look, the cops are on their way so we gotta go. We're taking Beach's jet to Austin."

"Sarah—"

"No, seriously, Mimi, I don't have time to talk about this right now. I'll call you when I get to Austin. I'm okay, and I love you. I know Dad is probably freaking out right now, but I'm with good people. I'll call you as soon as I can."

Hanging up on my stepmother, I shoved my phone back into my boot, mentally reminding myself to check all the messages that had piled up while I was on the run.

Beach gave me a quick scan, then nodded. "Let's go."

He opened the door and there were three big, scary-looking men waiting for us outside, all wearing Iron Horse vests. Beach had his on as well and I was once again facing a different man than the one who'd rolled around with me in bed. That man with the smiling eyes was gone and in his place stood a stone-faced beast without an ounce of warmth on his face. In a group of dangerous men, he still put off the darkest vibe and I was drawn to him in a way that probably wasn't healthy.

I wanted to close the distance between us, hold his hand and try to absorb some of the endless comfort he so easily offered me, but I didn't allow myself to do anything but look. When his gaze swung around to meet mine, the edge of his lip curled up the slightest bit in a smile and something eased in my chest when I realized he wasn't hiding his affection for me in front of his buddies. When he squeezed my hand lightly then winked, more of my tension fell away.

"Come here, baby. I want you to meet the boys. You're gonna be seein' a lot of them in the near future."

Jury was still out on that, but I decided to make nice. Instead of telling him to fuck off, I smiled and allowed him to pull me to his side and slap a possessive grip on my upper ass.

My smile grew strained.

"Sarah, you know Smoke already. He's my Master at Arms."

The handsome Spanish man with the sinfully dark eyes gave me his panty-dropping smirk and I gave him a little wave.

"Hey, beautiful." Smoke lifted his chin. "Glad to see you feelin' better. Nice underwear, by the way. Too bad it isn't white."

Nailing Smoke with a rather impressive glare, Beach took a step closer. "Mind your manners and your mouth 'round my old lady."

Still smirking, Smoke got a positively wicked smile. "Oh boy, Beach got himself a ball and chain."

"Smoke," Beach practically snarled, and everyone could see that the more possessive Beach got over me, the more it entertained Smoke.

Idiot was going to get himself killed.

By me.

Closing the distance between us, I smiled then slid my arms around his waist, easily grabbing his gun. I had it pressed against the side of his head long enough to whisper, "Bang" in his ear before I held the gun out to Beach.

He took it right away, laughing the whole time. Smoke looked both embarrassed and pissed, so I placed my hands on his shoulders then gave him a kiss on the cheek. "You're lucky I saw you out there, trying to fight your way to where Beach and I were. I thought I saw an ambush forming around you in the distance, but I was knocked out before I could do anything. I'm glad to see you're doing better as well, Smoke. I forgot to tell you yesterday, thank you for saving us."

He actually appeared stunned when I walked away and rejoined Beach. My man silently snarled at me with jealousy, but I calmly held his gaze before giving him a soft, lingering kiss on his lips. That shut him right the hell up, and when I pulled back, I found I'd somehow melted into his embrace, pressed close from hip to shoulders. Darn it, my body was being hijacked by my hormones.

"Sweet," he murmured while holding my gaze with a heart pounding intensity that lent his words the power to make my knees weak. "Such sweetness in a bitter world."

I barely held back a totally girly sigh of sparkly eyed delight. The kind fourteen-year-olds give over their boy band crush of the moment. With each moment that passed in his presence, I found myself getting tied tighter and tighter to him through the invisible bonds. Already my body was more comfortable with him than it had been with anyone in years. Maybe this was what it felt like to be able to have faith in a man again. I'd trusted my first boyfriend with all my heart and he'd crushed me into a million tiny shards. Maybe this bliss I felt while touching Beach was how it felt when you were with someone you knew was safe, someone who would die to protect you.

"Prez, we have to get moving," a man said in a tight voice.

Beach growled for a moment before gesturing to a familiar guy in his late forties with military-short dark hair peppered with silver and cool blue eyes. He had tattoos on his neck and they said something in Latin I couldn't figure out. As he studied me, I found him almost impossible to read so I gave him a small but polite smile. "You already know Vance, one of my Enforcers."

The deep gold in Beach's hair gleamed in the fading sunlight as he lifted his chin in the direction of a hot Asian man. He had the most exquisite bone structure, his jaw chiseled in a way any photographer would love. He also had a nasty scar going around his throat like someone had tried to remove his head from his body, which took away from his biker *GQ* vibe. "And this is Dragon, my tech specialist. They're all with the Austin chapter and are gonna be travelin' with us. Anything happens to me, you go with them. They'll protect you."

"Hi." I waved to them, keeping to myself the fact that if anything happened to Beach, I was out of here. "I met Dragon at Sturgis."

"Nice to see you again," Dragon said while Vance merely nodded in my direction.

"Sarah," Beach pulled me even closer until I was practically plastered to his side, "is gonna be your number one job to protect. She's important to me, so you really don't wanna fuck this up. *Comprende?*"

All the men murmured in agreement but I sighed. "While I appreciate the sentiment, I can take care of myself."

At this they chuckled, and I had to grit my teeth. Misogynistic assholes. Did they already forget me disarming Smoke? Morons. Just because I was female they assumed I was easy prey. Add the blonde hair to my big boobs and most men looked at me as nothing more than arm candy.

Yes, there are plenty of beautiful women out there who are dumb as a brick, but there are also smart ones. I liked to think of myself as being in the latter category, even if I'd never technically finished high school. Dropping out when I was sixteen was a life or death situation, and while I regretted it, I don't feel like I've really missed anything. My IQ was high enough that I could learn just about anything with the help of a few books and YouTube videos. My exacting attention to following directions made even the most tedious tasks easy for me. And when I learned something, it stayed with me forever.

Vance, the guy with the greying hair, ignored me as he spoke to Beach. "Who you want her to ride with?"

"Me," Beach growled. "Sarah is my woman, on the back of my bike."

They all went silent and Vance said in a quiet voice, "You sure about this? Pretty public gesture. Gonna draw attention to her."

"Yep."

I turned to look up at Beach. "Sure about what?"

"We'll talk about it later." He stepped away from me and slung his saddlebag over one shoulder, the duffel over the other. "Let's move."

I was tempted to argue with him, but my Spidey sense was tingling and I agreed we needed to motor on outta here.

As we made our way out to the parking lot, I was surprised to see most of the bikes were already gone. It made me pause for a moment to look down at the few men still in the lot, the tension filling the air like the heaviness before a storm. Shit was going down in this part of the world and I couldn't wait to extract myself from it.

By the time we'd reached Beach's bike, a small crowd of people were tracking us, and out of the corner of my eye I could see stern men watching me closely. Inwardly I sighed at the fact I wasn't wearing a bra because while my implants were big, they were super well done and my breasts were soft enough to wobble a bit with my walk. And the fact that I was wearing men's underwear wasn't lost on anyone, I'm sure. The warm air quickly took away the chill on my skin from the air conditioned hotel room and I sucked in a deep breath of a breeze flavored with exhaust, cigarette smoke, and a hint of weed.

Beach slung one long leg over the bike then helped me on behind him. He looked over his shoulder and gave me a small, satisfied smile as I wrapped my arms around him. Smoke handed me a black helmet with a face shield and I gladly took it. I've ridden on the backs of motorcycles before and knew a bug hitting my face at fifty miles an hour hurt like hell.

After sliding on a pair of dark glasses, Beach put on a matte-black helmet that was undecorated and turned on his big bike. I knew enough to recognize the Harley-Davidson brand name on it, but other than that, I just knew it was a kick-ass bike with a cool paint job. Definitely customized, and the motor was strong enough to vibrate between my legs in a not-unpleasant manner. Our trip back to the small airport wasn't a long one but I enjoyed the fresh mountain air swirling around me as I leaned into Beach's strong back.

As soon as we parked the big bike in the parking lot of the airport, Hulk yelled, "Hustler said he got a tip from an informant Los Diablos knows where you are and they're movin' in. They're pissed their Secretary got killed."

"Fuck," Beach muttered and grabbed my hand. "Go."

We jogged through the small building and onto the tarmac, my skin prickling as Beach's increasing tension rolled over me. I caught movement out of the corner of my eye and watched in astonishment as Smoke moved out of the hangar holding a submachine gun held in a very competent grip.

Beach slowed and I noticed for the first time a rather posh white and navy blue private jet. A group of men waited by the bottom of the stairs leading up to the jet and they were all armed with their weapons drawn.

They gave me brief looks, but mostly their gazes were locked onto the space around us.

We didn't pause to talk with them, instead Beach shouted out, "Let's move, everyone go, if your ass isn't in the plane you are getting the fuck out, now."

People didn't hesitate, scrambling to either leave the area or move to the plane. They of course made way for Beach, and when we reached the interior of the plane the stewardess, a woman in her early forties with a nice smile, greeted us. "Welcome, Mr. Rodriguez. What can I get for you?"

"Once we're in the air, feed everyone. We gotta move, so second that door is closed, I want us airborn."

She didn't even blink. "Of course, sir, I'll be back for your orders once we're at cruising altitude."

"Buckle up," Beach said in a loud voice as he tugged me down onto a dark grey leather couch with him.

The interior of the plane was nice, neutral with silver and gold accents. I remained tense but didn't protest when Beach buckled me in next to him. Hulk went to take the empty seat on the couch next to me but Beach shook his head.

"Nope."

Giving me a wink, Hulk nodded. "Gotcha, Prez."

I gently turned his face to mine. "Are we going to be okay?"

"Yeah, everyone's on and Los Diablos, if they show up, are in for a big surprise."

The big engines began to rev up and the plane's ventilation system kicked in, pressurizing the cabin. A little thrill of excitement filled me as we began to pick up speed, the moment between being earthbound and soaring among the clouds filling me with exhilaration. Despite all the bullshit I'd been through, I still had a deep and abiding love of being up in the clouds.

"You like flying, huh?" Beach asked with a bemused smile as he turned to face me.

"Yeah."

"Why?"

Still caught up in the sensation of the plane climbing, I couldn't help my grin. "Do you know how amazing this is? How long man yearned to be able to do this, to soar higher than the birds? I mean if you think about it, once you leave the ground, you leave some of your worries behind. They can't follow you where you're going, can't drag you down. It's a fresh start."

"Never thought about it like that," he said in a low voice before leaning forward enough to take his vest off and place it on the empty seat next to me. Cracking his neck, he rested his head back against the couch and sighed. "For me, it's a peaceful thing. Unless my enemies sprout wings, myself and my people are as safe as can be in this fucked-up world. When lookin' down on humanity all the bullshit seems so petty, it allows me to focus on what's really important, who's really important."

The stewardess announced we could take our seat belts off and I shed mine, then removed my boots with a sigh of bliss. "Nice."

Chuckling, Beach reached down and pulled my feet, clad in a pair of his too big bright white socks, into his lap. "Let me see if I can make it better."

"Oh, you don't…"

My words died in my throat as he clenched my feet in his big hands, pressing in just right. Magic hands. Tingles raced through me and I sighed then flopped onto the couch. As someone who wore high heels on a regular basis, having my feet rubbed was nirvana. Another soft laugh from him as my eyes closed, the relaxation sinking into me. It was a clean peacefulness, not one induced by drugs, and I reveled in giving myself completely over to the sensation. Then again, the amount of hormones that Beach's mere presence released in me was a high on its own, so maybe this feeling of warmth and safety *was* drug related, just natural ones.

"You're so good at this," I moaned in shameless delight.

"Had a lot of practice with my mom," Beach said in a low voice. "After my dad died there were some…legal issues with my family. Basically my uncle believed that more should have come to him than did, and lots of other family members felt the same, so my inheritance was caught up in legal battles. See, my dad had been aware of their scheming bullshit to get their hands on his money. And even though I was in and out of trouble with the law, and had firmly entrenched myself in the world of the Iron Horse MC, my dad knew I wasn't a dumbass."

I couldn't help but smile. "How the hell did you end up President of Iron Horse?"

"Prez," Smoke said in a low voice. "Our lawyer has some questions for you."

Pushing myself into a fully upright position, I turned to Smoke. "Lawyer?"

"Just a precaution, baby," Beach said as he stroked my calf. "Gotta make sure you're legally covered. Also called and talked to Marley. A couple brothers from an affiliate club out in Vegas are gonna watch over her and her boy. Also talked to your neighbors while you slept and they're aware you're gonna be outta town for a while and to keep an eye on your girl. Marley's packing some of your things up and sendin' them to me."

"What the fuck?" I tried to jerk my leg from his lap, but he gripped my ankle as my patience snapped. "Stop trying to take my life over!"

His lips thinned and Smoke gave me an incredulous look. Awareness filled me as I realized everyone on the plane had stopped talking and were staring at me, but fuck them. I wasn't going to let any man steamroll over me. I didn't care if Mr. Carlos Rodriguez was the

President of the Known Universe, I was tired of his heavy-handed bullshit.

"Yesterday two Los Diablos members tried to abduct Marley on her way home. If my guys wouldn't have been there, she would have been in a world of hurt." He glared at me. "So swallow your pride and let me help you."

"Help me? While I totally appreciate what you did for Marley, I feel like you're trying to take away every bit of control I have over my life. I will not allow you, or any man, to do that to me. I can handle this bullshit, stop treating me like I'm some fucking moron. Remember, I saved *your* ass and this isn't my first rodeo, dick, and I don't need your bullshit complicating my already fucked-up life. So leave me the fuck alone or I will vanish first chance I get."

Thunder rumbled through his rough features and I glared at him as he said, "That ain't gonna happen."

"Oh yes it will," I hissed, edging into the analytical space my brain slid into when I felt really threatened, my fear driving my anger. "I'm gonna walk out that door and be gone from your life so fast I'll be dust in the wind before you blink."

My face heated as my temper strained to get free and I tried to fight it, but oh, the temptation was there to really fight with him. I'm cursed with anger management issues that I'd inherited from both my parents and when I say I know how to fight dirty, I mean I *know* how to fight dirty. So bad that by the time the argument was over, I'd have said some hurtful shit I didn't mean but could never take back. Memories of my mother making men cry with her bitter words flashed through my head and I found the strength to calm myself.

Beach must have seen something that alarmed him in my face because he abruptly unbuckled, then stood and hauled me to my feet. "Right, see it's time we have a conversation. Wanted to wait until we got home, but you're forcin' my hand."

A bolt of apprehension went through me, memories of men beating my mother flooding me even as I tried desperately not to think about them. Deny, deny, avoid, avoid, that was my emotional motto. Probably not a healthy one, but when Beach jerked me into a rather large and plush bathroom with an actual shower and wide countertop, I was still tense enough that I ripped my arm from his grip and put as much space between us as possible. He frowned at me, pushing more of my triggers with his angry look, and I took in a shuddering breath, trying get a grip on my instinctive panic. The overwhelming urge to fight Beach making my body heat with adrenaline.

I was so busy trying to keep my shit together that when he touched my hand, I yelped and jerked away, going into a defensive stance.

He studied my raised arms, my spread legs, then my face for a long, long time. Seemingly of their own accord, my arms lowered and my heart began to slow. His gaze was so intense I had no choice but to fully live in the moment with him. Never before had anyone been able to drag me from my obsessive negative thoughts this quickly and I found myself looking at him with something close to wonder.

"Baby, I know you have a lot to deal with right now, and I promise you that as soon as we get to Austin things'll calm down, but you can't act like a bitch to me in front of other people." He held up a hand, cutting off my protest. "Not sayin' you can't yell at me in private when you got a concern, but you gotta keep your temper until we're not around people that'll see you running your mouth as a sign of weakness on my part. Considering I'm keeping you alive it would be in both our best interests if I don't appear vulnerable."

What I wanted to say was fuck you, but instead I muttered, "I understand."

Sighing, I moved past him to the sink, spying a black lacquered basket filled with toiletries.

He waited, watching me set about brushing my teeth with a puzzled expression. "That's it? You understand?"

I handed him the first toothbrush I'd prepared, noting the bemused quirk to his lips as he took it. "Yeah. In your world your reputation is a big deal, it keeps you alive. I'm more than familiar with living with badasses and their often erratic and nonsensical behavior. My dad and his friends are into that macho bullshit. Which it is, by the way, bullshit. I'll mind my tongue over stupid shit, but life and death situations I'm not going to play damsel in distress. I think we can both agree that isn't anything unreasonable."

He couldn't argue with that so he just stared at me.

I got another toothbrush and loaded it up with toothpaste as he scrubbed his teeth. Shit, he even looked sexy brushing. There had to be something wrong with me if I found toothpaste foam on his lips attractive. Bet he tasted all minty and fresh now.

He rinsed and spit, then gave me a considering look. "We good?"

"I'm tired. We can have more drama tomorrow, but right now I need to rest."

"We will, but first we need to clear the air a little bit between us 'bout how me and you work."

"We can talk about it tomorrow."

"Nope, we're gonna talk about it now, then crash."

"I don't want to."

"Too bad."

"See, and that's another thing. You keep bossing me around behind closed doors and we're going to have problems."

He washed his hands while looking at me in the mirror. "I'm willin' to compromise with you, Sarah. I want you to be able to stand strong on your own two feet, but also to have everything you've ever wanted."

"Why? Why would you be so nice to me and suddenly become my leather-clad fairy godfather?"

His lips twitched like he wanted to laugh, but his voice was serious as his said, "You don't get it. Taking care of a strong woman like yourself is a privilege a man has to earn. And once we get to our place in Austin, I'm gonna spank your ass for that fairy godfather bullshit."

"Ha," I squeaked. "Good luck with that one. And what do you mean 'our' place. I don't remember looking at real estate with you in Austin. If 'we' had a house it would be one that I picked out. You have a home, I have a home, and they are different buildings in different states."

Reaching past me, the heat of his body scorching against mine, he grabbed a towel and dried his hands. "Why you fightin' me so hard on this?"

The truth slipped past my tired lips. "Because I'm afraid to trust you."

His rough hands cupped my face, his skin still slightly damp and smelling of citrus soap. "Don't be. Whoever hurt you so bad in the past, I'm not them. My word is my bond and I swear to you that I want nothin' but the best for you."

"That doesn't make one ounce of sense."

"Hurts my heart to see you believe that, *mi corazón*."

Blinking fast, I looked away and huffed out a breath. "Whatever. None of this makes sense."

"No, it doesn't. The way I feel about you makes no sense at all, never felt it before in my life, but I like it."

He brushed his thumb along my throat, drawing my gaze back to him in time to see his eyes going half-lidded. "Haven't had more than a taste of you yet, but I know it's gonna be so fuckin' good between us."

A needy pulse flared to life between my legs even as I crossed my arms and gave him a good glare. "That is *so* not happening."

In a bold move that left me gasping, he pressed his fingers between my legs, then rubbed, making my knees weak.

"Warm and wet," he groaned out. "Sarah, it's gonna happen with us, but I'm not in the mood to share any part of you with anyone. Not even the noises you're gonna make when I fuck you, so we're gonna have to wait."

One of those noises escaped from me when his long finger rubbed through my slit, grazing my clit again and again. I wanted more, needed more, and tilted my hips to get it. Soon I was riding his hand, just the soaked fabric of his boxer briefs separating our skin. I wrapped my arms around his thick neck and pulled his mouth down to mine, raining soft kisses on his lips. My clit was so engorged and sensitive that the press of his finger through his boxers was almost enough to get me off.

Almost.

He must have sensed my growing need because his fingers slipped through the handy-dandy front flap of the boxer briefs, the sensation of his rough skin grazing through my wet folds enough to have me shuddering, then whimpering against his throat.

"Shhh, baby," he whispered. "Be quiet for *Papi*. I'm gonna make you come, but you have to control yourself for me. Be a good girl."

Those words went straight from my ears to my clit, which throbbed as he rubbed his thumb over the stiff nub. I choked back a cry, desperate for his fingers inside of me. If he'd give me some penetration I'd climax in a heartbeat. The more turned on I got, the more wanton I became, until I was whispering into his ear about how much I wanted his cock.

"Beg for my fingers." Beach teased me with the tip of one pressing against my entrance. "Beg your *Papi* to make you come."

Once again that naughty phrase aroused me something fierce, to the point where I was blushing hard, equal parts embarrassed and out of my mind crazy with lust as I said, "Please, *Papi*, make me come."

He began to rub his thumb faster on my clit, hard enough to rocket me to my orgasm. It happened so fast and fierce that my cry of delight at the tension finally breaking inside of me came out loud, echoing in the bathroom. With a growl, Beach shoved my face into his neck, muffling me. A ribbon of pleasure so intense it hurt tore through me as he continued to finger fuck me through my orgasm, praising me for how beautifully I released for him. It was all too much and I had to bite down on the muscled column of his neck to mute my cries.

Instead of bending me over and fucking me like I hoped he would, Beach held me close and whispered to me about how much he enjoyed giving that to me while he showered me with super-soft kisses.

As I came down, I became all too aware of my battered physical state. My body needed some serious rest and the little bit I'd gotten at the hotel didn't put a dent in my injuries. Right now said body was telling me it was time to find a bed, floor, or chair to sleep on while my stomach argued I needed food. My internal clock was all thrown off and I could feel the weight of the day trying to grind my spirit into dust.

Beach pulled back with a soft laugh. "You are dead on your feet, *mi riena*. Much as my dick hates me, I gotta give you time to heal before I take you. Your growlin' belly is tellin' me you burn through food like nobody's business. So I'm gonna take care of you and you're gonna let me do it because it is something that brings me great pleasure, yeah?"

I wanted to put up a brave front, but that orgasm had knocked the fight out of me. "Okay."

The word kind of slipped out, but I was beginning to see that behind closed doors, life with Beach was going to be interesting. In my relaxed and weary state, having someone to take care of me was nirvana. I can still remember when I got sick at my dad's for the first time and how it had changed my perception of my other family. I had the flu and all three of them, Mimi, Swan, and my dad, all took care of me without any complaint. In fact, I think they were happy I was allowing them to help me. I think I scared Swan when I broke into hysterical tears after throwing up, overwhelmed that she'd cleaned both myself and the toilet after I was done, then helped me rinse my mouth out. My fever had been raging at that point and I was terribly weak, which made caring for me a not-so-fun chore.

Most people would have thrown me in the shower and hosed me off, but she actually helped me take care of my long hair, exactly like her own. As she'd put conditioner in it, she'd chatted about how we needed to trade haircare tips because mine was so soft. That was it, the first time she'd spoken to me like the sister I'd always imagined, conversing away happily. I found out later she'd been scared by how sick I was, and what I thought was gossip was instead worried babble. Either way, I fell more in love with her that day than I ever had with another human being and I mourned the loss of our friendship.

Beach kissed my forehead, his scruff rough against me. "Come on, let's get some chow in you then bed. Got a long day ahead of us tomorrow so get your sleep tonight, you're gonna need it."

Chapter 8

Carlos "*Beach*" Rodriguez

Sarah had fallen asleep in her chair after inhaling a large club sandwich and plate of fruit. Dark circles stood out beneath her eyes, and a myriad of bruises had begun to bloom on her smooth skin. We were back out in the main cabin, but I'd kept her away from everyone, needing to shelter her from my world as long as possible. Once we landed I would have a metric shit ton of stuff I had to personally attend, which meant I wouldn't have a chance to settle her in anywhere personally. I fuckin' hated the world for interrupting us, but I couldn't put off business any longer.

I set down my cup of coffee with a weary sigh and stood, but before I could get to Sarah, Hulk was there. He was coming back to Austin to train with Big Al on a new hacking technique and I appreciated him taking the time to do this, but I didn't like him reaching for my woman.

When I went to stop him, he said, "Lemme get her up. Carrying a woman with your leg all fucked up is not a good idea. Hard to impress a lady when you're stuck in a wheelchair, Prez."

His voice was just loud enough so I could hear it over the jet's engines, but I nodded. My pride wanted to insist I could carry her, but the reality was I couldn't afford any more injuries and I was smart enough to admit that. Didn't mean I liked the idea of him touching her, but she needed to get back in the bedroom so I could do some business out here with the boys. 'Sides, Hulk had taken a shine to her and I knew my brother was not the kind of man who'd overstep his bounds with any woman. "Thanks."

The moment Hulk touched Sarah, she shot out of her chair and away from him, her hands raised in a defensive stance while sleep still filled her eyes.

We all startled, none of us expecting such a violent response from a sleeping woman. I mentally cursed myself for not realizing this would be her reaction, and hoped like shit she didn't kick my ass when I approached her.

"Easy. Just Hulk helpin' you to bed, *mi riena*."

She darted a quick look at me, then back to Hulk, then to me again and dropped her stance. "Right."

I reached out slowly and held one of her hands, lacing our fingers together until our palms touched. "You okay to walk on your own? You were out pretty hard."

She blinked at me a couple times before saying, "Yeah."

My poor baby was out of it. "Follow me."

The tension left her shoulders and she nodded, rubbing her thumb over the back of my hand in a slow, soothing manner. I got her back into the small bedroom with its queen-size bed, already turned down for the short flight. Slipping her between the sheets after getting her socks off, I lingered for a moment before turning the lights down to a low glow. Damn, she was sweet when she was tired like this. Her big pale blue eyes gazed up at me and my heart thumped hard at the sheer loveliness of my woman, bruised jaw and all.

"Aren't you coming to bed with me, Carlos?" she whispered and my dick jerked.

"No, I wish I was, but got some business to work through before I get the privilege of pullin' you into my arms."

She smiled and reached out, slowly stroking my cheek where a good bruise was swelling up. "You need to ice this."

"I'll take care of it later."

A stubborn set came to her jaw, but I already knew her well enough to anticipate a lecture I didn't have time to hear was on the way. To stop it, I brushed my lips softly back and forth over hers. I've never kissed a woman with lips as full as hers before and it was like kissing two incredibly soft pillows. Soon I'd have those lips wrapped around my cock and that mental image was not helping me get my ass out the door to let her sleep. Her fingers stroked over my neck to curl into my hair and her lips parted beneath mine, giving me a taste of her sweetness I could easily get drunk on. My whole body hardened with the need to fuck but I managed to pull away before my dick could get me in trouble.

"Sleep."

She pouted, tempting me to bite that plump lower lip of hers. "Fine, but only because I'm tired. You'll be back soon, right?"

"Yeah, baby, I'll be back soon."

This seemed to satisfy her and she wiggled around until she was on her side, hugging a pillow and watching me as I left the small bedroom.

Hulk and Gardner, one of my Enforcers from Austin, were waiting for me outside.

"I'll watch over her, make sure she's not disturbed," Hulk said as he stepped to the side, allowing me to pass.

I gave him a nod while Gardner walked ahead of me, his long dark brown braid tied back with a series of leather thongs. About thirty years older than me, Gardner had been one of the men my grandad, the former President of the Iron Horse MC, patched in back in the day. Man was completely loyal and knew how to keep his mouth shut, but liked to stay out of club business for the most part. He'd retired as much as a biker could, but shit like me getting kidnapped could pull him back into action. Without a doubt he was a surly son of a bitch, but he was loyal and had the club's best interest at heart.

In theory, everyone on this plane fell into that category, but all those fucking cops back in Denver waiting to ambush me let me know someone was running their mouth and making trouble for me. Nothing new, but adding the police into the mixture was unusual. Someone either really didn't give a fuck, or they were desperate enough to break the unwritten rule of the MC world that you don't bring in the government to do your dirty work.

I cracked my neck to the side before slowly sitting in a seat that faced the rest of the plane. A quick glance showed the flight attendant was up front, looking at her iPad with a big pair of headphones on. She'd been with me for around five years now and I trusted her, but I still had Vance close the small curtain between us and the galley.

Myself, Gardner, Smoke, Vance, and Big Al shifted around so we were all facing each other and I studied their faces. None looked happy and I knew the shit that had gone down back in Sturgis was a negative mark on Iron Horse. Having their National President snatched up didn't make them look good and they knew it. I was within my rights to punish them, but that wasn't gonna happen. I chose to go after Sarah instead of with them and that was on me.

I decided to start with Big Al. He actually wasn't big at all, around 5'7" and leanly muscled with curly black hair and dark eyes, but we didn't call him big for his body, but for his brain. Big Al was a certified hacking genius, a tech ninja who was one of the craftiest fuckers I'd ever met. Thankfully he worked for us and Smoke paid him well.

The gleam in the younger guy's eyes and a slight smirk tipped me off that he knew something. "What did you find out?"

Leaning forward so his elbows rested on his knees, Big Al gestured to the back of the plane. "I got the information you wanted on Sarah, and let me tell ya, Prez, you have no idea who the fuck you decided to place your patch on. Jesus, that bitch is not who the world thinks she is—at all."

"What the hell are you talkin' about?"

"What do you want first? You wanna know her dad is Mike Anderson, the arms dealer out west who we've done business with?"

"Wait, Crazy Mike?"

"The one and only. Or maybe you wanna know her stepmom is Mimi Anderson, aka Mimi Stefano, aka Lady Death."

"Jesus."

Pleased as shit he's shocking us, Big Al rolls on. "Or maybe you'd be interested to know she hooked up with

Morrie Rendbar, one of the top mob bosses and casino owners out in Reno, when she was sixteen?"

"What the fuck?" I said in a low breath, my disbelief echoing around the room.

"Sarah Marie Star, whose age is listed on all of her extensive documentation as twenty-three, is actually Sarah Jane Murphy Anderson, age eighteen—"

"She's eighteen?"

"Yeah."

"Jesus fuck."

I felt sick to my stomach. She was a fuckin baby, way, way too young for me. Christ, I was almost fourteen years her senior. I was in fucking high school when she was born. Bile churned inside of me as I frowned at a laughing Vance. "You find this fuckin' funny?"

The smile dropped from his face and he looked away. "No, Prez."

I plunged my hands into my hair and shook my head. "Keep goin', Big Al."

"Right, so from what I've been able to piece together, she's hasn't had the best life. Parents divorced when she was four, was supposed to be joint custody but her mom Billie took off with Sarah, leaving Mike with her twin sister Sue Wanda. Other than that, not much."

"Not much?"

"As you can probably guess, Mike Anderson made sure both himself and his girls were as private as possible. I really couldn't find anything other than the fact that Sarah did pageants and figure skating while living in Reno. Won a bunch of awards and shit, there was even talk of her making the Olympics but she blew out her knee when she was fifteen. Somehow when she was sixteen, she hooked up with Morrie—who was married at the time to a wife he has since divorced. Their affair lasted for awhile before it ended abruptly and she went off the grid again until she was almost eighteen. When she came back she had the new identity of Sarah Star. In less than a year, she became a performer in a high-class Vegas show, then won the World Pole Dancer of the Year and was in *Playboy*. Other than that, from the age of four to the age of fourteen, her life is a big blank page. Like when her mother snatched her, Sarah simply dropped off the face of the earth for ten years."

My head ached and it matched the throb from my leg. I hated taking pain killers, couldn't afford to be fucked up at what amounted to a war council, but damned if the Motrin I took earlier wasn't cutting it. I looked down at my knuckles and forced myself to focus on the big picture, not just my personal bullshit. I couldn't fucking wrap my mind around who I thought Sarah was, and who she really is.

Big Al grinned, his white teeth gleaming, and opened his laptop. "However, I can tell you what she's been doing since she became Sarah Star. Check this shit out. Your old lady is amazing. This ain't titty club shit right here, this is art."

He clicked on a YouTube video then enlarged it and turned up the speakers. We all held our breath as the music started up, a weird tinny piano, then some chick singer with a velvety voice started singing about the long days being over and the world getting better.

I wasn't sure what the song was about at this point, because I was entranced by the sight of Sarah wearing a small white summer dress and a bright, happy smile. She was all sunshine and innocence with her hair braided back and a wreath of tiny blue and white flowers threaded into it. As the camera zoomed in on her, I noticed her whole body sparkled with some type of glitter, making her look almost ethereal.

Instead of overt sexuality, her lithe movements were subtle and seductive. Her sensuality was in the way her body turned and how she flitted around the stage to the music, her movements graceful like a butterfly but also incredibly strong like a ballerina. Her entire body was tightly muscled, but not in a bulky way. No, she was all long, smooth lines and nicely rounded feminine curves. Stunning, the essence of everything a man would fight to keep for himself, no matter how wrong or taboo it was to want her.

The beat of the music changed and she skipped over to the pole, throwing herself onto it with an exuberant shout that rose above the music as she spun around with abandon. She flipped upside down, still spinning, and her golden braid whipped around her, gleaming in the now bright lights. My heart slammed as I took in the happiness pouring from her, the joy she shared so openly with the audience. The crowd of people watching were obviously loving the show because their cheers filled whatever auditorium she was in.

Extending her legs straight out, she then began to do this crazy hip undulation that made her legs flow through the air almost like wings. I didn't know where to look, at the elegant, sculpted muscles of her strong arms holding her suspended, or at her world-fucking-class legs and the white panties revealed beneath the dress.

The music slowed and she wrapped one of those impossibly long legs around the pole and swung her upper body out, her arms flowing gracefully with the heavy beat. Once again I'd underestimated her, had assumed what kind of pole dancing she did, and found myself totally wrong. Yeah, it was sexy as hell, especially when she ripped off the skirt of the dress, using the fluttering white fabric as part of her routine. When she did a quick drop from the top of the pole to the bottom while spinning, I wasn't the only man in the room who sucked in a quick breath of air.

"Close it," I muttered, aware of the arousal thickening both my voice and my dick.

Smoke let out a low sigh. "She's got a twin sister? She single?"

Big Al shrugged. "Couldn't find out much about her sister Sue other than she lives in Houston and she's some kind of super-reclusive genius. Has all kinds of degrees and graduated high school when she was thirteen. Other than that, she either lives a real borin' life or Mike Anderson is doin' what he can to keep his girl under the radar."

"So not too far away," Smoke said with an interested look that for some fucked-up reason made me feel protective of Sarah's sister.

"I want surveillance on Sue Wanda, but keep your dick in your pants. Got me? And if she spots you, tell her who you are, but keep your fuckin' mouth shut about me and Sarah. Far as you know, we met here in Austin when she was decorating one of my places. You pass that along to your boys as well. Understood?"

Smoke arched a brow, but didn't argue. "You want 'round the clock?"

"For the next two weeks. After that we'll discuss it to see if you think we need to keep someone on her. I do not want her to know you're there."

Snorting, Smoke gave me an arrogant look. "You know that won't be an issue."

"Normally, no, but think with your brain instead of your dick. This is Mike Anderson and Lady fuckin' Death's daughter. You think she won't be able to spot a tail? Whoever is gonna be on her is gonna need to know how to watch from a distance."

From across the way, Vance said, "I'll keep watch over her if you need it."

Smoke nodded. "When we get on the ground, head to the office and do what you need to start up a Gorman Protocol detail on her. Beach, is Sarah gonna be staying at your place?"

I hesitated. An hour ago I would'a said hell yes, but now that I knew how young she was, I knew I should walk away—but I couldn't. Not just 'cause she could very well be in danger, but my gut felt sick and hollow when I thought about her leaving.

Still, it would be best if she went and stayed with Birdie until I let the women I'd been sleeping with over the years know I was off the market. They were known to stop by from time to time unannounced, and I didn't want Sarah dealing with that shit. No, my girl would be better off with Birdie for a day or two, being smothered by the old woman's relentless affection.

So though it pained me to say it, I forced out the words. "Take her to Birdie's."

"Not to your place?"

"No."

Big Al pursed his lips and leaned back in his dark leather recliner, his gleaming eyes intent. "You withdrawing your claim on her?"

If I had a decent bone in my body, I'd say yes and let the boys know she was off limits, but I didn't earn my position as President of the most powerful MC in twelve states by being a good man. I'm selfish, I'm proud, and I know what I want. Or in this case, what I'm apparently obsessed with.

Looking my men in the eye one by one, I let them know I was completely serious about my claim on her as plainly as I could. "Sarah Anderson, Sarah Star, don't care what the fuck her name is, she is my old lady. That means one hundred percent hands the fuck off."

"Beach," Vance said softly with tension lacing his gritty voice. "She's young."

"That may be true, but the woman I just survived a kidnapping with didn't act like some stupid young bitch. I know brothers who wouldn't have been able to pull off the coldhearted shit she did without blinkin' an eye. Those were not the actions of some innocent young girl." It pissed me off he would even say that, but Vance's dad had left his mom for a fifteen-year-old girl so I gave him a little breathing room. "You know me. You've partied with me for years. I've been around your family and you mine. Have I ever come across as the kinda guy who would be interested in young, stupid stripper pussy for anything other than a fuck?"

A feminine inhalation somehow cut through the roaring hush of the plane and I knew by the looks on my men's faces Sarah was behind me.

Sure enough, when I turned around, I got sucker punched in the gut by her pale, bruised face as she stared at me with tears glimmering in her eyes.

Hating the look I know I'd put there, I opened my mouth to try to smooth things over but she beat me to it with a scathing snarl.

"I'm sorry to interrupt, but Beach, your phone is in the room and it keeps ringing. It woke me up and I think someone is trying to reach you for an important reason, so you should answer it. Oh, and if you try and get into bed with me tonight, I will castrate you. I assure you, I both know how to do it and have had practice, so don't test me. This young, stupid stripper pussy isn't quite as foolish as you think."

Her gaze hardened so fast I could feel a physical wall slam down between us and my gut clenched in response as her disappointment in me hit me on a visceral level.

"Sorry for the interruption, gentlemen, carry on with your shit-talking me behind my back."

With that, she chucked my phone onto the couch, spun on her heel, and slammed the door shut.

We all stared in silence at it before Hulk said, "Sad I'm gonna miss this."

"Miss what?" Vance asked with a sour look, clearly pissed for some reason as he stared down at his phone.

"Miss watchin' the Prez fuck up over and over again with that sweet young thing. You boys believe in karma? I do, and I believe that stunning creature is gonna give the Prez the fight of his life to win her heart." His dark face tightened. "Then again, not sure if you're worthy of something so sweet."

I had to resist the urge to pull my gun on Hulk. "Watch yourself."

He shrugged and made his way into the lounge area. "You want my advice on how to handle a woman like that? One who threatened to unman you and probably meant it? Unless you know her well enough to get in there and fuck her until she forgives you, you sleep on the motherfuckin' couch."

The way he enunciated those last two words made me grunt. I limped my way over to said couch, all too aware we would be landing soon where a dangerous jungle of problems threatened to destroy everything I hold dear. Without a doubt, the Iron Horse MC was being targeted and I had a meeting scheduled with various segments of my empire to shore up our defenses. This wouldn't be the first time we'd been targeted, but whoever was trying to take us down was being sneaky about it and I did not like having an enemy I didn't know.

Opening my phone, I saw nine messages from Sledge and I softly cursed, wondering what the fuck had imploded around me now. I listened to the most recent one.

"Prez, almost lost a load of fur jackets from the pawn shop but we caught the fuckers before they made off with anything. Turns out they're independent contractors…Russian contractors hired to target us. They'd heard we're movin' some high-quality jewelry for our friends and thought the fur jackets was it. That means word has gotten out. I've got shit locked down tight so nothing to worry about, but thought you might be curious 'bout this happening while you were up in Denver. I'll meet you when you land. Oh—and don't get pissed, but Scarlet made me promise to tell you that Sarah is one of the nicest people she's ever met and to be gentle with her. None of my business, but my little sister's known you since she was in diapers so she feels like she's got a right to interfere in your life."

With a weary sigh, I returned to answering messages on my phone as we began our final descent into Austin and I tried to figure out how to get the shit that I needed to get done finished as quickly as possible so I could clear the air between Sarah and me.

Chapter 9

Sarah

I let my expression go bland as Beach tried to feed me his bullshit again. He'd apologized about what I'd heard, explaining that I'd only listened to a tiny part of the conversation. I said I forgave him, but not really. I was still pissed and he was not helping the matter by taking off on me as soon as we landed.

"I'm sendin' you someplace safe for a few days to heal. Shit around me is bad and I need you somewhere I know no one'll fuck with you. Birdie's ranch'll work and I know you'll like her. She's like a second mom to me and she's been a biker since the 1960s, and is my mama's best friend. Birdie's also a little crazy, you gotta be if you're gonna be friends with my mom, but has a big heart and will love havin' your company. She lives for entertaining."

While Birdie did indeed sound like an interesting character, and I could use some down time to heal, I didn't like being shuffled off on a stranger in some kind of odd holding pattern while Beach went out and did his thing. I was not, am not, and never will be the kind of woman who is content to sit around and twiddle her thumbs while the world floats by. My mother did that, fogged herself out into a drug-induced permanent haze and gave up caring about anything but incoherent chemical bliss.

I needed to get out of here. "No, I'm going to get a hotel room and contact my father."

He grit his teeth. "Look, Sarah, I need you to go to Birdie's."

"While you run around doing what?"

"Club business."

His eyes shuttered and I snorted. "Give me a fucking break. You're going to pretend, *now*, that I can't handle the way the world works? That I can't figure out you're going to be out there seeking vengeance while I sit around with my thumb up my ass waiting for you to decide it's time to see me again? You are out of your damn mind."

A few throats cleared around us and Beach's nostrils flared with anger. "Don't test me. Not here, not now."

I took a step closer into his space, not liking that I had to tilt my head up to meet his amazing eyes in the bright lights of the parking lot of what appeared to be a somewhat busy regional airport. We were standing in the middle of a circle of men who were openly staring at me, and all wearing leather Iron Horse MC cuts. I ignored them, pissed beyond belief. Though it pains me to say, I've inherited my father's temper combined with my mother's razor-sharp tongue, and it took a lot of self-control to keep myself from saying something that would cut deep.

"I'm not trying to test you, I'm trying to make this easy for you." I lowered my voice further and leaned up then whispered in his ear, "I may be young, dumb, and a woman, but I've had enough of your shit to last a lifetime. We are parting ways, period."

A flash of violence gleamed over his roughly elegant face when he jerked back, so sharply it made me gasp. Without another word, he grabbed my hand and pretty much dragged me as far away from the group of people as we could get. When we were in an isolated section of the lot, he turned to face me.

"We do not, *ever*, share our shit in front of people like that," he growled back as his entire body stiffened and seemed to grow bigger. "You got a problem, you talk to me about it in private and we'll address it. Getting bitchy with the whole world watchin' is not smart. We do not have time to talk about this shit right now, but I promise you, Sarah, we are nowhere near done."

Despite my being supremely pissed off at him, I lowered my voice and turned my back on the people watching us, not wanting to give them a show just in case they could read lips. "Oh, that's cute, you think you can decide when I can end things. Not that there's anything to end."

Instead of becoming even more pissed, he chuckled low in his throat and whispered into my ear, his lips stroking my sensitive skin with each word, "Had my fingers up that sweet, wet pussy of yours, made you come so good for your *Papi*. I think that qualifies as us havin' something right there."

Anger mixed with arousal and, if we were alone, I'd be tempted to jump him just to relieve the lust he so easily stirred in me. "Fuck off."

"We are definitely havin' a talk about your mouth once you're healed up," he muttered while giving the lobe of my ear a stinging nip. I gasped then pressed into him, my hands automatically going to his lean hips to steady myself. "By the way, Birdie used to run a spa and from what I hear from the old ladies, her bathtubs at the ranch are the shit. Big enough to swim in with candles and all that chick shit you women love so much. So how 'bout instead of arguing with me, you go with Smoke so he can take you over to Birdie's house. Programmed my number into your phone; you need me, text me or call me and I'll talk to you as soon as I can, yeah?"

At this point he started rubbing his soft lips, surrounded by his thick blond scruff, along my neck in a way that felt incredibly sinful. "I should go home."

"Stay, just for a little bit. We'll take it slow, get to know each other without the fuckin' world falling down around us," he cajoled and kissed his way to my mouth, where he seduced my lips until they parted for him. "I realize this is movin' fast and even though I really wish

I could take you home with me, I have shit that needs to be handled. If it was just personal stuff, I'd let it suffer, but this is the safety of my people and I gotta take that into consideration. I don't just protect my brothers, but their women and children. It's not a responsibility I take lightly and right now, my people need me."

I closed my eyes and hung my head in defeat, forcing myself to take a look at the bigger picture for a moment and not just me, me, me. He softly stroked my neck with his rough fingertips and I leaned a bit closer, taking in his crisp scent and basking in his heat. In a history of fucked-up relationships, this…whatever I had with Beach, was a whole new level of dysfunctional—but I felt something for him that was new to me, something warm and bright, something I wanted more of.

Without a doubt I was making a huge mistake and my heart would crash and burn, but I couldn't walk away from the possibility of something amazing with Beach. With this in mind, I stood on my tippy toes and kissed my way across his face, gentle kisses meant to soothe. He responded instantly, a happy rumble escaping him as our lips met.

Damn, he tasted so good and I loved the way our bodies fit together as he kissed me with a deep tenderness that said worlds about his feelings for me. Or at least I thought it did. I tried to keep a clear head around Beach but it was next to impossible to resist his charisma. Or his talented tongue. Our bodies were drawn together in a way that defied logic and I returned his kiss while threading my fingers into his deliciously thick hair.

Then he added a temptation I couldn't resist. "Did I also mention if Birdie likes you, she'll make you some home-cooked meals so good, you'll swear you died and went to heaven?"

My stomach decided to hijack my mouth. "Does she do brownies?"

"Yep, frosts 'em with this kick-ass fudge frosting and everything."

"The frosting is kick-ass?" I asked with a slight smile, amused by the idea of this big, bad biker so clearly enamored with the wonders of fudge frosting.

"Taste and you'll see."

"I'd love to hang out with Birdie for one day, maybe two, but I won't wait around for you forever," I murmured and tried to ignore the way his smile made me want to both smack and kiss him. "You're right, I do need to rest up."

"Thank you."

Walking me back to the group, he gave me a semi-teasing grin. "Gonna be a good girl for me?"

I flinched before I could help it, my instinctive reaction to those words hitting my psyche like a blow. Good girl—I always had to be the good girl or no one would love me. If I wasn't good enough, I'd be alone with no one to take care of me. Goose bumps prickled my arms and my breathing sped.

Playing the flinch off like I was merely shrugging, I sighed. "Seriously?"

Leaning in again, he caught my chin and that stern expression came over his face again, nailing me to the spot even as the echoes of my childhood memories kept ringing through my wounded heart. "*Mi reina*, in my world, when a woman is claimed, her actions reflect on her man. If you do something that brings shame to yourself, it will shame me as well. Mind your manners so everyone can see the beautiful woman that you really are, not the cold bitch you can pretend to be. *Si?*"

"Uh, no, not *si*," I hissed back in a whisper as my muscles tensed and I forced my palms flat on my legs in order to keep them from gripping into fists. "In my world, here on earth, there is no such thing as claiming a woman. So I'm sorry if you think my behavior is going to somehow shame you, but—"

He cut me off by kissing me until I forgot what I was going to say, his tongue stroking me into submission before he pulled back. "Not sayin' that at all. Just askin' you to keep our private life private and allow Birdie to fuss over you a little bit."

"Okay," I whispered, aware of the now very impatient men waiting for Beach and staring at us. "You should go."

"You gonna go to Birdies and wait for me?"

"Yeah."

"Promise?"

"Promise."

Six hours later, I was glad Birdie's daughter-in-law was a few sizes bigger than me, because my belly was straining against the waistband of the pajamas I'd borrowed. They were black with hot-pink piping on the edges and I knew without having to ask that Birdie bought these for her daughter-in-law. I knew this because the guest bedroom I was staying at in the main house was decorated in a similar zebra/hot-pink theme. Thankfully the zebra pattern didn't extend into the super fabulous en-suite bathroom, and Beach had been right, the bathtub and girly bath crap Birdie provided me with were awesome.

Now, post a real home-cooked fried chicken dinner complete with all the fixings, I lounged in the big russet leather recliner near the lit fireplace, watching Birdie move quickly around her kitchen. I'm pretty sure she was the same woman I saw back in Denver wearing the Jack Daniel's robe and fuzzy pink slippers, but she looked different now. Biker babe chic for the seventy-year-old woman. In her case, a black tank top, tons of gold chains with different pendants, a crazy-big diamond tennis bracelet, and a pair of designer jeans studded with tasteful rhinestones on the back pockets along with kick-ass black cowboy boots. Her hair was sprayed into a crispy blonde helmet, the likes of which I haven't seen outside of teen movies from the 1980s.

She was sassy, she was brutally honest, and she was the shit.

Grabbing a wooden bowl full of apples, she moved over to the black granite countertop which separated the open-plan kitchen with its gold, brown and amber glass tiles from the living room dominated by deep browns and crimson red.

One of the reasons I'm so into interior decoration was because I found that people's homes reflected their spirits. If the heart and mind didn't love where they lived, it would never transition from a house to a home. Yeah, I know my own lack of a stable place to live as a kid was part of my joy in providing others with the perfect décor, but it was *only* part of it. I just loved interior design. Back when Swan and I had been tight, she'd watch those home improvement shows with me all the time and I'd valued that bonding time with her and our circle of close friends.

The glug of wine being poured drew my wandering thoughts back to Birdie, refilling her etched crystal glass. She was an odd woman and I hadn't quite been able to get a read on her yet. This is the first time we were alone, all the farmhands that had stopped by earlier to meet me and give me a once over had left. Picking up a big, shiny and sharp kitchen knife, she began to peel one of the apples in between sips of wine.

Concerned she was going to slice herself, I put down my own barely tasted glass and sat up. "Why don't you let me do that?"

"I've got it, little girl." She gave me a wry smile that folded up all her deeply tanned wrinkles. "My husband travels a lot doing his job as National Chaplain."

"Chaplin?" I frowned into my glass. "Iron Horse didn't seem that religious to me."

She laughed. "Maybe not in the traditional sense, but my husband is an ordained minister and he performs lots of weddings, and sadly lots of funerals, for Iron Horse. Not only in Austin, but all over. In fact, right now he's marrying a nice couple out in California, Skipper and Tracy. Good kids, strong foundation. They'll have a good life. *Mazel tov* to them."

"You're Jewish?"

"What?" She arched her carefully plucked brows. "You don't think Jews can be bikers?"

"What? No…"

Laughing, Birdie winked at me. "Just giving you a hard time, doll. Venom, my husband, is Christian, I'm Jewish, and one of our daughters is Buddhist while the other is agnostic. My son followed in his dad's footsteps and is a chaplain in the Army."

"Wow…that's really cool."

Birdie tilted her head to the side, a soft smile curving her lips. "It is, isn't it? Now, word is goin' around your Beach's old lady. Is it true?"

Uncomfortable beneath her sharp gaze, I looked away and took a sip of my wine. "Something like that."

"Something like that?" Birdie laughed softly and waved the knife in my direction, her diamond tennis bracelet sparkling. "There is no something about it. He's publically claimed you, not as his house mouse, or his sweet butt, or even a girlfriend, but as his old lady. That's a big deal and a huge privilege."

I tried to hold back my irritation. "Look, no man can claim me. I'm a person, not some old washing machine that's been abandoned on the side of the road."

Birdie let out a hoot that echoed through the large open space. "Girl, you know anything about the MC life?"

I thought about bullshitting her—never show weakness—but she seemed like the kind of woman who could sniff out a lie. In a way she reminded me of a cruder, older, blonde version of Mimi. So far she'd been nothing but nice to me, if a little crazy, so I decided to be honest.

"Not really. Before I landed the biker cover in," I cleared my throat, not wanting to have her turn judgmental on me for posing nude, "a magazine, I really hadn't ever thought about the biker culture. I know a little bit from Scarlet but that's about it."

"You talking about when you were in *Playboy*?"

Look, I'm not ashamed of being nude in a magazine, but this woman was old enough to be my grandmother and it didn't feel right talking about anything sexual with her. Different generations had different standards and I'm sure back in her day, any woman posing in a nudie magazine was instantly labeled a bad person.

Flushing bright red, I took another sip of my wine and mumbled, "Yes. How did you know?"

"Do you really think Miss March getting kidnapped with the Prez, saving his life, then getting claimed as his old lady wouldn't be news?"

"News? You mean I'm on the news? Oh shit, my parents are going to freak."

"No, no, what happened to you is club business and we keep club business locked down tight, but the brothers do gossip amongst themselves. No doubt Beach has airtight alibis for both of you. 'Sides, who is going to believe a pretty little thing like yourself would be capable of what you survived?"

This was true, most people saw the size of my breasts with my blonde hair and instantly put me into the "slutty bimbo" mental category and didn't count me as a threat. "Good point."

She tapped her long, hot-pink and sparkly red nails on the granite countertop. "Most important thing you need to know is what your role in the club will be."

I had to admit I was curious as to how Iron Horse worked. "What role?"

"Slick, you're the National President's old lady." I must have looked as confused as I felt. "That means you got a role to play, but one thing you need to realize right off is that to a lot of the old bastards who are patched-in members, you're a woman, which means you don't have any say. It's complete and utter horse crap, but it's the way of the MC world, or at least it has been. Iron Horse isn't as bad as some other clubs, but it'll take you some getting used to. Now, the younger guys aren't as bad, but you'll have to get used to being a second-class citizen."

"Sounds fun," I lied. "So my role would be what? Arm candy? A pretty bit of fluff who's supposed to flutter my lashes while the men run the world? Or wait, Beach will want me at home, barefoot and pregnant in the kitchen."

"Not quite that bad." She smiled and shook her head. "And like I said, the world, even the world of the MC, is changing. The dinosaurs may not like it, but that doesn't mean their kind isn't almost extinct. Now, your relationship and how you live it is between you and Beach, not my place to tell him how to run things, but I'm more than happy to give you my take on things. I've been with the club since before computers were invented and I've seen two of the former old ladies of the National President in action, the first being Beach's maternal grandmother, Gracie."

"Wait, Beach's grandpa was also a National President?"

"Let me give you a little bit of Iron Horse's history, make things easier to understand. Peg, Beach's grandfather, was a good man, and Beach's great-grandfather was one of the founding members. Boy's third-generation Iron Horse and about as tough as they come." She bent over, briefly disappearing before popping back up with a giant black Crock-Pot. "Gracie passed away first of breast cancer, God rest her sweet soul, and Peg not long after of a heart attack. After much debate, a man named Red was elected President."

"Why wasn't Beach elected?"

"Beach was only eighteen at the time, had just gotten patched into the MC. Just 'cause a man is born into the life doesn't mean anyone owes him shit. Respect is earned in our world, regardless of who your daddy is. So while Beach had already begun to prove that he had a good head on his shoulders, ain't no one trustin' a kid with runnin' Iron Horse."

"Makes sense. So did like Red retire and then Beach took over?"

"Hardly. Red had it out for Beach. Made the boy's life rough, giving him the shittiest assignments, runs that lasted months so he was away from the MC and Red as much as possible. Man knew Beach was his greatest threat and kept Beach on the road for years. Not only was Beach third-generation Iron Horse, he was also a natural born leader. Known that boy since the day he was born and even when he was a kid, he was always the one leading the children around." She almost patted her hair, then realized she was holding a knife in that hand. "Idiot couldn't have set it up better for Beach to take over as National President."

"What do you mean?"

"Think about it, Beach is *National* President, as in, he's the man all of our chapters look to. The man who took Red's place as National President wouldn't just be responsible for the Austin chapter, but all of them. The Chapter Presidents have control over their own chapters, but the National President runs them all."

"How many chapters do you have?"

"Twelve chapters in nine states at the moment."

"Wow, that's a lot."

"When you figure you got anywhere from 200 to 500 brothers in each club, plus the Prospects, it adds up."

"And all of them wanted equal representation from someone they felt knew them," I mused out loud. "Someone who'd spent time with them, someone they'd respect. Can't have respect without facetime."

"Smart girl." Birdie beamed at me, her eyes all but disappearing in the folds of her face.

I grinned at her. "Obviously at some point, Red went away and Beach came into power. What happened?"

Birdie paused mid-chop as she sliced a peeled apple. "Bad times. Red got the club into some things they didn't normally do, evil things, and there was a rift in Iron Horse. Rumors were flying around and I swear you could feel death creepin' up in the air like frost. See, Red picked weak brothers to do his dirty work, men susceptible to doing anything for a buck. Greedy fools. Every patched member of Iron Horse gets a cut of the club's financial holdings, and it's more than enough for any family to live comfortably on."

"Financial holdings?"

"Come on now, you really think a man like Beach, who has jets and helicopters at his disposal, isn't loaded? Your old man has his own wealth, which isn't anything to sneeze at, but the MC has assets worth tens of millions of dollars. Every patched-in member, or their widow and children, get a portion of the club's profits each year. How much you get depends on your rank, and the officers make hundreds of thousands a year."

"Wow."

"We got everything from real estate to investments in various business start-ups. Hell, back in the day, Iron Horse gave the seed money to my husband to get our ranch going. On the outside it may just look like bikers and danger and wildness, but don't fool yourself, behind all those tattoos and scars are some very smart and wealthy men who will do whatever they need in order to protect the brotherhood. So when people noticed problems with the club's bottom line, they started looking into it and found out Red and his old lady, Fancy, had been stealing from the club."

"No shit." I sat forward, fascinated by this biker drama that could give any of my favorite soap operas a run for their money.

"Yep. Not going into details, but it almost caused a war within Iron Horse before Beach…took care of Red and his crew. That was seven years ago, and I'm proud to say Beach has been one of the best National Presidents Iron Horse has ever had. He's a smart man who surrounds himself with smart people and has a real knack for seeing the value in someone." Birdie gave me a shrewd look while pouring a measuring cup full of what I thought was sugar into the Crock-Pot. "That's why when he told me he found his old lady, I knew you would be a good woman, and I'm glad I was right."

I flushed at the compliment. "Birdie, you have to agree that this is all moving a little fast. I mean Beach and I hardly know each other at all. We're practically strangers."

"You got the rest of your lives to learn about each other, child."

I made a feeble protest, not wanting to admit how nice that sounded, I said, "You don't understand. I have a life, plans, things I've worked hard for and sacrificed for that I don't want to give up."

"No one's asking you to give up your plans." She calmly stirred the contents of the Crock-Pot with a wooden spoon. "Five years down the road, where do you want to be?"

I've been dreaming about this for so long I spoke up right away. "I want to either be working in an establish interior design firm, or starting one of my own."

"You going to school for that?"

"I've been taking courses online in interior design, but now that I have more than enough money set aside to live on, I want to get a degree then hopefully start to work with a design firm. I'm not sure which one yet, but I do know that being someone's old lady isn't part of that plan."

"Why not?"

I frowned at her. "Because all the schools I've applied for are out in California, where I plan on moving. I don't know about you, but I'm pretty sure Beach doesn't strike me as the kind of guy who would do a long-distance relationship."

"No, he definitely isn't the kind of man to want that." Birdie was silent for a few moments. "Do you enjoy his company?"

"Who, Beach?"

"Yes."

I picked at my cuticles rather than look at her. "He's all right."

"Just all right?"

Her teasing tone made me smile, then sigh. "Okay, so he's the hottest thing I've ever seen, super smart and brave and awesome. And so far he's been really nice to me, but a lot of guys can be really nice at first then they turn out to be demons in human form who will do everything they can to destroy you."

"You had a lot of experience with men like that?"

I drained the last of my second glass of wine. "You could say that."

The only sounds that filled the air for a little bit were from Birdie moving around the kitchen while I stared at the fire and mentally flipped through all the men I'd seen use and abuse my mom and vice versa.

Stifling a yawn, I stood and stretched, then winced as my sore body protested the movement. "I'm going to head to bed. Thanks so much for all your hospitality and making me feel so at home."

Birdie gave me a small smile. "You're welcome, doll. Pancakes good with you in the morning? If not, I'll make whatever you like."

"Oh, you don't have to—"

She waved her hand at me while wearing a sour look that pulled her wrinkles together. "It ain't no bother. I've gotta eat too and there are always brothers dropping by with their bottomless-pit stomachs. Hasn't been a week gone by in the last thirty years where I haven't had a group of brothers at my table, not to mention hungry ranch hands, so I always make a hearty breakfast."

"In that case, pancakes would be wonderful. Thank you, but you'll have to let me do the dishes. I don't feel right with people waiting hand and foot on me and I hate sitting around. Let me know what you need help with and I'll gladly do it. I know you have the men who work here to take care of the ranch, but I have experience cleaning stalls and stuff. If you can find me some clothes you don't mind getting dirty, I'd be more than happy to help take care of the animals. Or anything else you need. My parents have a small farm of sorts—goats, chickens, and a llama, so I have experience taking care of animals."

Laughing, Birdie came around the countertop separating the kitchen and the living room. She stopped before me and held my shoulders, peering into my face so intently I was fighting the urge to squirm. "You just worry 'bout getting better and we'll deal with the rest tomorrow. Okay?"

I wanted to argue, but I had a feeling I wouldn't get anywhere with her so I nodded. "Okay."

"Sleep tight, honey." She gave me a gentle hug and whispered, "It's good having you here. I think you're gonna do Beach a world of good. He needs a strong, but sweet woman like you in his life. I hope you'll give him that chance. Just think about it, okay?"

"I'll think about it," I whispered back, wanting to blame the tears prickling my eyes on the wine, but knowing it wasn't true.

Chapter 10

Carlos "*Beach*" Rodriguez

We sat around the huge scarred oak table that one of the founders, a master carver, made for the original clubhouse in Austin back in the 1950s. That small shithole had long since burned down and we'd moved into a much bigger and nicer building, with lots of land around it. We'd even had a room specially built for holding church, and right now it was filled with pissed-off brothers. They did not like seeing me hurt, did not like the fact I'd been snatched from them like that, or the fact that we'd been ambushed, and they were hungry to dish out the pain.

Problem was, we had to figure out who deserved it.

I looked over at Smoke, sitting in his position to my right as my Master at Arms; behind him, Vance's gaze kept scanning the room. I sometimes wondered if he was pissed Smoke got the position and he didn't. After all, Vance was a distant older cousin on my mom's side, and there were some who believed you should trust blood over anyone. Then there was the fact Vance had outranked Smoke in the Marines so Vance felt he should automatically get the position.

That was bullshit. Just 'cause we shared genetics didn't make him the best man for the job. I also didn't give a shit he'd outranked Smoke. My Master at Arms was a genuine fuckin' war hero with more medals than I'd ever seen. More than Vance had earned in his ten years in the Marines.

Smoke was brutal, no doubt about that, but he could control his anger and make logical decisions when the pressure was on, something my cousin couldn't do. Vance had a temper on him and had made some enemies over the years, which disqualified him from the sometimes diplomatic nature of the Master at Arms position. I'd had to save my cousin's ass when we were younger enough times to know how bad his rage was. His hurt pride had written more than one check his ass couldn't cash, but he'd gotten a lot better. He was still arrogant as ever, but he didn't talk as much as he used to and I could always depend on him to have my back.

He must have felt my gaze, 'cause Vance turned to look at me and when our eyes met, there was a flash of something I couldn't read, followed by a cold, blank stare that was borderline disturbing even to me.

"Prez, got some info for you." Sledge's familiar voice came from my left.

I turned to the man sporting a freshly trimmed Mohawk, revealing the flame tattoos on either side of his skull.

Thorn bellowed, "Church is in session, all you shut the fuck up and listen to what your Vice President has to say."

Soon the only sounds in the room were breathing and the faint rustling of fabric and creak of leather.

Sledge nodded to the room, the big muscles of his tattooed arms bulging as he placed them on the sturdy table and leaned slightly forward. "It looks like there was more than one player that night at Sturgis. From what I can piece together, we had three separate groups. One that was clearly some Los Diablos, but I think they took the opportunity the first two groups' actions presented. The ones who tried to take Sarah were Russian. They both had *Bratva* tattoos all over them. I'm in contact with our Russian sources to see what they have to say, but right now we've got no fucking idea who they were and why they tried to snatch her."

I nodded, not surprised to find out we were having problems with our overseas rivals. One of the Russian mafias, or *Bratvas* as they liked to call themselves, had been trying to push Iron Horse out of some oceanfront property we controlled in California that was perfect for smuggling by land and sea. Since we basically told them that was never going to fucking happen, they'd been taking undercover shots at us. Nothing we could prove, but we knew it was them fucking with us. It might have been a full-out war, but we were allies with the Novikov *Bratva* and no one wanted to fuck with them.

"The second group, the ones that took our Prez," the room filled with anger and muttered threats, "we got no clue. Any evidence burned up in that van, and other than the descriptions that we got from Beach and Sarah, we don't got much. Cops got nothin' either, the site was swept clean by the time we got there. And by clean, I mean *clean*, like it never happened. Any idea who coulda done that?"

"Sarah said her dad had his friends on the way to get her. That could have been the vehicles approaching as we flew out."

Sledge let out a humorless laugh. "Damn, Beach, must be nice to have a father-in-law that'll clean crime scenes for you."

"Fuck off." I sighed and rubbed my tired eyes. "Got any good news?"

"Yeah," Hustler, one of my Enforcers and the owner of the pawn shop where we did a lot of business, both legal and illegal, said from farther down the table. "The buyers will pay our full askin' price for escorting their goods from New Orleans to the port in LA."

I let out a low whistle. When I'd made our counteroffer I went high, expecting them to try to lowball me. To know they were going to pay the full three million for an escort made me instantly suspicious. "We get a docket of what the cargo is yet?"

"Not yet."

"Find out what it is first. Not sayin' yes until they've assured us we aren't movin' any human cargo or crazy shit."

We sold drugs, we sold guns, we even sold willing pussy, but we did not and never will do human trafficking. That was the bullshit Red had begun to dabble in on the side, and my stomach still knotted when I remembered opening the back of a van parked in the clubhouse lot, expecting bricks of cocaine or weed, and instead finding three kidnapped young Mexican girls who were on their way to some pimp in San Francisco. They'd been beaten and raped repeatedly by Red and his men, then bound with duct tape and thrown in the van for transport.

"Got it," Hustler replied with a grim look.

After that it was a bunch of never-ending business that had to get handled and by the time we were done it had turned into a six-hour meeting. We split up and I dragged my ass to my room in the compound. The upper floor of the three-story building was split into ten different suites, with mine being the biggest. I nodded to the Prospect standing guard at my door before letting myself into my room with a weary sigh. My whole fuckin' body ached and I was beat and I needed some sleep, but I had to check on my girl first.

It was close to midnight, but I knew Birdie liked to stay up late so I dialed her house phone.

Sure enough, after three rings, the old lady answered. "Was wondering when you would call."

"Is she still awake?"

"Nope. She went to bed a couple hours ago. I've been checking on her and she's out like a light."

Sitting down on the edge of my bed, I began to take my boots off with one hand. "How was she tonight? You slip her a pill?"

"Fair to middlin'," Birdie sighed. "And you were right, she would rather sit and suffer in silence than ask for help. Foolish girl thinks she's going to muck out stalls tomorrow when she moves stiffer than I do and I've got a bum hip!"

Next to my bed I've got one of those mini fountains with soft lights, and I turned off every light but it. The moving reflections on the walls help me focus at night when I'm thinking and need a clear head. God knows my brain is just about crisped at the moment and my injuries were starting to bother me as well. Knew I should be taking a couple pills in order to sleep tonight, but like Sarah, I didn't want to. Never know who, or what, might come after me.

Collapsing back on my bed, I stared at the waving patterns on the clean white ceiling thrown by the water of the fountain, shimmering with faint golden light. "You think she noticed?"

"No, I only gave her a small amount and a couple glasses of wine. Fed her my fried chicken and you'd think I'd gone and made ambrosia for her. She's skinny, but she can put away the food when the mood sets her."

"She's strong—incredibly strong."

Birdie was silent for a few moments. "Honey, you gotta be careful with her."

I sat up, my entire body tensing. "What?"

"She's got a very gentle heart and has been hurt, I'd guess a lot, in the past. Her guards are up and even though it's clear she's fond of you, she fights it. Not saying she isn't strong, or that she can't handle the life, but she's gonna be skittish far as you're concerned."

Resuming my position on my back on the king-size bed, I relaxed again. "I know that."

"I know you know that, but I still had to say something. You're gonna need to entice her to stay here with you, Beach. Give her a purpose outside of being your woman."

Birdie had been married to her husband for fifty-seven years, and had set all of her kids up in successful marriages of their own, so I forced myself to push aside my impatience and listen to her advice. "Got any opinions on how I should handle this?"

"Did a little chatting with her and found out she wants to be an interior designer. She's been going to school online but doesn't have her degree yet. You're gonna need to show her you're serious about her being a part of your life, so it wouldn't hurt to use your connections to get her into any local college she wants."

"Done, what else?"

"You need a place, a new place, where both of you can live. If you move into your place it'll be just that, *your* place. You need her to put down roots and no better way to do that than choosing where she's gonna live."

"That's not gonna freak her out?"

"Not any more than she already is. May help 'cause she'll feel like she has control over her life. You are a very smart man, honey. I've watched you fight for what you wanted all your life and I know you can figure out a way to make it work." She sighed. "I've never seen you give up before, and I'm not gonna start seeing it now. Your nature won't allow it."

"What are you yammerin' on about, woman?"

Her voice came out unexpectedly soft. "Carlos, I was one of the first people who held you after you were born. I want you to be happy and I don't like seeing you alone at your age. This girl, she's a handful, but once you get her to settle down she's gonna make some man very happy, and I'd love for that man to be you."

"I'd love for that man be me too, Birdie."

"Now, question is, if you're trying to win her heart, why the hell are you all the way across town?"

"Good point, but as I'm sure you can understand there's been just a little bit of shit to deal with over here today."

"I do understand, and I appreciate how hard you drive yourself to keep Iron Horse safe, so you do what you need to do and I'll take care of Sarah."

"Thanks. I think I'll be able to come by tomorrow afternoon."

"Good, I can tell she misses you."

I give her a grunt, only willing to talk about so much with my Mama's best friend. "Thanks for the update, Birdie. You stay safe."

"Always do, sweetheart. Goodnight and we'll see you tomorrow."

I hung up and got about three minutes of peace before there was a knock on my door.

"What?" I yelled as my body sank into the comfort of my bed.

"Your girls are here."

Rubbing my face, I once again sat up and wondered if I should have gone to Birdie's place with Sarah. It would certainly be better than the conversation I was about to have. Feelings would be hurt, despite the fact the women on the other side of that door were experienced sweet butts knew it was nothing but sex between us.

"Let 'em in."

As soon as the door opened, Brandy and Sandy both rush in wearing short-shorts and tight tank tops that showed off their great bodies. Both are brunettes, but

Brandy has some Mexican in her, with her dark tan and brown eyes, while Sandy is as pale as cream with light green eyes. They've been my regular girls for the past year, I don't like to share my women with my brothers, but before that they'd been club sweet butts who've been around long enough to know the score. Hell, they loved the club so much they shared a room at the clubhouse on the floor below us.

"Beach," Sandy squealed as she comes flying at my bed. "We heard what happened, are you okay?"

Brandy slid onto the bed next to me, her breasts swaying enticingly with her movements. "*Papi*, I was so worried."

I untangle myself from their bodies with a small trace of regret. These girls are wild in bed, knew their place in the club, and were always there when I wanted them. Plus Sandy kept the other sweet butts in line for me, something that's gonna change once Sarah gets her feet under her.

At the thought of my beautiful girl, the appeal of the two women sitting on my bed withered away to nothing. It had been fun while it lasted, but like every woman before them, it was over.

Always said when I found my old lady I was gonna be totally loyal to her, and I meant it.

"Girls, I'm afraid our time together is done."

They both blink at me, Sandy's eyes filling with tears. "What?"

I ran my hand through my hair, wanting this shit over with so I could get some much-needed sleep. "Time for me to move on."

"Move on?" Brandy repeated, anger sparking in her dark eyes. "What do you mean, move on?"

While I don't claim to know my way around the fucked-up mind of a woman, I did have enough experience to know this shit wasn't going to go down well. "I got an old lady now."

"An old lady?" Sandy said through clenched teeth, her hands fisting. "You really do have an old lady? It's not bullshit, the rumors are true?"

I wasn't going to explain myself. "Yeah, I got an old lady now and that means we're done."

"I don't understand," Brandy whined. "We can still be your club girls."

Some brothers did that, had an old lady at home then a club girlfriend on the side. Hell, some had three or four of 'em. While it worked for them, cheating wouldn't work for me and I was real fuckin' sure it wouldn't work for Sarah. She did not strike me as the kind of woman who would accept her man fuckin' other women.

"Like I said, we've had some good times, but we're done. You can stay in your room on the second floor, and I'll give you next month's allowance, but then you're on your own. And you stay the fuck away from my old lady. You get near her and it's not gonna end well for you, history between us or not."

To my surprise, Brandy flew off my bed, anger turning her face red. "You can't do this!"

"Excuse me?"

Sandy screamed, "What's wrong with you? We love you! You can't throw us away you fucking asshole."

"First, bitch, I don't know who the fuck you think you are, but me stickin my dick in you—which will never fuckin' happen again—does not give you the right to get fuckin' lippy with me. Second, you don't fuckin' love me. You love the status that comes with bein' my regular bitch, and my money."

"That's not true!" Sandy yelled while Brandy began to cry.

"Bullshit. You love throwin' my name around to get free shit. How many restaurants do you eat at, every day, where you eat for free? Or bars where you drink for free?" Sandy's angry gaze darted away from mine 'cause she knew it was the truth. "You think I don't know about all the times you got an Iron Horse discount on shit 'cause of you droppin' my name? All the times you shoulda gotten speeding tickets that were swept under the rug? And you sure as fuck maxed out the credit cards I gave you every month."

Chewing on her lower lip, Brandy said nothing while Sandy silently fumed.

"That's what I fuckin' thought." I took a deep breath, calming myself. "Now, get the fuck out. You two have been friends of the club for a long time, but if you ever disrespect me like that again you will be banned for life and I'll personally make sure you will regret it. We clear?"

Sandy opened her mouth again, her crazy temper no doubt getting the better of her, but Brandy reached out and grabbed her arm. "We understand."

My gaze turned to sweet but not-so-smart Brandy. "Get her out of here."

She nodded, tugging her friend after her. "I'll always be here for you, Beach, always. When you want a break from your old lady, you just let me know."

Sandy wiped away her tears, smearing her thick black mascara over her cheeks. "We'll do whatever it takes to get you back. Anything."

My patience at an end, I stalked across the room to them and they scurried for the door. "You never had me, bitch, so there is no getting me back. You know I'm givin' you a break 'cause we got history, but that is what it is, history. Never put my patch on either of your backs, or claimed you for anythin' more than sex. Now, last warnin', get the fuck out and don't let me see you for a few weeks."

At that they left and before the door finished swinging, I yelled out, "Yo, grab Sledge!"

My VP appeared in the doorway a few minutes later, shirtless and chowing on a sandwich while some skank crawled all over him. "What's up?"

"Gonna need a ride to Birdie's place."

His wide grin made me want to punch him, but I was saving what little energy I had for Sarah. If I didn't get one more taste of her sweetness before I went to sleep, I knew in my gut I would regret it. I've always trusted my instincts, and when they told me my woman needed me, I paid attention.

The ride to Birdie's ranch was long enough for me to get a nap in, so when we rolled through the big gates leading to her main house, I was feeling a little more like myself. I sent off a few quick texts with instructions to leave me the fuck alone. Then I gave my officers the authority to take care of shit and for the first time in what felt like forever, I told them I was takin' the day off.

I'm not a dumb bastard and when Birdie says I need to do something, I pay attention. And if Birdie thought Sarah might take off, I needed to do what I could to bind her to me. If Sarah still thinks she's leaving before we explore this, she's delusional.

My breath eased out of me into the cool night air as I exited the car, giving the warm hood of the SUV a double tap before I started up the front riverstone walkway to Birdie's house.

Lotta good memories rolled through me as I took the front porch steps two at a time. When I reached the top,

Birdie was already waiting for me, wearing this crazy pair of black silk pajamas with gold sparkles around the collar and cuffs. I had to grin, loving that no matter what, Birdie always looked good. World could be falling down around her and she'd still make sure her hair was nice when she answered her door, be it for family or a repairman. I gave her soft, wrinkled cheek a kiss as I brushed past.

"Figured you'd be showing up." She smiled at me and crossed her arms.

"Hope you didn't wait up."

"Nah, never sleep good without Venom here."

"Where's Sarah?"

"The zebra guest room."

I inwardly groaned, hating that room. Birdie had designed it with a teenage girl in mind, but it had an amazing king-size bed with one of those massive memory foam mattresses. The thought of Sarah being in it had me hustling for the stairs, wincing the slightest bit as I moved up them.

"Slow down," Birdie said with laughter in her voice. "You'll do her no good coming to her crippled. No one wants a stallion they can't ride in their bed."

Shaking my head, I tried to block out Birdie's laughter as I carefully opened the door leading to the room Sarah slept in.

I didn't see her, only rumpled sheets, and went into the room figuring she'd be in the bathroom.

Once again, my assumption about her was wrong.

This was proven when her knife was at my neck and she whispered in my ear, "It's polite to knock first."

Laughing, I reached up and lowered her arm, having no fear she'd accidentally harm me.

Now purposely, on the other hand...

"*Mi riena*, do you have any idea how hard I am right now? Like you havin' that knife to my throat. You gonna let me return the favor while I'm fuckin' you? Hold some cool steel to your skin? Bet you like that little bit of danger."

Her sharp intake of breath made me smile. "Whatever."

So damn cute.

Turning, I examined her as she turned on the small lamp next to the bed. "What are you doing here?"

I made my way to her side, reached past her while inhaling her fresh scent, and turned the lamp off. "Stayin' the night with my woman."

As I stood back up, I paused to nibble on the tender lobe of her ear, taking in the electrical sparks I felt when my lips barely grazed her skin. It was like my entire being was centered on the feel of her, my brain devoted to the pleasure of touching her. Unable to help myself, I licked her neck, needing a taste. That made her moan and press her hips into mine, her arms snaking up around me.

"You smell like cigarette smoke."

"Sorry, baby."

"It's okay, I'm just not used to smelling it on you." She stiffened and pulled back.

"Don't smoke, babe, but some of my brothers do. Not gonna chase 'em out of the room for lighting up."

"Oh. Well, I think I should probably go sleep on the couch." Her voice wobbled with sadness and I had to resist rolling my eyes. "It's for the best."

"We back to that shit again?" I gave her ass a brisk slap, absolutely loving the way her curves moved beneath my touch. "I know you're gonna sleep better, here in the dark, with me at your side."

She abruptly sagged, her whole body melting into mine, giving me almost her entire weight. "True."

"So stop arguing with me and get back in bed. I meant what I said, we both need to heal. So though it's gonna kill me not to fuck you, we're just gonna sleep tonight."

"And tomorrow."

"We'll worry 'bout that tomorrow. You call your dad and let him know you're okay?"

"Kind of. I talked to my stepmom. I think she'll leave me be for a few more days, but soon I'm going to have to go home to visit them."

"I'm comin' with you," I decided instantly, knowing this was one solid way I could prove to her I was serious about us.

She ripped out of my arms and clicked the light on, the move violent enough to send the lamp rocking, casting weird shadows over the room. "You can't."

"Excuse me?"

"You can't."

"I absolutely can." I took a deep breath and began to tug my cut off, then went into the closet and hung it up, giving myself time to cool down. "Why?"

Her voice came out small, scared. I didn't like it. "Why what?"

"Why can't I come with you?"

"You're a way-older-than-me biker so my dad will kill you on basic principal," she said without hesitation.

I thought about who her dad was then shrugged. There as a good chance he just might do that. If not him, her stepmom might. Still, I was glad it wasn't 'cause she was ashamed of us or anything like that. I knew my lifestyle was something many women couldn't handle, knew it all too fucking well, and I couldn't help but smile at her.

Right away, those pretty blue eyes of her narrowed into slits. "What are you grinning about?"

"You. Fuckin' adorable baby I've got on my hands."

Before she could gear up to pitch a fit, I closed the distance between us and kissed her, seducing the anger from her, softening her whole body against mine. Those amazing tits of hers crushed to my chest and my dick was in heaven pressed up against her. As our tongues stroked, I moaned into her mouth and wrapped my arms around her, only breaking the kiss when she winced.

My jaw clenched when I realized I'd squeezed her bruised ribs. "Sorry, *mi corazón*. Didn't mean to hurt you."

She gave a shuddery laugh. "Before you came here, almost my entire body hurt. Now all I can think about is how empty I feel inside, how tight. I want to come."

"You're beat up."

"So be gentle."

It was close to fucking impossible to force the words out, but I had to say them. "I don't know if I can be gentle with you, babe. Want you so fuckin' bad, but you're hurt. Don't ask me to hurt you more. Not like this."

Her voice held rich amusement as she said, "Carlos, take off your clothes and come to bed with me. When I say I'm too tired to fight, I mean it. I think Birdie druggied me."

"Druggied?"

"It's like being high, but only a little bit. I'm just mellow instead of being trashed."

"You get high a lot?"

"I won't lie, I used to, but all I do anymore is smoke pot and that doesn't even really count. And I barely drink so I'm not too worried about it. Well, I had a couple glasses of wine after a massive fried chicken dinner, but that's not really partying. I still have a pooch from it. What about you?"

I tried to keep from laughing at her pooch comment. Sure enough, she had a tiny belly on her from eating too much. Truth be told, she could put on about twenty pounds of softness. She was fit, but fit to the point where I knew she'd had to sacrifice for all that lean muscle. I wasn't enough of a dumbass to say that to her, of course, but I loved how much she enjoyed the simple act of eating. Like it was something new and exciting.

She made everything new and exciting.

"Beach?"

"Sorry, mind was wanderin'. I'm more of a drinker than a smoker."

"How did I know you'd say that?" She smiled and helped me take my shirt off then stared at my chest. "You really are all man."

"Pardon?" With open appreciation, she closed the distance between us and rubbed her strangely calloused yet soft hands over my chest. "How come your hands are so rough, baby? Don't you wear gloves workin' out?"

"I'm a pole dancer, where do you think my callouses would be?"

Remembering the video I'd seen of her earlier, I smiled and placed my much larger hands over hers, feeling the delicate bones of her hands, so seemingly fragile beneath mine. "Good point. Watched one of your performances. Blew me away, my beautiful baby. Was not expecting it to be anything like that."

"What do you mean, 'like that'?"

I soothed her frowning lips with the thumb of my free hand. "I mean it was art."

Her eyes widened and for the first time I saw her true age in a way I hadn't before, the innocence she'd managed to retain beneath all her jaded disdain. "Exactly. You understand."

"I understand more than you think. Do you understand how important you are to me already?"

She looked away, her shoulders slumping the slightest bit. "I wish I was."

Frustrated and irritable from lack of sleep, I jerked my boots, then pants and socks off as I laid it out for her, hoping she was sober enough to remember this conversation. "I don't know why you can't believe this, someone in your past obviously fucked you over good, but I like you. I want to be with you, I want you to be with me. Yeah, I'm older and your dad may flip out about it, but a boy your age could never treat you better than I will. I get off on making you feel good, making you smile. I thrive on that shit. When you're happy, I'm happy, and you gotta believe I'll put work into making that so."

She slowly looked up at me through her pale lashes and tears glimmered in her eyes as she sniffled. "You're so awesome."

"Baby." Gathering her into my arms, I led my battered woman to the bed and got her situated before turning off the light and sliding in next to her. "I've got you, relax."

After a moment of pushing pillows around, we both turned to each other, our foreheads pressed together as we entwined our fingers. My thigh slid between her legs, my erection pressing into her stomach while her breasts pillowed against my bare chest. She smelled like some unfamiliar shampoo, but that faint hint of peaches was still there. So sweet.

I needed to sample her sweetness, had traveled all the way here in the dead of night to get just a sip. Shifting my head, I brushed my lips against hers, being oh so careful to take it easy. She tried to deepen the kiss but I pulled back and instead rolled us so I was on my back and her body was curved into mine, with her cheek resting on my shoulder. With a low groan, I readjusted my healing leg.

Right away she started to soothe me, her fingers stroking my chest as she said, "How are you feeling?"

"Now that I'm with you, good. Couldn't stay away from you tonight. Tried to give you your space to settle, but I was fuckin' miserable going to bed alone."

"I missed you too," she whispered. "You wanna know something cool?"

"What?"

"I'm not scared right now and I don't have the bathroom light on or anything." Her fingers stopped petting me and remained tense over my heart. "I travel with a nightlight."

"Why you so scared of the dark?"

She tried to draw away. "I don't want to talk about it."

Pulling her back, I hastily changed the subject. "If you could have any kind of house, what would it be?"

Ever so slowly, she relaxed her body back into mine and I marveled at how damn soft she was. "You ask the strangest questions."

"And?"

"Modern."

"Gotta give me more than that."

"Why are you asking me about my dream home?"

"You said we don't know each other, so I'm getting to know you. Person's house says a lot about them and

I'm curious as to what you like, where you could see yourself bein' happy."

For a long moment she was silent, her fingers tracing through my chest hair. "I'd be happy anywhere I'm loved. A building doesn't do that, it's the people who fill it that make a difference."

"So sweet," I murmured as I stroked my hand down her slender back, to the swell of her tight ass. "So damn sweet."

She yawned, "I'm plenty sour."

"But I get the sweet."

"Whatever."

"Goodnight, *mi riena*."

"Night, my king."

Chapter 11

Sarah

I wish I could say I was a good girl and listened to Beach about no sex, but as soon as I'd had enough sleep to refresh myself and get rid of the drugs in my system—thank you, Birdie—I set about seducing him.

How in the world he thought I could possibly resist the lure of finally getting him inside of me is beyond me. I mean, up to this point we'd done some heavy petting, but nothing serious. I wanted serious. I needed serious. And I wasn't about to let his good intentions cock block me.

Moving slowly in his arms, I began to play with the thick hair on his chest. Yes, he was a bit furrier than I usually fancied a man, but his blond chest hair was just so damn soft. And I knew it would feel amazing rubbing against my sensitive nipples.

Yeah, I needed to convince this man that we could do gentle, and that it would be amazing.

The smooth sheets slid against my bare legs, soft and warmed by our body heat. Beach lay on his back and I'd been sprawled across him, my face buried in his neck. He smelled so good there, and I loved it so much I fell asleep with my face snuggled against his skin. It was that delicious smell, a mix of cologne and sleeping man, that woke me up.

In the soft predawn light seeping in from the edges of the curtains, he looked like a grown man. Someone who held authority. The kind of guy others would defer to on instinct. Yes, he was way older than me, but damn he wore it well. My body pulsed to life as I examined his large frame. Wearing only his boxer briefs, he cut a figure any underwear model would kill for, and the bulge of his resting cock was big enough to make me shiver.

I didn't want him to wake up yet, so I kept my movements slow as I eased my way down, almost beneath the covers piled around his hips. It was warm beneath the sheets, darker and more intimate. And it smelled like us, a lovely fragrance filled with warmth and lust. Something in his pheromones hit me and I ached with the need for him to fuck me. Like my body knew his dick was the perfect dick that would fit me just right.

Evidently, my vagina had a Cinderella complex.

He grunted a little when I ran my hand over the warm cloth covering his dick. When he began to harden, I eased his underwear down enough to watch. Using the tip of my finger, I stroked him erect, loving the way his cock grew and filled. I licked the tip of my finger, then rubbed the sensitive spot right beneath the head of his erection above the metal ball of the piercing. To my delight, a thick drop of pre-cum wet the tip as his shaft jerked against my touch.

The covers lifted and Beach's rough voice strummed against my clit like a vibrator. "You made a mess down there. Clean it up."

Pushing him to get what I wanted, I gave him an innocent look. "What do you mean?"

His voice was nothing but a raspy growl. "Considerin' you made my dick wet with one finger, I can't wait to see what the fuck you can do with that bratty mouth of yours. Have at it, little girl, show me what you can do with it. Make your *Papi* proud."

I was so turned on by this point that my panties were saturated between my thighs and I wanted him desperately inside of me. If he was giving me permission to blow his mind, consider it done. One of my hobbies is sex. I love it, love doing it, love watching it, love hearing it. But most of all I love studying the different forms of pleasure around the world. Like this thing that I was about to do to Beach, a little trick I'd learned from reading the diary of a seventeenth-century courtesan.

I shifted around, moving so I lay between his legs, the covers kicked off to show my ass. Across the room from us was a dresser, and the view of the bed from that dresser was a good one. Which meant Beach was going to be able to see all sides of me. That sent another deep clench through my pussy and my hips twitched as I lifted them. Then I did something which caused Beach to make a choking sound then moan out my name.

First, I removed my pajama pants and soaking-wet panties. Next I leaned down over his cock and parted my thighs, tilting my pussy up so he could see me. All of me. Then I slid him all the way down my throat and relaxed to let him sink deep. The pierced head of his cock rubbed against me in an odd way and I struggled more than usual to take him all the way.

"Jesus." His legs parted farther to give me better access. "Shit. That's it, *Papi* wants his baby girl to take him like that. Suck it good for him."

Sick and wrong, but the way he said that went straight to my clit in a sharp buzz. My nipples pressed against my shirt and I slowly drew my head up, marveling at how much of him there was. I've been with some hung guys, but this man's dick was porno huge. When I had him all the way out, I grasped him with one hand, unable to make my fingers touch now that he was fully erect. The tip was shiny with my spit and I leaned forward to work the little slit at the top with my tongue.

I sat up, my thighs spread as wide as his allowed, my hips tilted to show my body to him. His groan of pleasure only added to my own arousal as he stared at me. His whole body was luscious and I wanted to lick his dusky nipples. "See how wet you make me? I need you to fuck me. Please."

His response was to pull me gently by my hair back to his dick, pressing himself between my lips and taking what he wanted.

The rough grunts he gave fueled my desire to please him and I gloried in making him feel so good.

Taking his time, he slid slowly in and out of my mouth, his breathing labored. He had what I thought of as a mushroom head on his cock, meaning it was wide, large, and perfectly shaped, with his barbell piercing through the tip. My sex literally quivered at the thought of gripping around him. The taste of his pre-cum coated my tongue, along with the indescribable flavor of man.

Yum.

I was so busy lavishing attention on his beautiful erection that I barely felt him sit up. But when his fingers slid over my pussy, I gasped loud.

"Oh, honey," he said in a slightly amused, highly aroused voice. "You're so swollen. And wet. You need something?"

"I need your cock inside of me, please. I need you to fuck me, *Papi*."

A spurt of pre-cum wet my tongue and he groaned as I sucked hard. "If I fuck you now, that means you spend a good deal of the day in bed. That means no talkin' 'bout you leavin', no talkin' 'bout how wrong this is or any of that bullshit you like to spin yourself up with."

I tried to pull up off his dick to argue, but he kept the fat head in my mouth, effectively muzzling me. "We're gonna lay in bed, get to know each other. I'm greedy for you, *mi riena*, I don't want to share you with anyone yet. People are gonna want my attention, so we'll probably only have one day where we're left alone together, but I want this time with you."

My breath came out in a gasp as he pulled me off his ridged erection. As soon as he was out of my mouth I whispered a husky, "Okay."

"Okay?"

I nodded and smiled when he crooked his finger at me.

"Come here." He cupped my cheek and studied my face in the brightening light. "Once you get in past those high walls of yours, sweetest thing I've ever seen."

"What?"

His rough thumb smoothed my lips, the crinkles around his eyes deepening before he replaced his thumb with his mouth against mine. So, so gentle as he kissed me, light strokes I felt down to the bottom of my soul. My body wanted to be closer to his so I crawled up a little bit, my ribs aching but the painkillers still working enough to make it manageable. My nipples tightened as his fingers brushed over them, my gasp swallowed into his mouth where he turned it into a groan.

"My cock is gonna fall off if I don't get inside of you. Get up here and ride your *Papi*, but do it nice and slow. Understood?"

"Yes."

"Yes what?"

I licked my lower lip then whispered, "Yes, *Papi*."

His growl of satisfaction rumbled against my body as I mounted him, his body stretching my legs open wide. Shit, he was so big beneath me and I took a moment to admire his scarred, strong body. He didn't have a six-pack, but he was solid in a way that had me stroking his body with reverent hands. His furred chest was so massive, solid, and I knew his heart was just as big. It thrummed against my palms and I closed my eyes for a moment, feeling his life beat beneath my fingers. Tears burned my eyes at the thought of all that we'd been through together to make it to this moment and I dashed one away as it escaped.

"Sarah," Beach whispered while he stroked my hips. "Don't cry."

"I'm so glad you're alive."

"Me too, *mija*." His fingertips ghosted over my ribs where they were injured.

He sat up a little bit, his cock pressing against my aching pussy and driving me mad. "Want this?"

My clit swelled further as the sensitive tip rubbed against his shaft. "Please."

"Put me in."

Right away I slid up his cock until I reached the tip, then titled my hips to try to get him lined up. I realized that wasn't going to work, he was too hung. I swear my pussy was dripping wet with need by now, and when I reached between us the crest of his cock was well lubed. It made it easy to press him against my entrance, but I only had the head partially in when his hands caught my hips.

"Eyes on me."

I met his gaze and had to close my eyes, overwhelmed by the tenderness in his expression.

"Baby, eyes open." I complied and he snarled, "Fuck, your pussy is so wet.

I sucked in a hard breath through my nose as he stretched me wide, my entrance burning. Christ, I've been with endowed men before, but no one like this. He could hurt me if he wasn't careful. A thrill went through me at the thought, demented creature that I am, and I let gravity take me a little farther down his cock. He was only halfway in when the ball of his piercing rubbed against my well exposed G-spot, hard.

"Oh fuck!" My entire body trembled as my legs shook. "Fuck!"

"Yeah," Beach growled out. "Take it. Come on my cock."

To reinforce this order, his fingers rubbed my clit hard and fast, sending me rocketing into an orgasm that had me covering my mouth to hold back the screams.

While I climaxed, Beach continued to work his way into me, swearing and snarling about feeling my pussy suck on him like a hungry little mouth.

He was so dirty.

My heart was still thundering in my chest when my pelvis finally met his all the way, leaving him seated deep inside of me. It almost hurt and I shifted gingerly on him. I swear I could feel those piercings of his as I slid up and down the slightest bit. That sensation made me moan, low and deep, so I did it again. Beach's body moved restlessly below me and I could feel his need to take over, to control the situation, but he was fighting it for me.

So I could get used to him.

So he wouldn't hurt me.

Because he cared about me.

I let out a fluttering sigh as I rose up as far as I could, but he was still half buried inside of me. Without going to my feet I couldn't get the leverage I needed, but that was a no go because it would hurt like a bitch. With a groan, I sank down, my head rolling back as my butt met his thighs. I felt so lazy, indolent with pleasure as I took the most leisurely, yet intense ride of my life with Beach watching my every move.

His attention on me was its own aphrodisiac and I drank in his silent adoration, showing myself off for him, giving him everything I had. He held my gaze while he reached up and cupped my breasts, running his thumbs over the tips. I wanted to look away, but he was so damn good-looking it seemed like a crime to not appreciate him. He had tattoos on both arms all the way down to his fingers, but his chest was bare. On his right forearm there was a big tattoo of the stylized horse of the Iron Horse MC and I loved the contrast of his ink against the creamy skin of my breast. He pinched my nipple and I twitched on top of him, grinding my clit against his pelvis.

"Naughty baby," he growled out as he sifted his hand through my hair then wrapped it around his fist and pulled me down slowly. "Kiss me."

With the hand not gripping my hair, he grabbed my ass and lifted his hips, rubbing me in such an amazing way that I practically fell on him, my mouth hungry for his. While he wouldn't let me kiss him hard, he did allow me to taste him, for our tongues to duel as long as I kept my mouth gentle. It was getting harder to do as he began to take more control despite being beneath me.

To be honest, I loved being pinned to him like this, allowing him to do as he wished with me. It was completely freeing in a way I've rarely experienced, a clean and pure surrender to a man who would take care of me. I knew he'd take a bullet for me, knew I could count on him when it got rough, knew he was strong enough to protect me and I cannot tell you how much it turned me on. I could trust him, at least with my safety, and it was heady stuff. That trust allowed me to whisper, "Bite me, where my neck meets my shoulder."

He didn't hesitate, instead jerking my head to the side so the line of my neck was exposed, then sinking his teeth into that sensitive bundle of nerves and muscle. Right away my whole body clenched down and I began to writhe on him, fucking him with everything I had while only being allowed to move a couple inches in either direction. His hand on my ass held me tight and I didn't fight him, the feeling of clutching his cock with my internal muscles so damn satisfying.

My clit was so sensitive by this point that the rub of his body against mine had me seeing stars.

Beach licked at the bite mark on my body, the pain so damn brilliant. "Bite me when you come, Sarah."

I whimpered then began to kiss his neck, licking the skin and circling my hips while he thrust up. The taste of his salty skin was addictive and as I lightly set my teeth against him, he began to tense beneath me. I could feel his cock getting bigger and knew he was about to climax, his thrusts bouncing me as he fucked me hard.

It was enough to send me over the edge and I pressed up on my arms, wanting to watch him come.

"Carlos," I gasped as my body tightened even further.

His deep blue gaze met mine, pupils huge with lust, and he stared at me as our orgasms consumed us, each struggling not to lose our connection in our bliss.

The last of my contractions swam through me and I collapsed on his chest, my cheek pillowed by his fur and my body still attached to his.

As I felt something leak out, I sat up with a gasp.

"Shit!"

"What?" Beach asked as he sat up as well, his hands going around my hips.

"No condom!"

He blinked up at me, then blew out a long breath. "Shit. You on the pill, right?"

"Not the pill, the shot, but that doesn't prevent STDs!"

"Babe, I always wrap my shit up, but we'll get tested. You clean?"

"Yes, I'm usually very careful. Like super careful." My stomach clenched and I rolled off of him, hissing as my body protested the quick movement. "Shit!"

"Easy." He rose off the bed and came over to my side as I slowly stood. "What are you doin?"

"I need to get cleaned up."

He nodded and let me go. When I stepped into the bathroom, I found him moving in behind me as I went to close the door. "I said I need to get cleaned up."

"Me too. Babe, you get so wet when you come you flooded me."

"Shut up!" I shrieked as my face turned no doubt flaming tomato red.

"Why? It's fuckin hot."

As if to prove this fact, his cock twitched, then began to thicken again.

Jesus he was endowed.

"I need to get clean," I announced, deciding I was done with this discussion.

Once the water was to my liking, I stepped into the glass-enclosed space, not at all surprised when Beach followed me in. I also wasn't surprised when bath time turned into sexy time, but I was surprised Beach was able to give me three really fucking good orgasms before we returned to bed.

Chapter 12

A knock came at the bedroom door, waking me from a deep and restful sleep. Warm, I was so incredibly warm and comfortable, hating whoever had torn me from dreamland. And I felt better. Way better. Yeah, I was sore, but nowhere near as bad as yesterday. I was even breathing easy. Damn, now I had proof Beach's big dick had magical healing properties.

Maybe I should build a shrine to it.

The knocking interrupted my meandering and pervy thoughts.

Beach's arms tightened around me and he muttered into my neck, "Go away."

The knocking came again, more insistent this time, followed by a very familiar voice. "Sarah Jane Anderson, open this door right now."

I let out a little shriek of irrational fear at the sound of my stepmother Mimi's voice, and Beach was instantly awake, reaching for the gun he kept next to the bed.

"No," I yelled to both the man and the people at the door, "wait!"

But neither of them waited, and Mimi stepped into the room then got an eyeful of a naked, semi-aroused Beach holding a gun on her. She stood, frozen, her dark eyes wide as she took Beach in, her pretty cheeks flushed.

Even though my stepmom is pushing sixty, she is still hot and dressed to impress in hella-cute skirts and tops. Today was no exception, a pretty black silk blouse coupled with a green, blue, and black color-blocked skirt and heels.

Shit, I should have known she'd hunt me down after my less-than-frequent phone calls.

Behind her, a small woman I've never seen before pushed past a stunned Mimi and glared at Beach, who was now lowering his gun. She had short hair, a light brown with hints of grey, along with lovely eyes lined by the kind of wrinkles you get from smiling in the sun a lot. Petite and dressed in jeans and a mint-green t-shirt, she still packed a punch with her presence. "Boy, what the hell is wrong with you, pullin' a gun on Sarah's mama? Have you lost your damn mind? And put some clothes on! She's going to think I raised a nudist."

I was tempted to hide under the covers but remained frozen, not wanting to draw anyone's attention to me.

"Baby," Beach muttered. "Toss me my pants."

That snapped Mimi out of ogling everything that was delicious about Beach, and there was a lot to ogle. Not only was he full of golden-god hotness with a nicely built body, his junk was pierced so there was an extra something "oh my" to look at. Now, Mimi is very happily married to my father, but she appreciated a handsome man so I could understand why she was distracted. However, when I moved on the bed, it drew her gaze like a lioness spotting a stupid, wounded gazelle who'd just had sex with a much older leopard.

Mimi's dark gaze met mine and I had to quell the urge to hide beneath the blankets. "Yes, Sarah, could you please give the gentleman who just exited your bed his pants."

Before I could move, I had to ask the most important question. "Is Dad here?"

"Would Beach still be alive?"

"Good point."

I darted for his pants at the end of the bed and tossed them to him, along with his underwear. Before I sat back down, Mimi was at my side, her cheekbones standing out as her face tensed. Oh boy, Mimi was pissed, and that didn't happen very often. I guess after a lifetime of being an assassin, your standards of what's considered a big deal changes. That was one of the reasons I got along so well with Mimi, she usually handled my bullshit without freaking out like my dad.

I frowned up at her, not sure why she was suddenly so mad, but then I realized when I'd moved she'd seen my bruised ribs. Her body trembled slightly and I watched as she began to stroke her thigh, where she no doubt had one of her knives stashed. Yes, one of. Mimi was a master at looking feminine while carrying enough weapons to outfit a small hit squad. The fact she was seeking comfort by touching her beloved knife was not a good sign and I tried to figure out ways of blowing off the impending eruption.

Thinking I'd finally pushed her too far, I whispered, "Mimi?"

Something about my voice had her looking up at me, her gaze haunted and filled with pain. "You're hurt."

Oh crap on toast.

She lost her fucking mind when Swan or I got hurt.

"Not—"

Her voice shook with suppressed emotion as she whispered, "Someone injured you."

"Mimi…"

Shit, if I didn't get her calmed down fast she was going to go on a path of vengeance, and that was bad. It would mean people would die, and I'd get pulled into some mafia bullshit that I'd never manage to escape again. Hell, Mimi's dad, my mafia boss grandfather Roman Stefano, would finally marry me off to one of his men like he'd been threatening too since I turned eighteen. Not going to lie, he has some really hot men, but even though I've had sex with a few of them, none of them were anything but fun while it lasted. Not that grandpa needed to know that; he'd quite literally geld them.

"Meems," I pulled out the big guns and used the nickname I used to call her when I was younger, one that always made her eyes sparkle, "I'm okay. It's just bruised ribs, and some bumps, and some other stuff. But no major injuries."

She studied my face up close. "Are the men who did this to you dead?"

"Yes."

The fire in her eyes dimmed slightly. "Good, and I don't want you to spend one damn moment dwelling on those deaths. You did Lady Karma a favor disposing of them."

"I know."

She gently hugged me, then reached out and brushed my hair back from my face. "Of course you do. Now, care to explain who the man with an earring through his penis staring at us is? And why he was in your bed?"

I mentally groaned as I turned to find Beach watching Mimi closely. I was certain Mimi knew who he was, no way my dad hadn't dug up everything he could on Beach, and what she was really asking was who the hell was he to me? I didn't have a clue, but I knew Mimi well enough to know that if I didn't answer to her satisfaction, she was going to make trouble.

Drinking in the sight of him with his jeans on and nothing else, his magnificent muscles tensed, how protective he was of me, made me want to sigh like a besotted idiot. He was so good-looking even the presence of my family couldn't keep my body from heating. As if he could sense my gaze on him, he gave me a quick, reassuring look that warmed me from the roots of my hair to the tips of my red painted toenails.

Because of my arousal, my voice came out slightly husky as I said, "This is Carlos, but he goes by the name of Beach. He saved my life, took wonderful care of me, and has treated me like a queen since the moment we met. I promise you, he's a good guy."

"Of course he is." The short woman who'd come in with my stepmother smiled at me, with Birdie, today wearing gold lamé with jeans, watching from the doorway. "I raised him right."

"Sarah," Beach said with a hint of laughter in his voice, "I'd like you to meet my mother, Mouse."

I waved at her, clutching the sheet to me as I forced a smile. "Uh—nice to meet you. Forgive me if I don't leave the bed at the moment to shake your hand."

Mouse's smile grew bigger and I could see shades of Beach in her features. "Don't you worry about it. We thought you two would be up by now."

Beach slid back into bed with me, sitting on top of the covers before pulling me to his side so I lay curled into him. Normally I love cuddling, but it was totally awkward with three moms in the room. They all watched us with that intense mom stare that makes you feel like they know ever single bad thing you've ever done and are waiting for you to confess your sins.

Letting out a soft chuckle, Beach kissed the top of my head then said, "Ladies, think you could give us a few minutes to get presentable? Sarah is getting uncomfortable with the audience."

They looked at each other, then looked at him, then back at each other, then nodded in unison.

Jesus, they shared some kind of creepy mother ESP.

Birdie smiled merrily at us. "Come join us downstairs when you're ready. I have a nice late lunch laid out with cupcakes. It's all sandwiches and sides, so don't worry about rushing down. You take your time getting ready, Sarah. No need to hurt yourself rushing around."

"I'll take care of her." Beach lifted his mouth from where it rested in my hair. "Those cupcakes got fudge frosting?"

"Of course, with cookie filling. Oh, and we have homemade cinnamon applesauce."

My stomach growled as my mouth began to water, loud enough that everyone heard.

Laughing, the women left the room and my ears rang in the silence for a moment.

"Well, Mimi likes you," I said in a voice that sounded faint even to my ears.

His chuckle vibrated against me and I began to pet his chest, unable to be around him when he was shirtless without wanting my hands on him. "Ya think?"

"Are you alive?"

Another chuckle that made my nipples hard while I stroked him slower. "Last I checked."

"If she didn't like you, you'd be gone before you even laid eyes on her."

"I'd say you're exaggerating, but I know that woman. You don't fuck around with Lady Death, and you definitely don't screw with her daughter."

"She's…very protective of me. Something happened in her past that she told me in confidence, which made her this way, so trust me when I say you need to cut her some slack."

"Something bad."

"Yeah. Real bad."

"Bet your dad's protective of you too."

"He's insane," I said instantly, leaning up so I could look him in the face and try to impress upon him the seriousness of the statement. "For reals."

Instead of arguing he merely nodded. "Heard that about him."

My stomach soured a bit as I waited for the judgement I usually got over the fact my father was an illegal arms dealer to enter Beach's face, but he continued to study me closely. "What else did you hear about me?"

"Not gonna bullshit, had a background check done on you. Your neighbors think you're the shit, your roommate thinks you're a guardian angel come to life, and the people you work with sing your praises for being such a nice person. There isn't a day that goes by where you haven't helped someone. Your parents may not be the best examples of humanity, but you make the world a better place and that's a rare fuckin' gift."

I really didn't want to ask, unsure what they had learned, but I needed to know. "What about my birth mother?"

"Married and divorced five times. She's currently livin' out in Carmel, California, right now with number six, a banker. Bet all that movin' around and shit was tough on you." He looked troubled as he smoothed my hair back from my face. "You still talk to your mom?"

I was at once disappointed and relieved. Disappointed because I hated lying to him about my family, but relieved I didn't have to explain Billie to him yet. She was so toxic even the thought of her made me feel slightly ill. I wasn't ready to discuss my past, not yet. Deep in my heart I knew nothing good would come of lying to him, but I decided to keep quiet for now. I wanted to give whatever was going on between us a chance to grow stronger before I let him know just how screwed up I really was.

Right or wrong, I loved the person I was in Beach's eyes and was too scared of losing him.

"No, I haven't seen her in a couple years."

"You have a fallin' out?"

"Something like that."

I'd inherited jewelry from my maternal grandmother and my mom had broken into my house and stolen it, then sold it for drugs. The memory of watching the tape from the pawn store with my once-stunning mother on it hawking my grandmother's Tahitian pearls hurt. After that I'd cut ties with her forever, and so far I'd managed to avoid her. Marley despised her and made sure the security at the gated community I lived in knew I had a restraining order against my mom. Not that she made any effort to see me after she realized I'd never give her any money and was totally over her shit.

"Her loss. And I do mean that. Already know having you in my life is like the sun shining down on me, warming me up, even in the dead of night. Bet she misses your light."

Tears burned my nose and I looked away, unable to stand his earnest words and how dead wrong they were. "Beach, you really don't want me in your life. I'm a bad person."

He closed his eyes, then opened them again and he stared right at me when he said, "I'm sure you believe that bullshit, but no, you aren't. Don't know who put that negative poison in your head, but you're amazing.

Fucked up you can't see that, but I'll help you get there. It'll be my privilege to help you see how beautiful you are, inside and out."

"Don't put me on a pedestal," I hissed. "I...I was a real bitch when I was a teenager. Did stupid shit with stupid people. Drugs, drinking, sex—you name it, I did it. I...I hurt people. Innocent people that had never done a thing wrong to me."

"What *mi riena*? Talk to me. Promise you I won't judge."

I decided to tell him one of my secrets, not the worst, but still a big one that could potentially run Beach off. "I had an affair with a married man."

At that he tensed, but his gaze remained remarkably calm. "You know he was married?"

"No!" He winced at my shout and I leaned forward and gave him a kiss on the cheek as an apology before leaning back. "Sorry. No, I had no idea he was married. He kept his family out in Connecticut. Nobody talked about them around me or anything."

"How old were you?"

I squirmed uncomfortably, not used to talking about that period in my life with anyone. "Does it matter?"

"Yeah, baby, it matters."

"Young, okay? I really don't want to talk about this right now."

He studied me, then nodded. "We got time. You come to me when you're ready and I promise you, no judgement."

My eyes swam with tears and I blinked them back, knowing Mimi would go back into freak-out mode if she noticed I'd been crying.

"Sure."

He searched my face while his big hand smoothed up and down my hip, relaxing me and allowing some of the tension in me to release. "That shit's in the past. Who you are now, what you do with your life, who you chose to be, that's important. 'Sides, we all got skeletons in our closet."

Actually, it was more like I had a zombie in my closet. A living, breathing, drug-addicted waste that used to be my mother. Pure shame burned through me at the thought of Beach knowing some of the shit I'd done with her, and even though I know I should tell him about her, I just couldn't.

Still, I had to try to warn him again I was flawed, imperfect, and for him to not idolize me. That was what Morrie had done, worshipped me like a goddess until he found out I was underage. Then I'd come crashing back to earth from the heavens, my heart irreparably damaged by the fall.

With this in mind I forced myself to say, "I know you don't understand, but believe me when I say you're better off without me in your life. Trouble follows me."

He laughed and curled his arms behind his head, leisurely examining my body as I inched towards the bathroom. "Hate to break it to you, but I'm not exactly a saint and my lifestyle ain't exactly trouble free."

"Yeah, but you're a guy. Different standards."

"So let me get this straight, you were a bitch when you were younger."

"Yep."

"And now you're not."

"I try really hard not to be. I don't like the person I was, Beach. It took some hard lessons to wake me up to the shit I was living in. Mimi taught me about karma, and the rule of three."

"Know what karma is, but never heard of the rule of three."

"Whatever you do to someone else, comes back at you three times harder, good or bad. I learned that the hard way when I was younger and decided I was going to give people all the good I could in hopes of balancing off the bad already sitting on my soul."

His deep blue eyes softened, as did the lines around his mouth. "I already know your soul is good, 'cause I can see it shining in your eyes."

I rolled said eyes, but still secretly felt pleased at his words. "Whatever."

"No, you can 'whatever' a lot of stuff, but you need to know it's true. You're a good woman, best I've ever met, and I don't care about any of the bullshit you're getting ready to spew about us being strangers. I know you, in here." He pressed his hand over his heart.

This was all getting too intense for me. I needed an escape so I crossed the room quickly while saying, "I'm going to take a shower."

"You got five minutes to do what you gotta do before I join you in there."

I paused in the doorway, turning back to find him looking like sin incarnate, stretched out over the bed and giving me that killer smile of his.

Refusing to be distracted by the need to rub myself against him like a cat in heat, I added some frost to my tone as I said, "No, I'm taking a shower, by myself."

He gripped himself tight and my knees went weak at the sight of his hella-big erection pressing against his jeans. "Thought of you all soapy and slick, washin' that beautiful body of yours, no fuckin' way I'm missin' this. Go wash up for your *Papi* so he can lick you clean. Haven't had the chance to properly worship that pretty pussy yet."

Dammit, my clit twitched when he said that and I glared at him, pretty sure he was conditioning me to get horny whenever I heard the word "*Papi*". Or was it the thought of him "worshiping" my pussy that had my need for him tightening my belly. I had a feeling he was really, really good at pleasuring a woman with that dirty mouth of his.

"Five minutes," he warned, and I shut the door on his laughing face then proceeded to brush my teeth, use the bathroom, and wash as fast as humanly possible before he came in.

I was working the conditioner through my hair when the shower door opened and a naked, aroused Beach crowded me into the corner. His gaze was positively feral and his upper lip curled as he muttered, "God damn you're the sexiest thing I've ever seen."

In the brief time we'd been apart, I'd already begun to question what the hell I was doing with Beach, but as soon as he touched me, I was melting into him despite my best intentions to remain aloof.

He held me and a tiny bit of guilt moved through me as he cuddled me close, knowing his ass was probably cold from letting me hog the hot water. Slowly he rubbed his rough hands over my sensitive skin, arousing me to the point I found myself reaching out to the tiles in front of me to brace myself while he manipulated my clit. With each rub I ground my ass against his erection, all thoughts of anything but Beach impossible. He drowned out the world with his presence and easily enslaved me with his highly skilled touch. Little electrical pulses zipped from my swollen nipples to my clit while he pinched them.

"Fuck," he hissed then dipped down to rub his dick against my entrance. "You sore?"

"Um…a little."

"Too sore to take me?"

I should have said yes, but my pussy somehow hijacked my body and instead I said, "No."

He began to press into me and it burned, but I endured it. His hands flexed on my hips and he stilled, a hard tremor running through him before he pulled out.

To my surprise, he smacked my ass, hard, like not-fucking-around hard.

"What the hell!"

I gave a half-hearted effort to wiggle out of his grip, but he held me tight. "Do not lie to me about shit like this, Sarah. You and me are only gonna work if we got honesty between us. That means no lying about shit like me hurting you."

The distress in his voice had me turning in his arms and blinking up at him before lacing my arms around his neck, my thumbs stroking his skin. "I'm sorry."

"Don't be sorry, be honest. Why didn't you tell me it hurt?"

"Well, it stung, but it wasn't bad. I've had some bad injuries—try fucking up your knee and tell me how that feels—so a little burn isn't even worth mentioning. I'm sure it would have felt good eventually. You're really well-endowed and my body will have to get used to something that size being inside of me. I'm just kinda on the tight side naturally, you know? If we're not careful your dick could get stuck inside of me like a finger in one of those Chinese Finger Torture toys. You know, the cheap tube things you get trading in tickets from play ski ball?"

He closed his eyes and I got the distinct impression he was praying for strength.

I tipped my head back and started to rinse the conditioner out of my hair. "Wash up, I don't want to keep our moms waiting. I already feel like a skank around your mom for walking in on us naked in bed."

"First, my mama doesn't think you're a skank." I started to protest, but he gently put his finger against my lips. "Second, I don't care how good you are at ignoring pain, *mi corazón*, you will not do that with me. Understood?"

I snorted and pulled my head away, then grabbed the soap and began to molest, I mean wash, his chest. "You can't make me."

He grumbled and arched into my touch like a big, happy lion. "I don't want to make you do anything. I want you to be happy. Ignoring pain is taxing, I know this, and I don't like to look at you and know you're in discomfort. If I inadvertently hurt you during sex and you hid it, I would be disgusted with myself for having gone too far. I like kinky shit, pretty sure you do too, but I can't play rough with you unless I know you won't let me inadvertently hurt you."

"You spanked me, that hurt," I said in a decidedly pouty voice that irritated me.

"That's an on-purpose hurt," he said with a totally serious expression. "Correction instead'a pleasure."

"Whoa, whoa, whoa—correction? As in you were correcting my behavior with a spanking?"

"Yep."

I considered clawing his back while I washed it, but felt it would be a sin to harm such incredible ink over beautiful muscle. "You are out of your damn mind."

"You put yourself in danger, you do somethin really fuckin' stupid, I will spank you to remind you that you do *not* do shit like that."

"Oh hell no!" My shout echoed loud in the shower. "You are not going to treat me like that."

He blinked at me, genuinely surprised at how upset I'd gotten. "Like what?"

I drew in a tight breath, my anger threatening my self-control. I would not give in to it, I would not be my parents and lash out anytime I got upset. I was better than that, please, God, help me be better than that.

Taking in a deep breath, I slowly let it out and pushed some of my anger out with it. "I will never be your perfect puppet to play with as you wish. That will never, ever happen, and if that's what you need in a relationship, *adios*."

"I never said I wanted anything like that."

"What do you call spanking me if I break *Papi's* rules?"

"I call that trying to keep someone I care deeply about alive."

"What?"

To my surprise, he began to run his fingers gently through my hair. "If I did something stupid, something you asked me not to do, something that endangered my life, wouldn't you want to spank me for doing it?"

I couldn't help it, I started giggling at the utterly weird idea of spanking Beach. "No!"

The lines around his mouth deepened as his lips lifted at the corners. "You wouldn't wanna tan my ass?"

"I want to do a lot of things to your ass, it's superb, but spanking is not one of those things."

"That's what I figured, just wanted to double-check."

I stared up at him while he gave my neck a gentle massage that had my knees weakening. "We have the strangest conversations."

"You're not lyin'."

"Beach, for reals, I need to be independent."

"And you can't do that with a man?"

"I...suppose you can, but I don't know if I can."

"When's the last time you had a steady man in your life?"

"Umm—over a year. Everything got really busy and I didn't have time to breathe, let alone have a boyfriend. It all happened so quick, winning the title, then *Playboy*, then the tour. I barely had time to see my family, let alone a boyfriend."

"Sounds like you were handling a lot of shit while standing on your own two feet, *mi nina linda.* Proud of you for that, but I don't think losing your independence is your problem with relationships. Think it's fear."

"What?" I tried to scoff, but my voice came out winded. "Fear of what?"

He studied me for a moment, then shook his head. "We don't got time to deal with this right now, but we'll talk about it."

As he stepped out of the shower I was tempted to chuck a shampoo bottle at him. "Oh, I see, when I say we need to hurry it's ignored, but the instant you think we need to get out of the shower it's go time."

He laughed, the bastard, while toweling himself off, and looking sexy as hell doing it. "I swear, you could argue the color of the sky if you got a mind to. Get a move on. Don't want Mimi comin after me."

"You're lucky you're alive right now," I huffed.

"Don't I know it."

He tossed me a towel as well and we dried off quickly before returning to our room. While Beach dug through the duffel bag he'd brought with him for clothes, his muscled back all too distracting along with his damp golden hair. Turning away from temptation, I went to the dresser to see what was in there. Last night, Birdie had mentioned one of her daughters-in-law was a little bit bigger than me, and that I could borrow whatever I wanted until we could go shopping.

I found a pair of dark grey yoga pants that were more like capris on me, along with a sports bra that barely fit my chest, but kept the girls in place. It's one thing going braless in front of a bunch of bikers, quite another to do it in front of Beach's mom. I'd been so shell-shocked about Mimi's appearance that I hadn't even processed the first impression I must have made on Mouse.

"Shit," I hissed. "Your mom is going to think I'm a psycho and a slut!"

Not looking up from his phone, Beach muttered, "Babe, told ya, she's gonna love you 'cause you saved my life. Stop worrying and stop callin' yourself names, I don't like it."

"Stop worrying? Are you insane?" I ran my fingers through my wet hair while towel drying it as best I could.

"I got this covered."

"Absolutely bonkers."

With a sigh, he put his phone into the pocket of his dark, well-fitting jeans then put on his shoes and socks while I toed on a pair of slightly small, bright yellow flip-flops that matched the happy face on my t-shirt with the words "Myrtle Beach Spring Break 2012" on it.

Great, I looked like a hungover white trash tourist while he was all biker hotness.

He held out his hand to me. "Ready?"

"No, but I don't have a choice."

Pausing, he turned serious for a moment and cupped my chin, making me meet his deep blue eyes. "If you don't wanna see them, we'll leave, right now, no questions asked."

I leaned up on my tiptoes and gave him a soft, sweet kiss. "Thank you, but I need to face Mimi or she'll chase me down again."

He kissed me back, then rubbed his nose slowly against mine in an affectionate gesture that melted my heart.

Who knew I'd love Eskimo kisses so much?

"No matter what happens out there, I want you to know that you're mine and I'm not giving you up."

"Beach—"

"Mine."

Exasperated, I threw my hands up in the air, "Just because you say it's yours doesn't make it yours. Didn't you learn that in kindergarten?"

He laughed, a sexy-as-hell arrogant laugh that made me yearn to feel him deep inside of me again even as I wanted to strangle him. "You keep tellin' yourself that."

"I've reconsidered my stance on spanking you," I announced in a haughty voice.

At that, Beach burst out laughing, his head thrown back and his arms clutching his stomach. It was a beautiful sight and I swore I felt him dig even deeper into my heart despite my best efforts. A giggle escaped me before I stopped it as I began to laugh with him, our eyes meeting, which sent us off into another peal of laughter.

We only stopped when he crossed the room in two big strides and kissed me but good, our tongues stroking together while we both made happy noises that were something between a laugh and a moan.

I think I'm falling in love with him.

I waited for the panic, but it wasn't there.

Weird.

Slipping his hand into mine, he lifted our joined fingers and kissed my scarred knuckles. "You got nothin to worry 'bout. I'm gonna make this right."

Sighing, I kissed his bristly cheek. "You need to shave before you go down on me."

He stared at me. "You tryin' to make my dick hard?"

"What?"

It was obvious he didn't believe my wide-eyed innocent act. "Brat."

"Whatever."

Chapter 13

Carlos "Beach" Rodriguez

A fine tremor ran through Sarah's hand into mine and I paused as we left our room, making her face me. "Baby, swear, it will be okay."

"Right." Her brittle smile was so obviously forced I could only sigh.

"You don't believe me now, but you will."

"Right."

Giving up on soothing her, I led us downstairs and into the kitchen, her breaths coming hard and fast. Even when she was trying to cut herself free in the back of that fuckin' van we'd been in she hadn't been this scared. It set off warning bells in my mind and my protective instincts roared to life, wanting to tell everyone to piss off and leave us alone. Unfortunately, saying that to my mom would result in years—no, *decades* of guilt being thrown my way on a regular basis.

No fuckin' thank you. Woman already has it out for me 'cause I haven't given her any grandbabies yet. Then again, I've never been with a woman she thought was good enough for me.

Birdie spots us first and a wide smile fills her weathered face. "Morning, lovebirds."

Sarah winces while Birdie laughs and my mama shakes her head. "Honestly, Sarah, like I was telling Mimi, I did raise him better than this."

Before they can embarrass Sarah further—she's looking like she wished she could run out the door—I cut them off. "Mimi, can I have a word with you, please?"

She tilts her head to the side, the faintest hint of grey at the temples in her still dark, long hair. "Sure."

Sarah just about jerked my arm out of its socket when she pulled me down to harshly whisper into my ear, "What the hell do you think you're doing?"

Fighting the urge to laugh at the look of utter panic on her face, I cup her soft cheeks gently, then rub my nose against hers. "We're not going outside to dual, promise. I need to clear the air between us so we both know where we stand. It's a good thing, not bad."

"You swear?"

Normally I'd think a girl was batshit crazy if I had to promise not to try to kill her stepmom first time we talked, but I understood her fears. "I swear."

She leaned up on her tiptoes, then rubbed her nose slowly against mine.

Never thought rubbing my nose against someone else's could be sexy, but everything Sarah did seemed to make my dick sit up and take notice.

In an effort to keep my cock under control, I stepped back and went over to the door, holding it open for Mimi. "If you don't mind?"

She stood with a truly deadly grace then gave Sarah a quick hug as she passed, kissing her cheek before whispering into her ear, then giving her shoulder a squeeze.

The moment we were out back and down the porch steps into the massive yard, the smile fell from Mimi's face. "You're lucky I don't gut you."

Glad we weren't going to tap dance around each other, I grinned. "'Appreciate that."

"It doesn't mean I like you."

We began to stroll in the direction of one of the fenced-in fields butting against the far side of the lawn, the horses inside enjoying a leisurely afternoon grazing.

"Need to let you know right now I really couldn't give a shit less. My main concern is Sarah, as long as she's happy, I'm happy." She stopped walking and glared at me, but I continued in an even voice, "She loves you deeply, so I'm gonna do my best to be civil with you, but I will never kiss your ass. Long as you're good with that, we'll get along fine."

She closed her eyes and tipped her head back, speaking to the sky as she said, "My husband is going to kill you."

I shrugged. "Maybe he'll try, he wouldn't be the first or the last."

Lowering her face again, she studied me closely. "What do you want from my daughter?"

"Like I said before, I want to make her happy."

"You're almost old enough to be her father."

"She may be younger than me in age, but both you and I know that woman is way older than her years. The hard things in life touch us, change us, and shape who we are. Can you really imagine her with some young dipshit her age? Do you really think he'd have what it's gonna take to be her man?"

"You may have a point, but there are a million men I'd chose for Sarah before you."

"That may be true, but none of 'em would make her as happy as I can."

Mimi pointed her finger at me, anger and concern twisting her regal face. "You have no idea what she's been through."

"She's fragile, I understand that, but she's also amazingly strong. Mimi, she saved my life and she did it as coldly, as professionally, as any seasoned hitman I've ever met. Not gonna lie, wish I'd been in the position to do the rescuing, but it was her courage that saved us while I was pretty much mummified with duct tape. Yeah, my boys brought in the chopper, but that was the easy part. She did all the hard work, so I don't just want her to be happy, I *need* it. I need to give this to her."

"You have no idea what you're taking on, but you'll learn." She blew out a frustrated breath. "She is fiercely independent and I'm afraid you'll try to crush her spirit."

I couldn't help but laugh. "Sarah would carve my ass up if I tried that. 'Sides, why would I want to crush a butterfly?"

It was funny to hear Mimi snort with laughter and realize where Sarah had picked that up. "Women's panties must fall off around you."

I didn't bother to deny it, instead moving the topic back to where I wanted it. "She's safe with me. I'll move heaven and earth to protect her."

"She doesn't need you for that. Her father and I—"

"You know as well as I do that she will not stay at home with you, isolated out in the middle of nowhere. She'd go insane, and there is no fuckin' way I'm letting her go back to Las Vegas. So it's either she stays here with me, where I can have constant protection on her, or you can hope that she doesn't do something that gets her ass dead, which I will never fucking allow."

"She may be physically safe with you, but she needs stability. She needs a man who will let her try to be what she thinks of as normal. I think we both know you can't provide that."

"Bullshit. I've experienced enough to know how to protect what's mine. Also know how to cherish it, and recognize a gift from God when I get it. Your daughter will never know anything but love from me. More important, I have tens of thousands of men who swear their alliance to me across the world. Mutual friends in cold places."

"I know." She crossed her arms and I couldn't help but wonder if she was reaching for a knife. "As far as our friends go, they stay out of whatever happens between us, on both sides. This is a discussion about family and it stays within the family. Understood?"

I watched her close, taking in the tension that was more worry than anger. Her words were abrasive, but she was the daughter of a mafia boss so it was natural she would pick up some of his attitude. Shit, I needed to keep in mind that no matter what else she was, Mimi was first and foremost Sarah's stepmom and I needed to respect her concern. I needed to reassure her, not make an enemy of her.

"I know you researched me. You ever find mention of me making any woman my old lady? Find anything beyond dating? Never. All my years as a biker and never once have I had a woman wear my patch, but I was ready to put it on Sarah's back the moment I saw her."

"There are so many things I want to say, but I can't." To my surprise, Mimi had tears in her eyes that sparkled in the golden sunlight. "I'm afraid you're going to break her heart, but I promised her I would never interfere with her love life. If I do, she'll be dust in the wind, and I can promise you she's more than capable of hiding so well even *you'll* never find her."

I rolled my eyes. "Her fake identity is good, but it's not bulletproof."

"I know that, but what you don't understand is that her identity when she disappeared was so good, we had no clue, not one, where she went. We didn't know anything about Sarah other than the fact that she was alive. And we only knew that because she'd send me untraceable emails. Two a week, all saying the same thing. 'I'm alive, I'm fine, I love you and I'll see you soon.' You must understand, Carlos, if you push my daughter into a corner, she will run and hide somewhere neither you, nor I, will be able to find her."

I did not like the thought of that happening one fucking bit. "Understood."

"I can see that doesn't make you a happy camper, and I'm not particularly thrilled with the notion either. So while I'd like to cut your throat then burn your body and scatter the ashes, instead I'll try to give you a little advice to attempt to save some heartache between you. If Sarah can truly fall in love with you, if you can truly make her as happy as you say you will, then I wish you all the luck in the world. She has suffered in her life, and I don't mean that word lightly, so you have to understand she has a hard time accepting affection, and you'll need a great deal of patience. Do you have that in you to give?"

"I do."

"Even when she's being vile to you?"

"Even then. Just words."

"She can be mean, cutting, and so heartless with her words they slice into you as neatly as any knife."

"I'm sure she can, but she hasn't used the sharp side of her tongue on me yet."

"Sometimes things…trigger her. She isn't even aware of what she's doing. I've seen it once or twice, and it's terrifying. If that happens, hug her, reassure her, remind her she's in the here and now. Keep her mind occupied on something other than trying to relive memories long buried."

My breath came out in a low sigh as I fought the growing pit of nausea in my stomach. "PTSD?"

"Yes."

We'd reached the fence and Mimi smiled at the horses grazing nearby on the deep green grass. They were fat, spoiled animals and lived a good life. Birdie had babied the hell outta them since her kids moved out, and they no doubt expected us to be carrying some kind of treat for them and then fawn all over 'em.

A dappled grey mare by the name of Cha Cha butted her nose against Mimi's hand and she laughed. "Shy, aren't they?"

Another horse joined us, Titan, a big blood-red Morgan who was as affectionate as a puppy. "Birdie has 'em thinkin' they're humans, treats 'em like they're the grandbabies she doesn't have yet."

Mimi stilled and Cha Cha let out an uneasy whinny before Mimi returned to stroking her. "Speaking of grandchildren, I do not want any anytime soon."

I yearned to tell her to fuck off, that it was none of her business, but managed to censor myself. "That's a discussion for me and Sarah to have, but I will tell you this, I want her to have a chance to live her life a little bit before we do talk about kids. We need to work on us before we bring any baby into the mix."

"Good." Mimi looked back at the house, her eyes unfocused as she rested her cheek on the horse's outstretched neck. "Let me be clear—if you hurt her, I will end you."

I chuckled. "I hear ya. Come on, we better head back before Sarah worries herself into a frenzy."

Mimi slipped her arm into mine and smiled as she said, "I don't trust you, I'm not sure if I like you, and I'm pretty sure my husband will hate you, but none of that matters."

"Why's that?"

"Because my daughter looks at you like you hung the stars in the sky for her pleasure. I've never seen Sarah look at anyone like that, man or woman."

Before I could school my expression, my eyebrows flew up. "Woman?"

"Sarah is one of the least judgmental people you'll ever meet. She bases her opinion of someone on how they act, but she likes to give everyone a chance. It's probably why she could look past your age, the way you dress, the criminal vibe, and see the man beneath. She can also overlook gender and has had a few girlfriends she's brought home to meet us. But never any men."

"Mimi, all due respect, I think this is Sarah's business to tell me, not yours."

"Oh my, you do have a backbone. You'll need it if you're going to make my daughter happy."

The door opened before I could respond and Sarah stood there in her t-shirt that hung tight in the chest and loose everywhere else. Her big breasts pushed against the worn fabric and my body felt lighter just looking at her. She was so beautiful it brought me pleasure to stare at her and drink her in. Then she smiled at the sight of us walking arm in arm and I could almost feel the relief pouring off of her.

"Time to eat."

I dropped Mimi's arm and strode up the steps then grabbed Sarah and stole a kiss. "I'm starving."

Cheeks pink, she avoided Mimi's eyes and hurried inside.

We ate quickly and fielded questions from both our mom's, our hands meeting beneath the table as I slid my fingers between hers. I couldn't be near her and not want to touch her. She was too filled with the kind of warmth a man could get addicted to. My mom and Sarah were getting along great and it did my soul good to know they'd be friends. Mimi was still giving me the occasional odd look, but I ignored her.

A text alert came from my phone, the chime letting me know it was one of my Enforcers, Hustler.

Excusing myself from the table, I went back outside, taking a quick look around before calling Hustler.

"Hey Prez."

"What's up?"

"Got someone at the clubhouse who wants to talk to you."

"Whoever it is, they can wait."

"It's Kostya Boldin."

My gut clenched and a sour taste entered my mouth at the mention of Kostya's name. He was here to talk about moving some of the Boldin *Bratva's* merchandise. I wasn't quite sure what it was yet, other than it wasn't drugs or people, and that left either cash or weapons. Anything else they could get through their legitimate business empire.

No, they'd only need us for the really dangerous shit, and it made the hair on my arms stand up. If

Kostya was here, I needed to speak with him face-to-face, no matter how much I wanted to spend the rest of my life in bed with Sarah.

"Got it. I'll be there soon."

"You bringin' Sarah?"

"Why?"

Hustler cleared his throat. "Some of the boys are gonna be partying it up soon. Pup graduated from EMT school yesterday. Might get a little rough around here."

I sighed. Knowing Pup, there would be pussy crawling outta the woodwork tonight. Maybe I should just leave Sarah here, but I got this feeling in my gut that I needed to keep her close right now. Not just 'cause I want her with me for personal, selfish reasons, but because Mimi's words were rattling around in my head. That and the genuine fear she'd shown when she talked about Sarah running off.

"Sarah's comin'. She partied with us up in Sturgis so she understands how wild we get."

"Yeah, but we both know when the boys let loose at the clubhouse, it ain't for the eyes of old ladies."

"Rather be honest with her about it than bullshit her."

Hustler gave a choked laugh. "Okay, it's your funeral, man."

I might give Hustler's words some consideration if he wasn't such a screwup in the relationship department. He picked these fucked-up, broken women to latch on to. Right now he was doing our brother Trick's little sister Veronica, but they weren't monogamous and he was still nailing his regular pussy on the side. Smoke's sister-in-law was a nice enough woman when she was in a good mood, but she could get evil. Then again, none of that shit was any of my business. I had enough going on without worrying about other people's relationships.

"Make sure my room is ready, and cleared of sluts. I am off the fuckin' market and I don't cheat. Period."

"Know that, brother."

"I'll need you and Hulk to watch over her."

"You got it."

I knew Hustler would try to charm her, but I was equally sure Sarah could handle him without missing a beat. Damn it was nice having a strong woman. Took a burden off me to know she wasn't some cute little baby bunny who could get easily killed. Any man who took her on would regret it, but I'd rather her not have to endure any bullshit.

"Just keep the bitches away from her. I know how women are, they'll want to test her, and a lot of them might feel the need to give her shit. Your job is to intercept them and keep her entertained."

"So I get to hang around Miss March all night guarding that slammin' body of hers? Can't say I'm sad about it."

"Fuck off. You best respect her or you will be in a world of fuckin' hurt. She's wearin' my patch tonight."

"I'll let Hulk know."

We exchanged goodbyes, then I headed inside, my body warming at the sight of my girl looking at me with a worried expression. "We're going to the clubhouse?"

I jerked my head in surprise. "Yeah, I was gonna tell you to find something warm to wear on the back of my bike. How'd you know that?"

"Sarah can read lips," Mimi chimed in as she braided Sarah's hair back in a tight French braid. "And so can I. If she's going to be on your motorcycle, she needs her hair braided or it's going to knot up."

Birdie spoke up from the living room. "Got Peaches bringing over some clothes for her."

"Why? What she's wearin' is fine."

A million invisible daggers of disgust hit my skin as all four women whipped around to look at me. "What?"

My mama's voice came out tight as she said, "You are not taking her to meet all those club members, for the first time, without giving her a chance to make a good first impression, are you?"

That was one of those riddles women liked to give men in order to drive them crazy. "Mama, she's so beautiful, all she's gotta do is breathe and she outshines every woman around her."

Sarah cleared her throat, bringing my attention back to her. As she looked up at me with her hair pulled back tight from her face, I marveled at the perfect symmetry of her features and her big blue eyes. Lost in how pretty she was, my senses dulled by admiring the woman that was mine, I missed how her big blue eyes weren't flashing with adoration, but rather with irritation—with me.

"It's sweet you think that, but I am not the kind of woman who will ever not enjoy being a woman. I like dressing up, I like looking good, I like wearing nice clothes and looking professional, or sexy, or whatever else I may be in the mood for. The fourth bedroom in my house had to be converted into a wardrobe. The whole damn thing. Gives me a tingle just to think about it. Anyways, if I was back home, I'd be going through my closet trying to find the perfect thing to wear so you're proud to have me on your arm. Since I'm stuck here, with you, I'm at the mercy of the fashion gods to find the right outfit to wear for this occasion, but I will be damned if I go to your clubhouse in fucking flip-flops!"

My throat was tight with the effort to hold back my laughter. Damn, she could go off when she was pissed. It was fuckin' cute. She lost me for a bit while she rambled about chick shit, but I honed in on the last part. "I'm proud no matter what you look like."

"Yes, but you like to show me off. I could tell that about you right away. You back your words up with actions, and in this case, you get off on men looking at, wanting, what they can't have. You like to have the best toys that no one else can play with, what they covet and you own."

"Goodness," my mama said from where she'd been wiping down the counters with a wide smile. "She knows you, Carlos."

Sarah leaned forward so Mimi could finish the long braid. I wanted to hold on to it while I fucked her from behind. Hard.

A giggle came from behind me and I knew Birdie was eating this shit up. I didn't let anyone talk to me this way, ever, but I couldn't bring myself to interrupt her while she was on a rip because it was fucking hilarious. Hiding my smile was getting harder and harder as she wrinkled her nose at me.

"And since I know this about you, I want to make a good first impression not only for you, but for me. For all intents and purposes I'm meeting part of your extended family tonight. Oh, and don't forget all the sweet butts that'll be there. If you think I'm sporting the white trash tourist look around those women, you are out of your mind."

The women all looked at me with loathing, like it was me who was personally inviting the club bunnies to come frolic.

"Those harlots," Birdie chimed in, "would cut Sarah down if she showed up in that outfit, patch or not."

"Birdie, we're bikers. No one gives a shit about fashion." They all sighed in disgust at once and it put my back up a bit. "What? It's true."

"You men don't," my mama put in with a lip curl, "but I guarantee you those loose women at your clubhouse do. Looks is everything to them, so to have Sarah stroll in there all dolled up will put them in their place. And if that doesn't work, Sarah's assured me she can fight quite well in high heels. Mimi over there even showed us a couple moves. She does yoga and let me tell you, that shit pays off. Limber little thing. Bet that'll work out well for me getting my grandbabies sooner than later."

I held up both my hands and began to back out of the room. I was done with this conversation, D.O.N.E. done. "I'm gonna go get dressed, do some business back in the office parlor. Y'all have fun up here. Keep in mind we don't got a lot of time, hour at most before we will have to go, no bullshittin' around."

"Got it," Sarah said in a strong voice, her gaze locked on mine. "Chances are someone may be there tonight who was part of the failed plot. I'll keep my eyes and ears open. I will also be carrying your Ruger SR40 in a belly band. Well, it's actually a yoga tank top rolled down and modified, but it works. I'll have two extra clips with me."

Once again, she gave my view of reality a little shove that kept me off balance. Why was it so hard for me to believe that she is both perfect, and lethal? Life and death. She's a woman of extremes right now and I wonder if she'll ever balance out and find a happy medium. I wonder if she can even see the chaos she swirls in so adeptly. I can calm those seas, give her a safe and protected harbor in the storm. I'll never take away her guns, but I hope to someday be able to take away her need to wear them everywhere.

"Always prepared, though I'm hopeful we'll have a nice relaxin' night."

I gave Sarah another kiss, ignoring the way the women tittered as we stared into each other's eyes, then went to get ready for the next round of bullshit in my life. Being with Sarah was like finding moments of true peace in the unrest of my world. It was a rare and precious commodity, something I swore I'd never feel again after some of the shit I've lived through. There have been months, years, where I haven't felt a moment of calm before I'd get a small respite from the violence to carry me through. With Sarah, I lived in peace, enjoying it and adjusting to the relief it was trying to give my fucked-up psyche.

Our lips met a few more times before we tried to drag ourselves away.

"We're gonna be one of those," Sarah said in a breathy voice.

"Those?"

"Yeah, those PDA couples. You seem to like snuggling up to me in public."

Smiling down at her, I enjoyed the teasing fire in her eyes. "Looks like it."

"Hmm, I've never been in one of those relationships before."

"Stop bein' so damn cute and get ready. I wasn't kiddin' when I said we gotta move."

Birdie peered out the window, her golden hair shinning in the sun. "Peaches is pullin' up right now. Good lord, she has enough clothes with her to open her own store. Oh, she brought her chaps! Girl, you have to wear those."

Giving Sarah a wink that made her smile, I turned away and took out my phone, taking care of business while my girl fancied herself up.

Chapter 14

Sarah

I tried to relax as I left the house with Beach, holding his hand as he led me to where his brothers were waiting. They'd all roared up to Birdie's ranch about ten seconds after I was done getting ready and I hadn't had time to crap my pants about how many people were out there. At least two dozen bikes and let me tell you, it was impressive to see them all move in unison as they circled around the massive bricked courtyard out front of the main house.

It wasn't until I held Beach's hand in mine as I strutted next to him, in a pair of stretchy jeans that fit like a glove and black leather chaps, that I realized I was the only chick in a massive sausage fest.

Everywhere I turned were hot, and not-so hot, and really-not-hot-in-any-way-shape-or form bikers of every age, from a cute black guy who was probably in his late teens like me, to a man with a braided white beard that hung down his chest and six teeth.

And they were all staring at me.

While I'd like to think it was because I looked cute with my makeup done, and a tight black mock turtleneck half-shirt showing my belly, they were all staring at the fashion accessory Beach had added to my outfit.

A black leather vest that fit me perfectly with "Property of Beach" expertly sewn in bright white thread on the back.

Yep, somehow in the last five minutes, I'd officially become Beach's old lady.

I couldn't help it. Birdie had stayed up all night getting the vest ready for me and she'd been positively beaming when Beach slid it over my shoulders. As if that wasn't bad enough, Mouse had begun to cry like she'd just seen us get married, welcoming me to her family and telling me how thankful she was to have me in her life. Mimi had kept quiet, but when I finally turned to her, all she'd done was sigh, then give me a big hug. Beach had gotten a glare and a handshake.

My...boyfriend? Or was it old man, or my biker husband? Either way, he'd looked at me with so much affection and pride, I couldn't take it off.

So now, in a moment of what had to be lovesick stupidity, I'd become forevermore known as the Property of Beach Rodriguez by my own impulsive choice.

Fuck me.

Beach's hand tightened around mine as he led me to a super-cool looking black bike with flame-colored pin striping and the Iron Horse MC logo on the gas tank. I don't know much about motorcycles, but even I could tell it was old and in pristine condition.

Next to the bike stood a curvy woman dressed in an oddly attractive retro outfit. Baggy khaki pants paired with black riding boots and a cute, almost military-looking jacket. Her helmet was dark brown with a faint trace of sparkles and I instantly adored the red lipstick she wore so well. The jacket was unzipped a bit to show her chest, and I noticed she had an interesting heart-shaped lock tattooed between her breasts, with flowers embellishing it.

"Maggie," Beach said with a fond grin that creased his face. "Thanks for bringin' my baby."

Smiling at Beach, Maggie turned her friendly brown eyes on me. "So this is Mrs. Beach Rodriquez. She's absolutely gorgeous. Well done."

I flushed at the obvious heat in the other woman's gaze, and Beach growled. "Mine."

Maggie laughed, her voice loud and clear, before she shook her head at Beach. "Hulk was right, it is gonna be fun watchin' you around her."

With a sigh, Beach gently knocked on her helmet. "I mean it, hands off."

"You know I'm teasing. Besides, I'm a happily married woman now and you know my wife would kill me if I so much as commented on your woman's body—which is outstanding." She turned her attention away from Beach then winked and held out her hand to me. "Nice to meet you, Sarah. I'm Maggie, Beach's cousin."

"Nice to meet you as well, Maggie."

Sliding his arm around me, Beach guided me to his bike. "Let's go."

After putting a black helmet with a face shield on me, he then put on his own black helmet that was made of this neat stuff that kind of looked like graphite.

The ride wasn't a long one, but I enjoyed spending that time pressed close to Beach and watching the world's reaction to our passing as if we were a parade or something. Beach and I were at the front of the long line of bikes, along with some older black man with long grey dreads who rode next to us. His patch said "Road Captain" and I wondered what that meant but quickly lost interest as I sank into Beach's big, rock-solid body cradled between my thighs.

Even though we were out in public, I felt like we were moving in our own bubble of privacy, and the ride on his bike took on an intimate mood as I cuddled him close. We were so tightly pressed together that I moved with his every breath, and soon found myself matching his inhalations, our bodies shifting as one while we roared down the highway. Occasionally he'd reach back and give my thigh a quick rub before returning both hands to the gleaming handlebars of his vintage bike.

When we took an exit outside of the city, the sky had darkened to the point I could easily see the mass of lights up on the side of a hill we were driving towards. We'd passed a gas station right off the freeway, but other than that there was really nothing out here. It was amazing how barren the land could get outside of the city and I had a sudden yearning for my dad's place out in the country. I swear the air out there was sweeter, and the sun shone brighter without all the chaos of civilization.

We passed through two sets of gates, and I had to smile at the way the men guarding them chin-lifted to us, but didn't wave.

The paved road we drove up was smooth beneath the tires of Beach's rumbling bike, and I eased my grip up as we slowed and got closer to the three-story building surrounded by freshly mowed grass and woods.

Made up of deep red brick, the building had a sharply pitched slate roof and, oddly enough, a huge playground off to the side. All of the windows had bars on them and a pair of double doors on the main level were thrown wide open, letting the parking lot see what was going on inside the building as darkness fell. I blinked in shock as we drove past the open doors of the clubhouse to the side of the large paved lot, trying to tell myself I hadn't just seen some old dude's balls. No, it couldn't be. It had to be some liver-spotted Silly Putty stuck between his legs covered in dog hair.

The bike slowed and I scrunched up my shoulders, trying to banish that visual from my head.

Once the big motorcycle was quiet, Beach got off then helped me, his eyes intent on me as I took in the club.

His rough fingers caressed my chin and he leaned forward, rubbing his nose against mine as he said, "If I kiss you, is your lipstick gonna rub off on me?"

"Nope."

He chuckled as I closed the distance between us, going up on my tiptoes as I combed my fingers through his thick hair.

A few sharp whistles rent the air, along with some catcalls, as Beach gripped my ass with both of his big hands and lifted me closer, nipping my lower lip before releasing me with a wolfish smile.

While I knew he'd enjoyed the kiss, I was also aware it was a very branding move on his part. "What, your name on my back isn't sign enough that I'm your girl? Need to give a little visual evidence?"

He chuckled, but whispered in my ear, "Watch the snark right now, *mi corazón*."

I wanted to argue with him, but I knew now wasn't the time or place, so I just nodded. According to Birdie, I needed to play the role of a good old lady if I wanted to make a good first impression, and I did. While this world was new to me, and these people strange, I wanted them to like me because I cared about Beach and he cared about them.

"Good." He looked over my shoulder. "Hustler, stop starin' at my woman's ass and get over here."

The handsome Latino man with a goatee and hazel-green eyes who headed our way seemed familiar, but it wasn't until he opened his mouth that I remembered where I'd seen him before. He was the guy who wanted Beach's well trained sloppy seconds.

While most women would have swooned over his charming smile, I didn't buy his bullshit for a moment. "Can't help my eyes gazing on perfection."

"You can if I rip them out," I informed him.

Hustler raised his hands in a placating gesture while people around us chuckled and Beach sighed. "Sorry, sorry. I won't look."

More people poured out into the parking lot and many of them called out greetings to Beach.

"Sarah." Beach caught my attention as I noticed the ratio of scantily dressed women joining the men, some of them with their tits hanging out and fresh hickies on their bodies. "Babe."

"What?"

"I got some business to handle with people who have already been waitin' here for me a long time."

"Okay." My attention was fully on this chick who squatted against a tree at the edge of the parking lot, taking a piss. "Nasty."

"What?"

"Sorry." I kept my gaze on his. "What's up?"

"Hustler is gonna watch over you while I take care of some business."

"No way am I hanging out with Perv Merv over there. Is Smoke here?"

"Awww, come on," Hustler said in an affronted voice. "I'm not that bad."

"I remember you. You were the guy at the party at Sturgis who wanted to double-team me with Beach. So excuse me if I don't feel like being your drinking buddy tonight."

"Baby," Beach said in a low voice, "go with Hustler."

"Does it have to be Hustler?"

"Go with Hustler," he repeated in a stern voice that made my hackles raise.

"Whatever."

All the guys around me laughed and my temper wanted to spark, but I wasn't stupid. The vast majority of these men were macho-pig badasses. Now, a guy being a badass is hard enough to deal with—they're moody and stubborn bastards—but add in macho-pig and you had a guy who thinks women are delicate, meek little things who need a man to protect them. And if you weren't a delicate, little meek thing, you were a bitch. Let their first impression of me be a delicate one and they'd forever underestimate me, which would work in my favor.

My pout was ruined when Beach snatched me close for another round of ass-grabbing and kissing that left me weak-kneed and smiling.

"Go with Hustler," he whispered against my lips.

"Fine."

"Stay out of trouble."

"Fine."

"Don't antagonize anyone."

"*Fine.*"

"And have fun."

"Whatever."

With that, he turned me around and gave me a swat on the ass that stung like fire and made me give a girly shriek.

I turned to glare at him, but he was already surrounded by serious men talking in low voices.

Sensing the not-so-friendly vibe coming from that way, I sauntered over to Hustler who smiled at me. "What's your poison tonight, beautiful?"

"I'm not drinking anything but bottled water."

"Why?"

"I've been roofied four times."

"Four?"

"Four. And a couple of those times was when I had a bodyguard with me. So, in a place like this, I'll take a sealed bottle of water, but that's it."

"Understood. So you don't party at all?"

"I smoke weed, but nothing else."

A bright, gleaming smile lit his face and he rubbed his hands together with a slap. "I know someone you need to meet."

Half an hour later, after searching through hordes of people, I'd managed to draw the ire of just about every slut in this place. I'm not saying all the women there to party with the club and have fun were catty, some were super nice, but I'd seen more than one bitchy snarl thrown my way.

In my life, I've had my fair share of women who hate me on sight, especially ones who considered me competition at the strip club, so women being spiteful is nothing new to me. While I was used to the maliciousness, I wasn't ready for the genuine sadness and yearning I saw on a lot of those women's faces as they took in my leather vest with "Property of Beach" stitched on the back.

There were a lot of broken dreams that night and I couldn't help but feel a little guilty for my part in crushing their hopes.

Beach had been a biker for a long, long time and no doubt in those years, more than one woman had lost her heart to him and his giant dick. That didn't mean I was giving him up because they were bummed, and while I understood their disappointment, that also didn't mean I'd put up with any jealous bullshit. The few women who had thrown subtle, venomous comments my way found out quick I can more than hold my own.

By the time we made it outside, I had Hustler and Hulk with me. We'd met Hulk on our quest for "the chick with the weed" and he'd given me a big hug that felt nice, even though Hustler kept complaining Beach was going to cut his dick off for letting Hulk touch me.

Hulk had merely laughed at Hustler's warnings and I'd told them all to calm their panties. In a weird way, Hulk, in all of his massive-black-man gloriousness, felt like an old friend and I needed that right now. It seemed as if it was taking Beach forever to get done with his meeting. I mean, I understood he was an important man with life or death matters to decide, but that didn't mean I wasn't missing him, and uncomfortable without him here. I just hid it well by not barfing every time I witnessed some icky sexual act between two icky people.

I'd seen more than one dude standing around getting a blow job like it was no biggie, talking with his buddies who were also getting sucked off. I'm not a prude by any stretch of the imagination, I loved a good orgy and had participated in a few, but they were loving orgies. I know that sounds bizarre, but at the hippie commune my friend Indigo had grown up in on my dad's property, orgies were a regular thing, though they didn't call them that. They believed in free love, in sex being natural, and all that fun swinger stuff. While I didn't have sex with anyone other than whoever I was dating at the time, I'd enjoyed watching everyone get all caught up in a big puppy pile of lust and affection from a safe distance.

Big happy piles of affectionate sex were not what was happening here.

The majority of the sexual acts going down around me were so beyond casual it seemed like there was no emotional connection. It was truly just sex, and as I noted some guy screwing a woman doggy style in a shadowy corner of the yard, I wondered if either of them actually found it gratifying.

We walked past the couple grunting in the shadows, but unfortunately it was still bright enough that I noticed the guy pumping away had a really hair ass. Like really hair. Yeti hairy.

"It's like watching a bear hump a blow-up doll," Hulk muttered.

Unable to help myself, I burst out laughing as I turned away to smack Hulk's solid arm. "Oh, that's so fucking wrong."

We reached the side of the building and as soon as we did, Hulk yelled out, "Yo, Poppy!"

A very pretty Hispanic woman in a long, flowing pink dress glided over to us with a smile. She looked as out of place as a debutant at a biker rally but didn't seem bothered in the least by the hard partying going on around us. Behind her lurked two big white dudes with dark beards wearing black bandanas on their heads and leather cuts that noted them as Treasurer and a guy named Crabs. My mind went to nasty places right away with that name and I pitied the guy for having it. I mean I realize his nickname probably wasn't referring to crotch lice, but at the same time, I had to fight a frown of distaste.

They scanned the area while the lovely dark haired woman in her early thirties closed the distance between us. She smelled like patchouli and marijuana, an oddly comforting combination that I associated with Indigo's people. I took in the flower tattoos on her wrists, the swaying silver moon earrings, the bright smile, then noted the lack of a patch covering her slender shoulders. There had been quite a few women wearing patches similar to mine here tonight, but they'd been mostly outside, away from the shit going down in the clubhouse. This woman, with her perfectly tanned skin and wavy black hair, for sure wasn't a sweet butt, so I was curious as to what her role was within the MC.

"Are you Sarah?" she asked with a light Hispanic accent.

"I am."

"Oh, it's so nice to meet you. My name is Poppy and I work with your old man." At some point the parking lot and exterior building lights had been turned on and as she turned her head, I could make out a piercing winking in the side of her nostril. "By the way, you have my pity. He can be a real pain in the ass."

I couldn't disagree with her about him being a pain in the ass, but I wasn't sure how I felt about her expressing pity for me. "Pardon me?"

"Don't get me wrong, Beach is a great guy, but he's intense. I know lots of women would kill their BFF for a chance to win Beach's heart, but I have a feeling he's one of those consuming lovers." She gave a mock shiver. "I have no room in my life for a man who thinks he can run it."

Okay, she definitely wasn't one of the old ladies or the sweet butts. They all talked about Beach as if he was a God slumming among mortals on earth. I swear grown women were reduced to giggling teenage girls by the mere mention of his name. It was disconcerting to hear the guy I'd pledged my troth to was viewed as a deity, to say the least, so having someone treat Beach like he was human was refreshing.

"Poppy, I think you and I are going to be friends."

"She leads the research and development branch of our medicinal marijuana division up in Colorado," Hulk supplied helpfully from next to me. "Ms. Poppy has a green thumb like you wouldn't believe."

Poppy gave me a wink before shaking her head at Hulk. "Actually, I hold degrees in agriculture and biotechnology. I'm doing research and development for Iron Horse because they let me do pretty much whatever I want and pay me well to do it, better than I'd make in the public sector, for sure."

"She's growing designer weed," Hulk clarified, earning another frown from Poppy while Hustler went to grab some beers.

"It's not just stuff to get you high," she huffed. "I'm also working on medicinal strains and ones with as little THC as possible. I specialize in strains for people going through chemo. And I'm developing a killer plant that will solely combat the effects of nausea. That can sometimes be the worst, ya know? The constant feeling like you're going to barf every minute of every day. Makes doing anything other than lying there and praying for sleep impossible."

Her eyes gleamed as she said this and I studied her more closely. "Have you gone through chemo?"

"Yeah, twice." She got quiet and I stumbled for something to say, hating that I'd made her remember a hard time in her life that took the happy sparkle out of her eyes.

"I'm sorry."

"Don't be." She gave herself a physical shake. "Really, I'm good now, thanks in part to the research I've been doing with medicinal plants. If you ever come up to Denver again you'll have to come visit me on my farm. I've got a massive greenhouse with some of the rarest plants in the world."

"I'd love to."

"Can I come along?" Hustler strolled up, two beers in his hand and the force of his most flirtatious smile aimed directly at Poppy. "Poppy grows the best damned weed this side of the Mississippi. Won the Cannabis Growers Cup for the last two years out in Amsterdam."

"Wow, that's really impressive."

Hulk gave Poppy his panty dropping smile, "You have any with you?"

She flung her hand out dramatically, the small silver bells on her bracelets chiming. "Hello? Have we met? Of course I do."

Hustler smiled even bigger as he handed her a beer. "You gonna share with the rest of the class?"

Her gaze bounced back to me and she took a step closer, her soft brown eyes sparkling with mischief. "Oh, I've got something you're going to love."

"That sounds ominous."

She giggled, then looped her arm through mine and pulled me away from the building and over to the now roaring bonfire where the picnic tables were. The men who were watching over Poppy cleared a picnic table for us and even cleaned it off…kind of. By cleaned I mean they threw away the empties and removed the ashtrays. Still, it was a place to sit down and even though we were the focus of a lot of attention, I ignored everyone in favor of Poppy.

She was a little odd, but I liked odd people.

Plus, she didn't take any shit from the guys.

"Hustler," Poppy snapped, "you better keep your eyes off Sarah's ass or I'll tell Beach."

One of the men she'd come with snickered, the one with the vest that said "Treasurer", and she glared at him. "You want me to tell the Prez you were letting a man openly eye fuck her?"

The big guy shuffled and I had to bite back a laugh as I reassured her, "It's okay, I'm used to it."

"Of course you are. You're insanely beautiful so even I took a moment to admire the view, but a quick glance is one thing, memorizing every curve of your ass for jack-off material is going to lead to an ass kicking if Beach catches him doing it."

"Okay." I licked my lips, wondering if everyone in Beach's world was a little odd.

"Anyways," she huffed out and dug into the pocket of her dress, "I have two different kinds with me I think you'll like. One that's good for mellowing out, and the other that's good for sex."

All at once, every guy around us was watching us with such an intense focus, I had to resist the urge to squirm. "Ummm, let's go with mellow."

"Right, but I'll give you a couple joints of the other one to try."

"And it's only marijuana, right? Not laced with anything?"

"Absolutely. I don't need to taint my babies with any bullshit chemicals to give you an amazing high."

I couldn't help but arch a brow. "I don't know. I've smoked some pretty good shit."

Her smile was smug as she pulled a pre-rolled joint from a neat silver cigarette case, perfectly done up like a cigarette with a filter and all, then passed it off to me. "Enjoy. It's a nice, really mellow buzz."

Hulk handed me a lighter and I took a hit, then passed it back to her but she held her hands up. "I'm good. I have some business to do tonight that I'll need to be feisty for. Some of these guys hate dealing with women as equals but because I'm the best at what I do, I don't have to put up with their crap and they know it."

I nodded, my anxiety lessening as I held the smoke in before passing the joint off to Hulk with the warning, "You can take a hit—but not one else. Especially Sir STD Lips over there."

I'd lifted my chin in Hustler's direction and he got this righteous look on his face. "I do not have STDs."

"Dude, I saw you kiss at least six of those sweet butts with tongue as we were in the clubhouse. Yuck. Any one of them could have had some random hairy-assed guy's spooge on her tongue."

Hustler turned a little pale while everyone roared with laughter. "They wouldn't do that."

"Right, because all women like to see you tongue it up with any slut who flutters her lashes at you." I took a deep inhale of the joint after Hulk passed it back to me.

Looking disturbed, Hustler rubbed at his mouth, then laughed. "Nah, every woman I'm with leaves my bed satisfied. They know if they want more they're gonna have to be on my good side."

We bullshitted for a little longer, laughing together as my anxiety disappeared with the fabulous high I got off of Poppy's weed. I had no idea how much money she was being paid to grow this shit, but whatever it was, it wasn't enough. This was by far some of the strongest marijuana I'd ever had, but I didn't feel out of control, only happy. It was actually really nice out here if you ignored the random sexing, and the men who stopped by to introduce themselves to me were all cool guys.

I shifted on the bench as my full bladder made itself known and asked Poppy, "I need to use the ladies' room, do you know where one is?"

"Of course, but we don't want to use the one down here. We'll go up to the officer's floor."

"The what?"

"Sarah, that leather vest of yours is like a key to the executive bathroom. We don't have to pee where all the skanks and brothers squat—trust me, it's foul. We get to go upstairs to Beach's private rooms. Bet you Beach's bathroom is sick."

Hulk must have overheard us, because he and Hustler were at our side before I could blink as I stood.

"Where you goin'?"

"Bathroom."

Poppy looped her arm through mine. "Don't worry, I'm taking her up to Beach's room."

The men looked at each other and nodded, as if they had any say in the matter.

"I have to pee, so move."

Giggling, Poppy and I slowly made our way through the crowd. It was way too packed to just barge through to get to the stairs leading to the upper levels, and we got stopped constantly by people who wanted to meet me. By the time we'd made it halfway, I was close to doing the potty dance but we were blocked by a wall of dudes. Evidently someone was having sex with someone else nearby, 'cause these guys were cheering them on and shouting 'suggestions.

Lifting her lip in disgust, Poppy tried to lead me around them, but we ended up blocked again. The crowd moved our way and Hulk, along with Hustler, pushed them back, but we were still getting squished and jostled around.

Someone shoved into me and I looked over my shoulder, seeing two skanky brunettes looking at me with hate in their gazes.

Nothing new here, so I glared at them, but got distracted when Poppy pulled me. "Come on, I see a break in the crowd past the two bitches eating each other out."

Wrinkling my nose, I followed her until we reached the stairs. Two big guys—one black, one Hispanic—guarded the bottom of the stairs. They let us past as soon as we reached them and we were a few steps up the stairs before Hulk said.

"Oh shit."

Pausing, I turned around to look at him a couple steps below me. "Oh shit what?"

"Tell you when we get upstairs."

We reached the landing and Hulk grabbed my hand, dragging me behind him. When I passed Poppy, I heard her say, "*Dios mío!* Oh no!"

"Oh no what?"

Hulk pulled me into what looked like an office with a wide wooden desk and a big computer, flicking on the light as he stared at me.

Seeing his eyes so big and the way he was staring, I started to freak out. "What?"

"Sarah—oh God, sweetheart...someone cut off your hair."

"*What?*"

His words made no sense and I reached back, finding my braid...or at least part of it. From just below my shoulders, my braid, which had reached to almost my butt, ended abruptly, the soft ends bristly against my fingers.

Horrified, I tried to pull it around to look at it, but it was too short. "Someone cut my hair off?"

"Honey—" He started to approach me but I held up my hand.

"Someone cut my hair off!"

"Sweetheart—"

"Someone cut my fucking hair!"

Poppy said in a low voice, "Hulk, are there cameras downstairs? Should I have someone get Beach?"

A banging came from the door and Hulk opened it up to reveal Hustler standing there with a panting woman. She was shorter and curvier than me, with wide brown eyes and big hair, and her dress was as tiny as could be, showing off her fabulous figure. Something about her was familiar and I tried to place where I'd seen her before.

"Sandy did it!" she told Hulk, her chest heaving as if she'd run up the stairs. "I didn't notice until after. I swear I didn't know she'd do it. We were just here to party."

"Bitch, have you lost your fuckin' mind?" Hustler growled and shook her.

"I didn't know she was going to do it! One second we're standing there talking with Vance, next thing I know she's pulling a big pair of scissors out from her purse. I didn't even realize what she was doing until she did it!"

"Why?" I asked while trying to keep my shit together. "Why would she do this?"

My hair. It was gone. I no longer looked exactly like my sister.

The woman's eyes flicked to me and they were angry. "'Cause me and her were Beach's women before you showed up."

"You mean that crazy bitch cut my hair off because of *Beach*?"

Hustler shoved the woman into the arms of another brother. "Get her the fuck out of here and find Sandy. You better run, Brandy, 'cause when Beach finds out, he's gonna lose his mind."

My distressed morphed, heated and twisted into anger. "I want her—Sandy, now."

"We'll—"

"Listen to me, either you help me find her or you are going to have to hide that bitch for the rest of her life because I will hunt her down and get her. Where's Beach?"

"He's in a meeting," Dragon said as he entered the room, his gaze going right away to my slowly unraveling braid. "Let us take care of this. Swear that cunt will pay for what she did to you."

I had a feeling what they meant by "pay" and what I meant were two entirely different things.

"No, she's mine." I took a gamble. "Either you give her to me or I'll go to Beach right the fuck now and let him know what happened on your watch."

"Yo, Hustler, we got Sandy," a strange guy yelled from the hallway.

"Bring her in here," I said, seething. "I want duct tape and a chair I can bind her to."

Dragon arched his brows, his full lips pursing. "Not sure the Prez is gonna be down with that."

"Not sure I give a fuck."

Hulk said in a weary voice, "Take Sandy down to the holding cell. We'll be there in a minute."

Not long after, I had Sandy taped to a folding chair in the middle of a suspiciously empty concrete room in the basement with a drain in the floor. Without a doubt, this was a room where they took unwelcome guests and I tried not to get creeped out by all the blood likely shed here. Normally I'd beat the fuck out of Sandy and call it a day, but I had a feeling if even one drop of blood was spilled, these men would be on it like a pack of wolves and kill her. Or hurt her in ways I didn't even want to think about.

No, the punishment had to fit the crime, and while she'd hurt my soul by cutting my hair, she hadn't hurt my body.

But she would pay.

Sandy sat in the middle of the room, her green eyes spitting fire at me while she raged. She was drunk, and torqued up on coke, so she had a lot of energy to waste on trying to get out of the tape. I kept the door to the room open, knowing I had a chance to send a message here that I needed to take.

Yes, I was furious this piece of trash who Beach had been fucking decided to take out his dumping her on me, but more importantly, I had the attention of these men and we needed to lay some ground rules. This was one of those "what would Mimi do" situations and I tried to channel her as I sneered at the woman and took out one of my knives. Word would spread about how I handled this situation and if I showed any weakness, I was going to be fighting off bitches for the rest of my time with Beach, however long that may be.

Before I could take a step closer, Hustler was there, his hand grasping my forearm. "What are you going to do to her?"

"Don't worry about it."

"If you're gonna kill her, I need to clear the room."

I glared at him, disturbed by the casual way he'd said that. "I'm not going to hurt her."

He didn't look reassured, probably because I was in scary-motherfucker mode, but he let me go and I crossed the room to where Sandy glared at me.

"I'm only going to say this once, so let me make myself clear." I ran the dagger under her eye, brushing her lashes and half hoping she'd sneeze and kill herself. "Whatever you do to me, I'm gonna do back to you three times as bad. Doesn't matter what it is, you will pay the debt you owe me—and bitch, you owe me big."

She said some not-so-nice things behind her gag, but I just smiled, stood, then grabbed her hair. "Listen to me. For the next three weeks, you're going to shave yourself bald every day."

Her muffled scream as I sawed through her hair was gratifying, but even more so was watching the men in the room wince as I laughed and hacked her hair off. There was nothing but ultra-short, uneven stubble left by the time I dusted my hands off and smiled. At this point, Sandy was sobbing and leaning forward as much as the duct tape would allow, snot and tears mixed with makeup dripping down her face.

I almost felt sorry for her, but tucking my now much-shorter hair behind my ear cured me of that emotion.

Giving her cheek a hard slap, I shouted, "Look at me, bitch!"

She did, her eyes almost swollen shut from her tears, so I got right in her face, letting my anger go as I yelled at her. "Every day when you shave your head, you're going to think about *me*, think about the results of your evil action. When people stare at you, I want you to remember who I am, and I want you to know deep down in your soul that I will find out if you don't and I will make you hurt. If you try to run, I will hunt you down and take great pleasure in making the last few hours of your life filled with pain. And believe me, bitch, there is nowhere you can hide that'll keep you away from me."

With that, I spit on her face, then turned and froze when I noticed Beach leaning against the wall just inside the doorway, his impassive gaze focused on me.

"Hey," I said with a small wave that caused some of Sandy's hair to fall off my arm.

"Hey," Beach said back while everyone stared at us.

There were quite a few women mixed in with the men looking in from the hallway, and they gave me some thumbs up and encouraging smiles.

Well, good to know the old ladies of the club were as crazy as I was.

Beach tipped his head in Sandy's direction. "Want me to finish it?"

And there was proof the old men were crazier.

"If I wanted her dead, she would be."

He studied me, then nodded. "She is very, very lucky you got to her before I did. If that bitch doesn't do what you told her, I'll make sure she regrets it."

Sandy sobbed and I ignored her. "You done with your business?"

"Yep." He straightened and came over to me, brushing some of Sandy's hair off my shoulder. "You need a shower."

The adrenaline high of the last half hour was wearing off and I sighed. "Are you going to wash me?"

Heat flared in his gaze and he leaned down and slowly rubbed his nose along mine. "Yep. Gotta keep my old lady happy so she doesn't shave me bald in my sleep."

"Damn straight."

Chapter 15

Carlos "Beach" Rodriguez

As we left the room, I cut my eyes to Hustler, who was fuming with anger. When he noticed me looking, a wave of remorse moved through his gaze and it was obvious he felt like shit this had happened on his watch. Hulk shared the blame as well, but Hustler was on flank and had apparently been distracted by Veronica throwing drama. He needed to quit that bitch, but for whatever reason, he kept goin' back to her, hopin' this time she'd stay on her meds.

Poor bastard, but that didn't mean he wasn't gonna get some form of punishment from me that would send a message. Sandy could have just as easily had a knife, or a gun, and the knowledge she could have ended Sarah's life instead of cutting her hair burned through me. My gut clenched at the mental image of Sandy stabbing a knife in Sarah's back, making me want to rage, but I needed to keep my control right now. Even if

I was screaming on the inside, I had to be calm for Sarah.

"Hustler," I said in a low voice as we passed him. "Tomorrow, we're havin' words."

He closed his eyes and nodded while Sarah tensed even further next to me.

I needed to get her away from everyone, and quick. She was going to lose her shit, I felt it like a storm building heavy in the air. Her hand gripped mine hard enough that it almost hurt, and her free hand kept lifting up to touch her hair, to finger the short strands that barely brushed her shoulders, where it had fully unraveled from her braid. Guilt that I'd been distracted by business when I should have been with her churned in my gut and I tugged her quickly behind me as we took the stairs to my rooms.

When we passed Sledge, I looked him right in the eye and nodded once. The disrespect Sandy had shown me couldn't stand. Man or woman, what she'd done to my old lady was unforgivable. I'd let Sarah have her vengeance, as fucked up as it was, and a few months down the road Sandy was gonna disappear. No one threatened my old lady and lived.

I had a feeling Sarah wouldn't have too much of a problem with bitches getting lippy with her after this bullshit. The horrified looks on the women's faces, old ladies and sweet butts alike, would have been funny if I hadn't watched my woman laugh in a bitch's face as she shaved her bald. There was more than a little bit of crazy in Sarah, and I needed to remember that.

That crazy was pushing at the surface as I led her into my suite in the clubhouse.

I flicked on the lights and she froze, then looked around with wide eyes. "Wow…this is not what I was expecting. It's beautiful."

"President gets the biggest suite."

"Suite," Sarah muttered, "this is a luxury apartment. You have an almost-kitchen and a living room. Nice color choices, the black with the teal and sand is a good combination, and I love how whoever decorated pulled it together with your couch. The pillow choices are a little feminine for your space…I would have avoided the velvets, but the harshness of the minimalist decorations needed to be blunted somehow. Oh, I see what they did now. The pillows match the thick velvet drapes. Bet they darken the room wonderfully if you want to take a nap. I wonder if the artwork they used was local; I really like that tree scene. Is your bathroom to the right?"

I shook my head to clear it of her rambling, a smile tugging at my lips despite the recent drama. "Bathroom's to the right."

"Good. Can I smoke in here?"

"What?"

She spun around to face me, Sandy's dark hair still sticking to her despite her attempts to brush it off. "Smoke, as in light up. Can I smoke in here?"

"Lemme open a window, but yeah."

"Thanks."

I led her over to the couch beneath one of the windows, leaving her to the task of getting comfortable while I opened it.

"Lighter?"

Silently, I went into my kitchen to grab one, wondering when that icy façade of hers was gonna crack.

Taking it from me once I returned, she fished around in the small inner pocket of her vest, then pulled out what looked like a pink cigarette.

"What the hell is that?"

Before she answered me, she lit it up and took a deep inhalation before letting it out. "Gift from Poppy."

"Shit, what did she give you?" I didn't recognize the hearts on the paper, and the smell of the weed had a hint of cloves to it.

"An aphrodisiac." She offered me a hit but I shook my head, wanting my mind clear for dealing with her.

"What?"

"Never mind." She settled back onto my couch with a huge sigh, holding her arm up and frowning. "Yuck, I look like I've been rolling around on the floor in a salon."

I sat next to her and gently grasped her chin, turning her head so I could see her watery eyes. "I'm so sorry this happened to you."

After taking a deep drag of the joint, she turned her head so she wouldn't blow the smoke in my face then let it out in a rush. "She did it because she loved you."

"No, *mi corazón*, she never loved me."

"She thinks she did."

"Don't let that bitch make you believe she did what she did to you out of love. I know Sandy, and her actions are the results of her hate and envy."

Closing her eyes, she finger-combed her hair back, her breath hitching. "She cut my hair."

I went to hug her, but she pushed me back and sat up, taking one more hit before standing and going over to the sink and wetting the end. Her shoulders had a slump to them that killed me, but as she gave me her profile, I realized how elegant she looked with her hair shorter like this.

When her wounded gaze met my own, I held my hand out to her.

"*Mi riena*, come here."

"No."

"Why not?"

She curled her lip in disgust and for one brief moment I thought she was lookin' at me like that and I though my heart was gonna break, sure she was gonna leave.

"I'm hairy, I need a shower."

Studying her as relief crept through me, I nodded, determined now more than ever to bind her to me in every way possible. "Go, shower. When you come out, I want you ready for me, so wash that little pussy real well. Gotta take care of some shit real quick, but I'll be back before you're done. Wash that tight asshole of yours real good while you're at it."

She gaped at me, then gave a visible shiver that went straight to my cock. "Okay."

"How about, 'Yes, *Papi*'."

Her pupils visibly dilated and I didn't miss the way she pressed her thighs together. "Yes, *Papi*."

Then she smiled and even though hurt and anger still haunted her face, there was also a hint of happiness and lust.

While she quickly went into the bathroom and shut the door, I went outside into the hallway and found Smoke waiting for me.

My Master at Arms moved away from his position leaning against the wall and made it to my side. I glanced down the hallway to make sure no one was close enough to listen. "What did the Boldin *Bratva* say after I left?"

"Kostya Boldin was pissed off until I explained your old lady was in danger. Motherfucker went all soft on me for a second and said he understood that family comes first, and hoped everything is alright."

"Great, but did that slick bastard give you the manifest?"

"Part of it. All weapons. Big ones."

"How big?"

Smoke's voice got real low and he stepped closer to me. "Missiles."

"Shit."

"Yep. And the Israelis are hinting they have something even bigger, but won't give me any information other than to say it is plants and some kind of herbal liquid. They swear up and down it's not a biological weapon. They want Poppy to be part of the ride-along to insure the plants survive the journey."

"What did she say?"

"Well, Poppy was a little freaked out, having witnessed your old lady go psycho barber on that cunt Sandy, but she agreed to be part of the transport."

"So we're gonna be movin' missiles and fuckin' plants?"

Smoke shook his head with a wry smile. "Life is fuckin' weird."

"And they're gonna pay us millions to do this."

"Yep."

"Fuck." I took a deep breath, greed tempting me to give the thumbs up, but I had to be careful. "Tell 'em we'll have an answer for them by tomorrow evening."

"Of course. They're partying with Tom Sokolov so I don't think they'll have an issue with extending their visit by a day."

Knowing Tom was probably treating them like kings with the best pussy and drugs money could buy, I'd bet they weren't in a hurry to leave.

I looked over his shoulder, noticing Vance standin' at the top of the stairs with Dragon on the other end of the hall. "I don't want to be disturbed until late tomorrow morning. Sledge can handle shit, but I need some time with my girl."

Smoke's dark gaze softened. "She okay?"

"No, but she will be."

"Right. Go take care of your old lady, I'll brief you in the morning."

I clasped his shoulder and squeezed it before returning to my room. The faint scent of my soap and shampoo filled the air and I took in a deep inhalation before moving to grab the black leather bag I kept beneath my bed. From it, I took out a red elk-hide flogger and a pair of black leather cuffs with sheepskin lining. I debated adding nipple clamps, but figured I was gonna push her enough tonight. I needed to take her out of her mind for a while, focus her on physical pleasure and fight back the sorrow eating at her.

When Sarah came out of the bathroom, her eyes were red and I knew she'd been crying, but she gave me a wavering smile that tugged at my heart something fierce.

Her hair was slicked back from her face and I once again admired her adorable freckles. "You're so beautiful."

She lifted the hand that wasn't holding up her towel to lightly touch her hair. "Thanks."

"I mean it. You're so gorgeous you bring me to my knees." I stood and took off my cut, then my shirt. "Come here."

Just as I predicted, she came to me right away and snuggled close, her hand stroking my chest hair and sending little sparks of pleasure through me.

"Is that a flogger on the bed?"

"Yep."

"And restraints?"

I indulged myself in stroking the smooth, muscled skin of her back. "Yep."

"Nice."

Chuckling, I was glad I wouldn't have to talk her into playing with me. "You gonna let me cuff you?"

"Absolutely."

"Flog that pretty ass?"

"Please, *Papi*."

"You are a naughty baby. Drop your towel then take the rest of my clothes off."

She did as I asked without protest and I grit my teeth when her breasts came into view. The tips of her nipples were already hot pink and I could see the way her pussy was puffed up and wet. This woman was ready for my cock and I hadn't even touched her yet.

After removing my boots and socks, she made quick work of my jeans, leaving me standing in my boxer briefs while she let out a happy purring sound.

Lightly running her nails over my thighs, she rubbed her face against my shaft, her lips parting on a sigh. "I love your dick."

"It loves you back."

She giggled, then began to place teasing kisses along my length, each brush of her lips making me twitch. "Can I see it, *Papi*?"

"Uh-uh, you gotta earn this dick." Her eyes gleamed as she looked up at me, kneeling back on her heels just as pretty as you please. "Get on the bed. I want you on all fours in the middle."

I loved the fact that she didn't appear fearful or apprehensive in the least. She trusted me to take care of her, to do her right and not hurt her. It was a heady feeling and I couldn't stop myself from smoothing my hands over the round globes of her perfect ass. Millions of men wanted this ass, but I was the only one who got to touch it, and that thought had a little bit of pre-cum wetting the tip of my aching erection. I placed a kiss on each cheek before licking my way down to where her tight thighs met her ass, soothing the soft skin there with my tongue.

This close to her pussy, I was drowning in the musky scent of her arousal and I took a deep breath, my cock pounding as blood rushed to it. Unable to resist, I licked my way slowly to her pussy, smiling to myself as she widened her stance and tipped her hips up, her pleading whimpers an aphrodisiac like no other. I was only going to allow myself a lick or two, just enough to get a taste, but the instant my tongue made contact with her wet folds, I turned greedy.

Lapping at her wet sex, I had to grip her hips to keep her in place, the taste of her driving me to take more, to take everything. When I sucked on the tip of her distended clit, she moaned and her whole body shuddered. I could sense that she was close to her orgasm, but I didn't want to give it to her yet.

"Mmmmm, please," Sarah murmured and wiggled her butt in the air.

"We got no safewords between us. You say no, it stops. Understood?"

"Yes, *Papi*."

"Good girl."

She giggled and wiggled her butt at me again. With a grin, I spanked her, hard, and enjoyed the way she squealed.

"Ouch!"

"Be still. Don't move. Can you do that for me?"

"Yes, *Papi*."

I worked her slow at first, soft brushes of the thick hide over her bottom and lower back, occasionally brushing between her thighs to stroke over her wet sex. Each time I did that, she'd shake and make these sexy, deep-in-her-throat noises, but she didn't move. Her control was excellent and I loved playing with a woman who did what I wanted, who gave me the tools to build her up to an unbelievable climax.

Increasing the strength of my hits, I sucked in a harsh breath through my nose and took in the scent of her, my body screamin' for me to fuck her.

Tossing the flogger aside, I greedily ran my hands over her bottom, loving the heat from her reddened skin. "What a dirty girl, all wet and dripping for her *Papi*."

Her gasp of pleasure as I ran my fingers through her soaked folds drove me to torment her further. "And this clit, so nice and hard for me. Allows me to do things like this."

I began to rub and pull at that sensitive bundle of nerves, smiling wide as she fought so hard to stay still, her yelps and groans giving away her struggle. The little bit of flesh between my fingers swelled further and her pussy wet my hand as she cried out with her orgasm, her arms giving out but her shaking legs keeping her bottom in the air. Desire tore through me at the sight of her cunt opened for my gaze and I couldn't hold myself back any longer.

With a snarl, I knelt behind her and pulled my cock out of my briefs, giving it a soothing stroke before I positioned myself at her hot entrance.

I sank into her grasping flesh, rotating my hips as I pushed in so my piercing stroked her internally.

She went wild below me, thrusting up onto my cock, forcing me into her. I reached around and played with her clit, pulling out and pushing back in, giving her more of me every time. Another orgasm tightened her inner muscles around my cock and I saw stars as her pussy tried to suck me in. A ragged gasp escaped me when I was balls deep in her steaming-hot body and I lay fully atop her, keeping my arms to the sides and holdin' off most of my weight.

Right away, she lifted so her back was pressed solidly to my chest, getting as much skin-to-skin contact as possible. I liked that I could kiss her shoulder without getting a mouthful of hair and nipped the smooth skin there, biting harder when she rocked her ass into me.

Our movements became harder, faster, and all too soon I was fighting the urge to come inside of her. I didn't want this to end, didn't want to give up the bliss of her body, the absolute perfection of her tight cunt. At this point I was holding still while she reared back into me, her head turned to the side and her face suffused with pleasure.

"Carlos," she whispered, "come with me."

Grasping her hips, I growled out, "Play with yourself."

She slipped a hand between us and not only did as she was told, but also reached back to fondle and squeeze my balls as I fucked her.

A hard and intense burn raced down my back and into my pelvis, making me cry out her name as she spasmed beneath me, her moans joining my own while I filled her up with cum.

Each spurt of me that went into her had my whole body jerking and by the time I was done emptying myself I felt hollowed out in the best way.

Collapsing atop Sarah, I rolled us onto our sides and held her close, still buried inside of her. "You're gonna kill me."

"Can't keep up with me," she panted, "old man?"

"I *am* your old man."

She sighed and tensed slightly. "What did I get myself into with you?"

Not liking the defeat in her voice, I kissed the side of her neck. "You got yourself a man who'll do anything to keep you safe, who'll always cherish you, and who'll love you until the day he dies."

Her pussy flexed around me, distracting me as she said, "You love me?"

"Babe…" I laughed, then winced as her pussy squeezed again. "You think I'd go through all this bullshit for someone I didn't love?"

"Well…but…we hardly know each other."

"When you gonna listen? We know each other," I placed my hand over her heart, "in here, where it matters."

Slowly she softened against me, but her occasionally twitching pussy kept me hard inside of her. "Beach…I…"

While I wished she would return the sentiment, I knew she wasn't ready and forced myself to be patient with her. "Didn't tell you that to pressure you into sayin' the same."

"It's not that I don't feel deeply about you, you're the most amazing man I've ever met, but Beach, I'm scared."

"Of what?"

"That you're going to get sick of my shit, then you're going to break my heart so bad it'll never heal." She sucked in a quick breath.

I wanted to demand that she recognize that'll never happen, but like Mimi said, I gotta be patient with her. "That's not gonna happen, and I'll prove it to you. May take five, ten, fifty years, but I'll prove it to you."

She was silent for a moment, then softly laughed. "I was trying to picture us together fifty years from now. I have this really weird mental image of you in one of those motorized scooters for old people with flames painted on the side."

With a wince, I slipped out of her and rose from the bed. "Stay here."

I returned a moment later to clean her up, loving how she lay back and let me take care of her. Before joining her in bed, I turned out the rest of the lights, leaving the fountain on for her. The watery shadows painted pictures of light over her magnificent body and I slowly ran my hand from the dip of her waist to the curve of her hip.

"You wanna know what I see when I think about us fifty years from now?"

She gave me a small, amused grin. "What?"

"I see us happy, surrounded by great-grandbabies on our ranch. You'll be sittin' on my lap while I sip a beer and watch our kids teach their kids how to play football."

Her gaze went misty and after I returned from tossing the washcloth into the hamper, she held her arms out to me. "Come back to bed."

I slid beneath the sheets with her, gathering her body to mine. We ended up in our usual position, with me on my back and Sarah curled into my side, toying with my chest hair. Her leg curved over mine and I waited for her to talk about whatever was keeping her awake.

"I want that, your fifty years, so badly," she whispered.

"You'll have it."

"Beach...what if I'm a bad mother?"

I sucked in a quick breath, alarmed at the sorrow in her voice. "Why the hell would you say that?"

"It's something I worry about."

"Impossible."

"What?"

"You are love, Sarah. You couldn't be anything but a good mother; it's in your nature."

"I like the way you see me."

"I see the truth."

She let out a soft sigh, her body relaxing more into mine. Seconds of silence turned into minutes, but neither of us fell asleep. Her voice came out soft with amusement as she said, "So, I had a fun time meeting your friends."

I couldn't stop myself from bursting out laughing, hugging her to me as she started to laugh as well. It took us a while to stop, and by the time we were done my stomach was sore. I tugged her back into place and she giggled, then yawned.

"Go to sleep, *mi riena*."

"Okay, goodnight, my king."

For a long, long time I lay there in the dark after she fell asleep, praying that I'd have the strength to slay Sarah's demons and the patience to win her heart.

Epilogue

Sarah

The next ten months at Beach's side were the best of my life. We fought, boy did we fight, but we always made up in the most spectacular fashion.

I had a few more problems with the sweet butts at the clubhouse, but after two of them tried to take me on at once and I put them both in the hospital, they didn't bother me anymore. I actually got along with a handful of them and enjoyed their company, even if I didn't understand why they'd want to be club property. With Birdie's and Mouse's help, I'd begun to take on the role of the old lady of the President, helping out club members when they needed it, giving the other old ladies someone to talk to about their problems, and occasionally babysitting the seemingly endless horde of kids the brothers had.

Being Beach's old lady was a full-time job, but he made sure that I still had time to go to school. I was taking some classes at a local art college in Austin twice a week and loving it. My life might not have been what my idealized version of normal was before I met Beach, but it was even better than my wildest dreams. Beach was right, I never would have been happy trying to be something I'm not, trying to make my wild spirit fit into a mold it wasn't made for. Don't get me wrong, not everything was all peaches and cream, but we worked on our relationship together.

Beach had an endless amount of patience for me and my various quirks. We bought the house of my dreams and Beach gave me full rein of decorating the place, making it perfect for us. I was in love, happier than I'd ever been, and had finally found a man who loved me more than life itself. Shit, even my dad begrudgingly liked Beach once they met and got over trying to beat the crap out of each other. I wished I could get Swan to agree to meet Beach, but so far she'd been super hesitant whenever I brought it up, despite my best efforts to let her know that Beach wasn't like the other losers I'd dated in my past. He treated me like his queen in every way, and I could only hope that Swan would find someone to love her like Beach loved me.

Everything was perfect, and I thought my luck had finally turned around...

Right up until the moment Beach answered a knock on our front door and found my battered and teary-eyed birth mother, Billie, standing on the other side with Vance, begging for our help.

Dear Beloved Reader,

Put that Ann Mayburn 'I hate cliff-hangers' voodoo doll down! Beach and Sarah's story will continue in Exquisite Karma, coming March 3rd, 2016 and it's available for pre-order now at select stores. Thank you, once again, for giving me the chance to entertain you and I hope you enjoyed the real story of how Beach and Sarah met.

Ann

Thank you so much for reading **Exquisite Redemption**! I hope you enjoyed the book, and would love it if you would please consider leaving a review. Not only does a review spread the word to other readers, it also lets me know if you've had fun visiting the world of the Iron Horse MC. I love to hear from readers and you can reach me through my website and through my Facebook and Twitter accounts. As always, thank you so much for giving me the chance to entertain you!

About the Author

With over thirty published books, Ann is Queen of the Castle to her wonderful husband and three sons in the mountains of West Virginia. In her past lives she's been an Import Broker, a Communications Specialist, a US Navy Civilian Contractor, a Bartender/Waitress, and an actor at the Michigan Renaissance Festival. She also spent a summer touring with the Grateful Dead-though she will deny to her children that it ever happened.

From a young age she's been fascinated by myths and fairytales, and the romance that was often the center of the story. As Ann grew older and her hormones kicked in, she discovered trashy romance novels. Great at first, but she soon grew tired of the endless stories with a big wonderful emotional buildup to really short and crappy sex. Never a big fan of purple prose, throbbing spears of fleshy pleasure and wet honey pots make her giggle, she sought out books that gave the sex scenes in the story just as much detail and plot as everything else-without using cringe worthy euphemisms. This led her to the wonderful world of Erotic Romance, and she's never looked back.

Now Ann spends her days trying to tune out cartoons playing in the background to get into her 'sexy space' and has accepted that her Muse has a severe case of ADD.

Ann loves to talk with her fans, as long as they realize she's weird and that sarcasm doesn't translate well via text.

CPSIA information can be obtained
at www.ICGtesting.com
Printed in the USA
LVOW04s0913080116
469677LV00026B/437/P